The Missing Dagger

By
Keith Hall

TRUST HOUSE PUBLISHERS
Taos, New Mexico

Published by Trust House Publishers
trusthousepublishers.com

P.O. Box 3181
Taos, New Mexico 87571
ISBN: 978-1-961110-43-4

Printed in the United States of America by Trust House Publishers.

260305

Contents

1

A Sad Occurrence

G WENDOLYN was troubled by the disappearance of her grandmother in the park. Gwendolyn and her mother Jenny had taken Grandma Gwen to her favorite park for her 95th birthday at her request. As usual, Grandma Gwen had kept up her tradition of dressing up every year on her birthday in the outfit she had worn in the other world she claimed to have visited. She had her bow and quiver of arrows slung on her back even though she had not used them for a number of years. She was also wearing her special necklace, had her sword strapped to her waist, and was carrying the dress she had worn as a girl. The only things missing from the entire outfit was her precious dagger, belt and sheath.

Standing at the edge of the woods by the park Grandma Gwen had just started walking into the woods. Gwendolyn and her mother had run into the woods after her, but she was just not there. There was no way that they could see for Grandma Gwen to have gotten far enough away to have not been seen as soon as they entered the woods, but she was gone. After searching for hours, they reported the incident to the authorities, but the grandmother was never found.

Suspecting foul play Jenny could not see any other way her mother could have just disappeared like that. Gwendolyn, however, was troubled in a different way. She did not see how it could be foul play as there was no way for someone to kidnap her grandmother and get her out of sight before Jenny and Gwendolyn got to where they last saw her. Gwendolyn had been close to her grandmother and had loved to hear Grandma Gwen telling her about the time she once visited another world by taking a path in the very park where she disappeared. The tale seemed too fantastic to be real, but Grandma Gwen had insisted that it really had happened to her, and she had shown her the priceless necklace as well as the other items.

Grandma Gwen had possessed a beautiful wooden box containing a leather-bound book which chronicled her activities in the other world she said she had visited. Grandma Gwen had passed this box and book on to her daughter Jenny on Jenny's 17th birthday as the start of a family tradition. Each girl was supposed to keep passing the box and book on to her first daughter on the daughter's 17th birthday. Jenny had in turn passed the box and book to Gwendolyn on her 17th birthday.

Beginning to wonder whether what her grandmother told her could be true Gwendolyn kept thinking more about this possibility. On her visits to her grandma's house she had often been asking questions about the other world. She had read the book several times and was intrigued by it. She had sometimes asked for more information than was recorded in the book about certain events. Grandma Gwen had always filled her in with much more detail. The interesting thing was even after a year or two if Gwendolyn asked about the same event her grandmother had told her the same details never forgetting something or getting the details mixed up.

Gwendolyn had been to the park where her grandmother's adventure began many times and was not surprised that she could not find a path anywhere in the woods. She was guessing that somehow her grandmother had found it again the day she disappeared. Gwendolyn knew the path was hidden to those without guidance. She also knew the dagger would guide the owner to the path. She was sad that the dagger had been lost somehow, but curious how her grandmother could have found the path without it.

Deciding that if she could succeed in locating the dagger she could try visiting the other world and see if her grandmother was still alive there Gwendolyn began earnestly searching for it. The only clues she had to go by were what her grandmother had told her and what was written in the book. Since her grandmother was no longer there to ask she had to go by memory for those bits of information. She had the book herself so she could refer to it any time she chose for possible clues. The only other possible source of a clue she could think of was the wooden box that held the book.

Thinking about all the conversations she had with her grandmother caused her to shed a tear or two, but also to smile as she recalled the happy or funny talks they had. After careful consideration she decided that there was nothing her grandmother had said that could help her to locate the dagger other than the suggestion her grandmother made for her to follow her instincts if she was ever unsure what to do.

Getting the box and book down from the shelf in her closet where it was kept Gwendolyn retrieved the book from the box returning the box to the shelf. She then spent her free time over the next few days carefully examining the book for any clues. She was convinced from reading the book that the dagger would guide her. She was unable to glean any clue from the book as to where the dagger could be or how to go about finding it. She was now becoming discouraged, but was unwilling to give up hoping that someday she would find the dagger.

Gwendolyn spent the next few weeks just doing her usual activities. She had told herself that maybe not thinking so hard on the problem and allowing herself to get back to a normal routine for a bit might clear her mind and allow her to better tackle the problem later. Her instincts told her that the clue to the dagger was in the box and since the only thing in the box was the book that was the logical place to search. She started analyzing what was written line by line. It took her quite a while to get through the book this way, but she finally succeeded in reaching the end. She was convinced that the events that were chronicled had been written as history and did not hold some type of hidden clue about the dagger in the wording.

Periodically getting the book out and rereading it over the next few years Gwendolyn was still trying to figure something out. At these times she would not consciously try to find a clue but would just enjoy the narrative. She was ready to stop if an idea came to mind and begin pursuing it, but nothing new presented itself. She was still unwilling to give up and her instincts kept telling her the box held the clue to the dagger.

On the evening of her 22nd birthday she got the box out to start rereading the book again. As she took it off the shelf she had a strange feeling telling her to slow down and think. Instead of following her usual routine of taking the book out and putting the box back on the shelf she just sat down holding the box with the book inside it on her lap.

Thinking about how Grandma Gwen faced and solved many difficult problems in Dreki's world she was reminded that General Hapsom had said he was impressed with her methodical approach to problem solving and her logical thinking. She also remembered that some of the problems had seemed impossible at first, but then they were solved by looking at the problem in a new way. Could that approach help her with her own seemingly impossible task?

Thinking about this for a while she then went over to her desk to get out some writing materials. Keeping the box in her lap she started jotting down her observations so far. She would then see if any new ideas came to mind while she was reviewing the notes. She began by writing that her instincts told her the box was the clue, the only thing in the box was the book, that she had read the book numerous times, she had read line by line all the way through, and she had not succeeded in finding any clues.

Analyzing each observation, she was making further comments about them as she went along. Her instincts had never changed so she left that as it was. The box was the clue. Here she sat pausing for further analysis. Did that mean "the box" or "something in the box"? Not realizing she was doing the same thing the Dartan council had done she made herself an upside-down tree to help her visualize the different choices. The first two branches now becoming "box" and "contents". Deciding to check the box itself for clues she began by examining the outside first. Although the wood was beautifully finished and had a fine lustrous glow to it there were no markings or carvings at all. Carefully looking at the inside of the top as well as the sides and bottom in the box it was as she suspected there was nothing there to give her a clue. She added that no clue was found on or in the box itself in her notes. Setting the box aside for the moment she proceeded with the book.

Since it was night and there was a bright full moon shining she took the book outside examining it by moonlight. She had been hoping that maybe moonlight would reveal some otherwise invisible marks or writing. Seeing nothing she brought the book back inside. She suddenly remembered something her mother had told her. Her mother told her that when she was younger her mom and some friends had tried painting their faces with eye drops. In normal light they looked just like usual, but under ultraviolet light the painted spots glowed a bright yellow. Gwendolyn tried to remember if she had an ultraviolet light source but could not recall any. Determining that she would have to get one and do the light tests before going further she returned the box and book to the shelf before heading to bed.

Buying an ultraviolet light from a store in the mall the next day and taking it to her room she got the box down from the shelf. Examining the box under the light she was disappointed that nothing was revealed. She then tried checking the book under the ultraviolet light but again got a negative result. Making notes on the negative results she decided to try looking at the box again under normal light but was not too hopeful as it was lined with a plush deep purple velvet that had no designs or markings on it. She picked up the box and started examining it one more time. There was absolutely nothing on the exterior or interior of the box to give her a clue. She was not sure if there was anything else she could try so she was going to call it quits for the day and try thinking about it some more later.

As she was putting the book back in the box again she paused as something just did not seem quite right. She sat for a while trying to decide what it was. She then put the book aside and started giving the box another examination. This time she did not try looking for any visible clue; she just tried to figure out what was giving her the feeling that something wasn't quite right. She finally noticed that the depth inside the box seemed slightly less than she thought it should have been. Wondering if it was just due to the batting under the velvet she tried pushing down on the bottom velvet until it was down as far as it would go. Comparing her palm position to the bottom on the outside of the box it seemed a little higher than it should have been. The difference was not easily discernible yet was more than could be explained by just the batting and thickness of the bottom piece of wood. She did not think the difference was great enough to account for the dagger, but perhaps there was a written clue in a hidden compartment.

She stopped pushing and grabbing a pinch of the velvet on the bottom between her thumb and finger she began gently pulling upward and noticed the bottom coming upward as well. With her heart beating faster, she continued gently pulling and eventually the bottom came out. She gasped at what she now saw. There was the dagger along with a handwritten sheet of paper folded over several times so that it just fit on top of the dagger! She saw that the bottom and top boards had been routed out so that the thickness above and below the dagger was not the full half inch of the boards themselves, but only about one-eighth of an inch thick. No wonder it had been so hard to detect the difference!

She knew she had found the dagger at last, but what was the sheet of paper? As she started reading the note she discovered it had been written by her grandmother Gwen. It complimented the finder on their ability to discover the dagger's hiding place. The note further encouraged her to let the dagger lead her on her own adventure.

Gwendolyn was anxious to see what would happen, so she began by strapping the dagger to her waist after retrieving the belt and sheath from the closet she kept them in. Sitting for a few moments she did not feel any different than before she had put on the dagger. She knew the only way to find out for sure was to go to the park so that is what she did.

Arriving at the park and making her way to the spot her grandmother had been in before she disappeared she then just started walking in the same direction her grandmother had gone. She had not gotten very far when she noticed what might be a path, but she started moving closer as it was hard to tell. The closer she got to it the clearer the path became. Once she actually stepped onto it, it was unmistakably a clear path going further into the woods. It was just like the description she had read in the book.

The further she went the more excited she became as she was somewhat familiar with what was coming. Watching for the side path to the left and turning on it as soon as she saw it she continued down the path. The door did not take her by surprise as she knew it was going to be there. The door opened for her without having to solve the puzzle, but she was not worried about that as she knew how to solve the puzzle anyway. After only a bit more hiking she was standing at the edge of Dreki's meadow!

2

Meetings

WELL," Gwendolyn said to herself, "now that I am actually here I will have to decide what to do first." Gwendolyn went out into the meadow a bit sitting down to try thinking things over for a while. After spending some time doing this she finally decided that since Dreki had not appeared in the sky like he did for Grandma Gwen she would have to be the one making the first move. Since Dreki's cave was the next logical place to look she started heading in that direction. Circling to the back side of the lake she found the wide path on the other side of it. Taking the path as it went uphill towards the mountain she was soon crossing the bridge over the stream. Knowing she should turn left when she got to the face of the mountain she smiled to herself as she did so. It did not take her long to find the cave, and she began calling out Dreki's name at the entrance.

Receiving no answer, she sighed to herself as she started making her way back to the meadow. She knew Dreki had not gone on a long journey or he would have put the door into the entrance of the cave. The question now was whether she would remain waiting there in Dreki's world or try going back home and hopefully return another day. She knew the basic rules of the path but did not know if multiple trips were allowed. Remembering that one of the rules was once the door was passed her grandmother needed Dreki's permission to return caused her to ponder this further. Did that hold for her as well or would she be able to pass with the dagger to guide her?

The only way to find out was to try testing it herself. Her plan was to follow the path back to the door and see if it opened. If it did she would know she could go back home at any time, but she did not know if she would be able to get back here. If it did not open she knew she was stuck here until she got permission. She figured she could see if the door opened but not actually try passing through it. That way she would know she could go back home if she got too hungry or if danger threatened.

Making her way back down the path to the door she stopped in front of it. Grabbing the lever so she could use it to undo the latch she discovered that the lever would not move. She tried just pushing the door open, but it would not budge either. "Well, that settles that!" she said to herself heading back to the meadow.

Looking around for the bushes with the berries because she knew they were edible and tasted good besides she found the bushes easily but was disappointed to see that the berries were all small and green. Unfortunately, she knew this meant she would starve long before those berries ripened. Taking a slow walk around the lake and looking for any other bushes or trees that bore fruit she had found nothing edible after completing a full circuit of the lake.

Gwendolyn decided the only reasonable option left for her was Dreki's cave hoping that there would be something in the kitchen area. If there was nothing there her only other option would be to try hunting. "Wait a minute!" she said to herself. "Is that really my only other option?" As she was heading back to Dreki's cave she thought hard about how Grandma Gwen responded to some of the challenges she faced to see if that could help her out.

Coming up with another idea as she was walking along she added it to her list of options. She was thinking, "If I can't find food in the cave perhaps I could make a fire and try sending smoke signals. That might get the attention of Dreki or one of his dragon friends."

No other ideas had occurred to her by the time she entered the cave, so she started heading for the kitchen area which she knew was in the back. Discovering that the kitchen was well equipped with pots, pans and utensils she knew that cooking the food would not be a problem once she found it. She did not see anything resembling a refrigerator but was not really expecting one in any case. She did find cupboards and drawers filled with cups, plates, bowls and silverware. She finally found some dried meats and vegetables after searching through several more cupboards.

"Yes!" she exclaimed loudly taking a pot to the laundry area and filling it about halfway with cold water. Taking this back to the kitchen she placed it on the stove. Next some dried meat and vegetables were added. She was laughing out loud when she found herself absentmindedly looking for the "heat control" for the "burner" on the stove top. After about 20 minutes she figured out how to get a fire going in the stove and had her stew cooking.

Since this was going to take a while and she felt a little guilty eating Dreki's food she decided to do a little cleaning while she was waiting for supper. She easily found what she needed in the laundry area managing to get the dusting completed fairly quickly. Checking the stew, she added a little more water as the dried meat and vegetables had absorbed quite a bit. Since the stew needed to stay cooking a while longer she was able to finish sweeping the floor. After the sweeping was done she finally sat down to her meal. It was pretty good but adding a little salt made it much better.

Making sure she cleaned up afterwards she put everything back where it belonged. She had only eaten about half of the stew so putting a lid on the pot she moved it off the heated burner. She was planning to finish the second half for her supper later that evening. She decided on checking out the meadow as she had not stopped to take a look at the Stone of Remembrance or anything else while she concentrated on looking for food.

She took a good look at the stone and pedestal when she arrived at that location. She did not find the stone to be particularly pretty but knew it was the meaning of the stone that was important and not the beauty or intrinsic value of the stone itself. The pedestal was indeed very beautiful, and she stood awhile admiring the intricacy of the carvings. Wandering about she saw a number of animals in the meadow or by the woods but did not see any dragons either in the air or on the ground.

When it started getting to be late afternoon she headed back to the cave. Building up the fire in the stove she started heating up the leftover stew for her dinner. Finishing her meal, she cleaned up afterwards. She was checking out the sleeping quarters when she heard a voice say, "It smells like stew in here! Is anybody here?"

Gwendolyn passed through the curtain into the main cave area and saw a dragon standing there. Gwendolyn said apologetically, "I am sorry Dreki, but no one was here and I got hungry, so I ate some of your food. I hope you don't mind too much?"

Dreki replied, "I do not mind at all especially since it looks like you took care of the dusting and sweeping I usually need to do after a trip away, but you have the advantage of me! You know my name, but I do not know yours. I can see that you are wearing the dagger that once belonged to Gwendolyn the Gracious and then to Gwen so I know you must be in her bloodline. Also, you bear a strong resemblance to Gwen. Can you please tell me your name, so I know what to call you?"

"I am Gwendolyn and the Gwen you referred to is my grandmother. I came here looking for her. She disappeared mysteriously in the park several years ago, but it has taken me a long time to find the dagger so I could get here. Have you seen her and is she still alive?"

Explaining that her grandmother was here and very much alive and well Dreki told her that she was now Queen Gwen in the kingdom of Pacem to the south. He also explained that due to the rules of the path Gwen was no longer an old woman, but a young girl again. Dreki mentioned that as soon as Gwen had gotten settled back in the cave they began visiting all their friends in Dartan, Vita and along the way to give them the good news that Gwen was back to stay.

Gwen had decided she wanted to try restoring the kingdom where Gwendolyn the Gracious had once lived and where she was now the rightful heir to the throne. She and Dreki had gone to see if it might be safe to return or if the plague was still active there. They had found that a few people had moved into some of the cottages in the surrounding area and had been fixing them up but were afraid to enter the castle after the first person took a careful look inside and saw all the skeletons there. Gwen and Dreki felt that if the cottages were safe the castle would be as well, so they checked out the castle and found it the same as when Dreki had gotten the dagger from there.

A few volunteers from Dartan and Vita had come and Dreki got a few of his dragon friends to help as well and the restoration was started. Gwen moved into the castle and was slowly cleaning it up and restoring it to the way it was before. The helpers took rooms in the castle to be living there until the restoration was far enough along for them to return to their homes in Dartan and Vita.

In the meantime, a search had been made by Dreki and his dragon friends for those who had left Vita returning to their homes. As they were found the progress on repairs of their homes was checked. Most had done well in getting their lands restored, but a few found the damage so severe that they were having a difficult time. These were asked if they would be interested in relocating to the village in Pacem. There were a number of cottages there that would be fairly easy to restore and were available for immediate occupancy. The dragons offered to carry the people there to have a look and either bring them back if they did not want to relocate or assist them in the relocation process if that is what they chose to do. All but one young couple opted to relocate and were assisted by the dragons in getting to their new homes.

Thanking the dragon for the offer the one young couple said they were willing to struggle through the rebuilding process as they both really loved the piece of land they had chosen to live on. The dragon said he would check on them again at the start of winter and if they did not have sufficient shelter and supplies to make it through the winter Queen Gwen said they could stay in the castle and return to their home to finish in the spring. The couple told the dragon to be sure and thank Queen Gwen for her generosity. When he was checking on them later they had made enough progress that they declined the offer of relocating to Pacem and said to thank Queen Gwen again for them.

The young woman then said that she did not know anyone named Gwen, but that Queen Gwen had a name very similar to a Princess Gwendolyn that had saved her from being given to a horrible man named Stultus and had killed Nequitia and freed the kingdom of Dartan, but that Dartan was quite distant from them. She said that she and her husband had been so anxious to get away from Mortem that she had not been able to express her gratitude before they left. She also said that it seemed a strange coincidence to her that the names were so similar even though the countries were so distant from each other.

When the couple found out that it was indeed Queen Gwen who had defeated Nequitia they asked the dragon if they could possibly be flown to Pacem to thank Queen Gwen in person. He said that he would make the arrangements and they could be picked up in two days spending the next day and night as guests in Pacem and then be returned home the following day. The couple then made preparations for the trip.

Arriving in the courtyard in Pacem the couple was surprised to see Queen Gwen there waiting for them. She smiled warmly at them and gave them a hearty welcome telling them not to worry about ceremony and to feel at home there. The couple felt a little uneasy at first, but after conversing with Gwen for a little while the three were soon chatting pleasantly filling each other in on what had been happening in their lives. A very pleasant visit was enjoyed by them all and Gwen said they were welcome to visit Pacem any time they chose.

Things were now going well in Pacem and quite a number of families had been settling into the abandoned cottages in the villages surrounding the castle. There were still some cottages in ruins, but all the skeletons had been given a proper burial. As more people settled they were gradually fixing up the abandoned cottages. A few of the relocating families had opted to move into the castle instead of one of the cottages and work there in exchange for food and lodging so there were enough people living in the castle for the cooking, washing and general maintenance tasks to be taken care of.

Gwendolyn had been listening carefully as Dreki shared the information with her but was having difficulty absorbing it all. It was hard for Gwendolyn to believe that her 98-year old grandmother was now younger than she was, but Dreki had already explained how that had happened due to the rules of the path. Thanking him again for the explanation Gwendolyn said it still might take a while for her to get used to having a grandmother younger than she was. They both shared a laugh about that.

Dreki said he was going to be fixing something for himself to eat and asked Gwendolyn if she wanted anything else. Declining his offer Gwendolyn enjoyed talking with him while the food was being prepared. Dreki took Gwendolyn to the area where he had stored the clothing Gwen had not chosen on her first visit and told her to find a few outfits she liked while he ate his supper. Gwendolyn was able to find a few things that fit her well enough and Dreki said that if they got to Glyka there would be plenty of choices there.

Conversation continued while Dreki was eating his meal shifting to what would be done to accommodate Gwendolyn into the household. Gwendolyn stated that she had no idea what she was going to do now that she was here. She said she had not really been thinking it through but just had a vague idea of finding her grandmother here, giving her the dagger, and then going home after visiting a few of the interesting sounding places she had read about. Gwendolyn asked if the kingdom of Pacem was far away or if it was within walking distance. Dreki told her it was a good day's walk, but much faster by dragonback. Gwendolyn was not sure she wanted to spend all that time learning how to ride and was anxious to see Gwen. Dreki then explained that since they were not going on a quest or facing enemies in battle there was really no need for all the training. She should be able to just ride along after a couple of short test hops followed by a few circles around the lake. Dreki suggested that they give it a try before breakfast and if Gwendolyn did OK they could see how her stomach felt after they ate. If she was still feeling good they would fly to Pacem, which would take less than an hour, and if she felt too queasy they would just hike. Gwendolyn agreed to the plan and after a bit more conversation they both went to bed.

Gwendolyn did not have any problems with the flying either before or after breakfast other than a very slight wobble after dismounting. She really enjoyed the view of the meadow from higher up and told Dreki he had chosen a really lovely place to live. It did not take long to get to Pacem and Dreki was soon gliding down and landing in the castle courtyard.

Since Dreki had previously made several trips to Pacem the girl in the courtyard was not surprised to see him landing there. She was surprised that Dreki had brought along a passenger though commenting that she had a remarkable resemblance to Queen Gwen. Dreki told the girl that they were related asking her to tell Queen Gwen that someone was here to see her.

Arriving and seeing who was standing in the courtyard Queen Gwen cried out joyfully, "Gwendolyn!" running up and hugging her. Gwendolyn hugged her back but then stepped back taking a good look at her.

Gwendolyn slowly shook her head exclaiming, "You do look exactly like one of the pictures in my mother's photo album, but it sure feels strange calling you Grandma Gwen even though I know that is who you are! It is going to take me a while to get used to this. Oh, before I forget I wanted to give you your dagger back. Here take it please." She then handed the belt, sheath and dagger to Gwen who accepted it graciously. "How did you find the path without it?"

"I have been wondering about that myself. I knew the dagger would be a guide, but I had passed it on along with the book. I had no thought of actually finding the path that day and was just remembering the first time when I saw a porcupine in exactly the same spot as the last time! Walking right up to him I began following him down the path. I was so excited seeing Dreki and finding out I was young again that I totally forgot about the porcupine for a while. When I was thinking about it later it occurred to me that since Dreki was surprised to see me he could not have sent the porcupine. So, I guess I don't know why he was there, but I am sure glad he was as I did not have the dagger to guide me."

"I guess we will never know about the porcupine, but I am glad I finally found where you hid the dagger."

"I am also glad you found it and came here! It is really good to see you. Since several years had passed since I came back I was not sure if you or perhaps your daughter or granddaughter would find the dagger while I was still alive. I had a feeling you might be the one as you always showed much more interest in hearing about my time here than anyone else." Gwen then strapped the dagger on getting a huge smile on her face. "You don't know how much I have missed this! Now I feel like myself again!"

"Do you mind if I call you just Gwen somehow 'Grandma Gwen' does not seem right with you being younger than I am now?"

"Of course! It would be awkward for me as well as I definitely don't look or feel like a 'grandma' anymore. By the way, what do you plan to do now that you are here?"

"I am not sure. I wanted to give you back your dagger and had a vague idea of possibly visiting some of the interesting places you and Dreki saw but had not really made any specific plans. Everything seems so peaceful, and everyone seems happy. I don't know what kind of adventure I could have in these circumstances."

Taking Gwendolyn and Dreki to an area in one of the castle courtyards with a large open garden where there were walkways with benches to sit on Gwen and Gwendolyn picked one sitting down with Dreki on the grass next to them. Enjoying pleasant conversation for quite a while there and answering Gwendolyn's questions about some of the events that had taken place on Gwen's adventure when she was there the first time the three passed a very pleasant morning. Gwendolyn asked if there were any plans to visit Dartan or Vita any time soon as she was interested in seeing them after reading Gwen's book.

Telling her that there were no plans Gwen said that did not mean they could not make some. Conversing for a while longer they started trying to figure out the best way to accomplish the journey. Dreki commented that for that length of a journey it would be best for Gwendolyn to have some flight training, and he would have to stop by his cave and put the door in place. The training would not need to be as extensive as what Gwen had received, but it definitely needed to be more than a few touch-and-go hops. Dreki mentioned he would have to find another dragon for the trip and it would be best for her to do the flight training with the dragon she would actually be riding. Dreki said he could easily carry two people, but the only dragon saddles available there were designed for a single passenger.

Gwen said that it would not hurt to try checking out the weapons and see if they could find something for Gwendolyn to use. Gwen explained that since they did not expect trouble this was more of a secondary concern and would probably only be needed if an emergency arose. Gwen then took her to the weapons section in the armory and had Gwendolyn start trying a few things. Gwendolyn found a sword slightly longer than Gwen's and a dagger that would work for her.

She asked Gwen if she could try her luck with a bow and arrow as reading Gwen's book had inspired her to do some archery back home. She had been on the school archery team but had never excelled at it since she did not devote as much time to practice as Gwen had.

Finding a bow for her Gwen took her to the range that was almost the same as the one Dreki had originally set up for Gwen's own training. When Gwendolyn saw how far away some of the targets were she said there was no way she would be able to hit them. Gwen explained that as she was learning archery with Dreki the farther ones were only put up for her after she had become expert at the shorter-range targets and she would not have been able to hit them either at first. Gwendolyn found it a bit of a challenge getting used to the bow and arrow at first since she was used to a modern compound bow, but after a bit settled down and was able to do fairly well. She mentioned that she had never seen Gwen shoot and asked if she would be willing to show her with the long-range targets. Gwen said that she would be glad to as long as Gwendolyn promised not to feel discouraged. When Gwendolyn agreed Gwen shot three arrows at the farthest target which all landed in the center of the bullseye with the fletching of each arrow touching another one.

Gwen then told Gwendolyn that it had taken several months of daily practice before she was able to do that, but that she was glad she had spent the time. If she had not made the effort to hone her skill to perfection the encounter with Nequitia might have ended differently. Gwendolyn said she was glad things were now peaceful and that she would not have to face anything like that. Flying off the next day to find another dragon willing to carry Gwendolyn on their journey Dreki headed out while the two ladies worked on Gwendolyn's weapons training. Gwendolyn was not nearly as skilled as Gwen was but was an apt pupil and made good progress in the use of the various weapons. Gwendolyn wanted to take a break and helped Gwen to prepare lunch. They enjoyed a nice leisurely meal with more friendly conversation.

Commenting on how beautiful Gwen's dress was Gwendolyn asked where she got it. She was told that it came from the royal clothier in Glyka and that King Firinne had said she could have more made for her any time she wanted a new one. Gwen said that it would not be a problem obtaining a couple for Gwendolyn when they got there as that was one advantage of saving the kingdom from Nequitia. Gwen also mentioned the fact that Gwendolyn being a princess did not hurt either. Gwendolyn gave a small gasp exclaiming that she had not even thought about that. "Now I understand how you felt when you got to Glyka! It is something of a shock when you first find out." They both shared a laugh over that.

3

THE DRAGONS RETURN

L ANDING in the courtyard just then Dreki began approaching with two other dragons. Greeting Gwendolyn, he said that both of the other dragons had volunteered and were anxious to be of help. Dreki introduced the two dragons to her as Slett and Hratt. He said the two dragons had decided to let Gwendolyn make the choice of which dragon she preferred, and she said it really made no difference as both dragons seemed equally nice to her. She finally asked if either had a mate back home with Slett saying yes, but Hratt replying in the negative. Gwendolyn then suggested that Hratt might be a better choice so that Slett would not be away from his mate. Everyone agreed that it was a good way to make the decision. Gwendolyn thanked both dragons for volunteering and waved goodbye as Slett was heading back home. Now that the choice of which dragon to bring along was decided plans for the trip could be made.

Neither the training nor the amount of equipment needed would have to be as extensive as what Gwen had for the quest she went on with Dreki, but still some planning was needed. The same dried meat and vegetables would work for this trip, but more would be needed due to the larger size of the party. This would not be a problem as now there would be two dragons carrying things. They decided that one large tent and one smaller tent would be brought along. The smaller one would always be set up for the ladies to sleep in and the larger one would only be used for the dragons' heads if it was pouring rain. The clothing needed would be much less as they were not faced with the possibility of dealing with the cold or multiple seasons.

The trip itinerary would follow Gwen and Dreki's original route, but hopefully not have any side trips to rescue anyone. It was too early in the year to gather hazelnuts, but they planned on stopping in that general location for a meal in any case. Gwen and Dreki would be in the lead as they knew the route and Gwendolyn and Hratt would be following. If something interesting showed up along the way they said they might make an unscheduled stop to check it out. This was planned to be a very relaxed trip as they were not worried about traveling during the winter.

Dreki was expecting that the flight training would only take about a week as they were not having to learn the sudden maneuvers as extensively as Gwen had. It would be good for them to experience a few unexpected turns or dives in case some unforeseen problem arose, but the training was mostly just getting used to takeoffs, landings, gradual turns, and glides. Weapons training was also accomplished at this time. The fact that Gwen assisted with the archery training gave Gwendolyn an excellent teacher and example to follow. One of the men in the village had previously been an accomplished swordsman in the Mortem army but had decided not to stay in Vita. He had felt that even though conditions would have been fine there now there were too many memories he was hoping to forget. He was of great help in getting his students above the novice level of swordsmanship. Even Gwen learned a great deal under his expert teaching. Now that sufficient flight and weapons training was accomplished they could gather their supplies and make trip preparations.

Gathering the supplies for this trip was easier than for the quest Gwen and Dreki had gone on. Knowing they could get to Glyka in less than a week they only needed to carry enough food to last that long. They had several planned stops already figured out along the route and they did not have to worry about not being able to set up a decent camp for any night. As was mentioned before, clothing for multiple seasons was unnecessary. Since Gwen had not claimed any of the treasure Nequitia had gathered while she was queen or demanded any reward for saving Dartan or Vita she was told that she could have anything she needed within reason at any time she chose. They would easily be able to replenish their food supplies for the return trip without having to worry about having to pay for them. Gwen did take along a purse with some coins she got from the Pacem treasury in case there was something special they wanted.

Waking early the morning they planned to start their travels the two dragons and their riders ate a good breakfast. With the early start it was a relaxed flight with them stopping for lunch a little before noon. Dreki and Gwen were not positive that it was the same clearing that they had stopped at on their quest, but Gwen was thinking it looked about the same and seemed somewhat familiar. Gwendolyn and Hratt both said it did not matter to them as it was new for them both in any case and besides it was a pretty spot to rest in.

Finishing their lunch, they were on their way again. Gwendolyn and Hratt were both enjoying the beautiful scenery and either Gwen or Dreki would be making a remark now and then as they saw something familiar from one of their previous trips. As sundown was approaching Gwen commented that she was hoping Daniel and Juliette would be home so she could introduce them to Gwendolyn and Hratt. Dreki said that they would be making a stop there in any case as the cleared area near their cabin was plenty large enough for them all to land in and set up camp.

They were getting close to their destination for the evening when suddenly Gwen exclaimed, "Oh good! I can see a column of smoke ahead. That should mean that at least either Daniel or Juliette will be home if not both of them." Once they got to the clearing and came in for their landing the group made their way to the front of the cabin. Gwen called out and in a very short time Juliette's smiling face appeared in the doorway. "Gwen I am so glad to see you and Dreki! Can you introduce me to your two other friends? You two ladies bear a strong resemblance."

Introducing Juliette to Gwendolyn and Hratt, Gwen mentioned that she and Gwendolyn were indeed related. Juliette remarked that Daniel had gone to check his traps but then smiled reassuring Gwen with a laugh. "He did not take the canoe this time so you can relax. He should be getting back any time now and we were planning to have a fish fry if his traps were successful. We are hoping you will join us for supper. If there are not enough fish we have plenty of other food."

Thanking Juliette for the supper invitation Gwen accepted graciously. She asked Juliette if anything was new since the last visit and Juliette said that they had enlarged the cabin by adding a couple of new rooms. Juliette then took Gwen and Gwendolyn inside to show them the additions while Dreki remained outside showing Hratt the grounds around the garden and the areas outside the cabin and down by the stream.

Juliette began by showing them a spacious room with a large window and comfortable chairs. It also had a fireplace and a table and chairs. Explaining that it was a multi-purpose room she said it could be used for reading, sewing, other projects, or just entertaining. She said she was excited to be able to use it for entertaining for the first time. The second room was small and snug. It had a nice rug on the floor, a wardrobe on one side of the room and a chest of drawers on the floor on the opposite side. Underneath the window was a cradle with rockers on the bottom. When Gwen looked back over at Juliette she saw she was smiling and had a rosy blush on her cheeks. The subject immediately changed to the expected arrival with Gwen and Gwendolyn both wanting to hear all the details. The ladies spent a good bit of time discussing the expected joys and challenges of adding the new member to the household.

Dreki and Hratt were just finishing up their rounds by making the stream their final destination in exploring the grounds when they heard whistling coming from down the path. In just a few moments Daniel appeared with a stringer full of large fish and a smile on his face. The smile got even bigger when he saw Dreki and he quickly came up to greet him. Dreki introduced Daniel and Hratt to each other as all three of them were heading back to the cabin. When Dreki mentioned that Juliette had already invited the dragons as well as their riders to stay for dinner Daniel said he was very glad. He was not looking forward to having to smoke most of the fish he caught which was what he thought he would have to do. He said that fish freshly caught, cleaned and fried was the best way to enjoy them.

Reaching the cabin, Dreki and Hratt obviously stayed waiting outside while Daniel entered heading to the kitchen with the fish. He called out to Juliette to come give him a hand if she could so they could get the fish scaled and cleaned. Juliette and the other two ladies came into the kitchen and with all four working together the job was done in only a few minutes. Daniel finished washing his hands and said he was going to join the dragons outside as four people trying to cook in the kitchen would make it too crowded. The ladies then began shooing him out teasing him about wanting to get out of work although Juliette remarked that he was generally very helpful when it was just the two of them there.

Daniel and the dragons had a pleasant talk outside with the ladies continuing their interrupted conversation in the kitchen. The supper was cooked and then served on the porch of the cabin. This arrangement was much better for including everyone in the dinner table conversation as they enjoyed the fish and other side dishes. The conversation continued for a while after the meal was finished, and the ladies finally headed to the kitchen to clean up afterwards. The men remained outside during the cleanup process but were again joined by the ladies when they were finished.

When the time came for bed the two ladies made use of the multi-purpose room by placing their sleeping bags on the rug there. Dreki and Hratt found places outside that suited them as well. All enjoyed an undisturbed quiet night's sleep and woke refreshed and ready for the new day. After breakfast and farewells the travelers were on their way again. As on previous trips there was nothing seen over the next few days that they spent extra time investigating. They enjoyed the relaxing flights and unhurried meals, even taking a few walks after the noonday ones. This was just to stretch their legs and enjoy the scenery rather than to be looking for anything specific. The evening camps were also set up in a relaxed manner as they did not have a schedule to stick to.

Keeping her eyes open to the north now Gwen was watching to see if the Mystery Mountains would be visible. She was hoping they would be and that she could point them out to Gwendolyn and Hratt. As she had been hoping they were clearly visible though shrouded in mist in a few places and she pointed them out to the other travelers. Looking over at them Gwendolyn asked if there was always that cloud of black smoke above one of the farther peaks. Gwen asked Dreki as she said she did not remember seeing the smoke on any of their other journeys. Dreki said he did not remember it either. They all decided they would start heading that way to check it out. Gwen pointed out the fact they just because they were checking on the smoke it did not mean they had to make a landing in the mountains unless they all agreed to it. Approaching the peak with the smoke above it they could see that there was more smoke continually being added to the black cloud above the peak. Gwendolyn said, "I believe that is an active volcano! Dreki, can we get a closer look or are the volcanoes here the kind that might erupt violently and be dangerous to us?"

"I am not familiar with volcanoes at all, and this is the first one I have ever seen. I would think that if we are not flying right above it or too close we should be fine. It probably would not be a good idea to be standing on the slope though."

Flying close enough to get a good view of the volcano they could even see some lava flowing out of the cone and down one side. They started making a slow circle around the peak and then continued their westward journey. They all agreed that the spectacular view was well worth the time spent on the side trip.

Entering the grassy plains Gwendolyn remarked to Gwen that they did indeed look a lot like the rolling waves of the sea. When they got to the patches of hazelnut trees they made a lunch stop. They would not be gathering any nuts as it was too early in the year for them to be ripe and Gwendolyn said she was a little sad that they could not enjoy them. Smiling broadly at her Gwen reached into her backpack and pulled out a small sack. "I was pretty sure we would be stopping here for lunch, so I came prepared. I brought some along for us to enjoy and we don't even have to crack them first!"

Gwendolyn thanked her and commented that they were indeed very delicious. They all enjoyed some of the nuts along with the rest of the meal and they were soon on their way again. Enjoying the pleasant flying weather and beautiful scenery they all watched for a grassy spot with a stream running through it. Once they spotted one they landed and set up camp for the evening. After the evening meal they stayed sitting around the campfire talking for a while. They planned on visiting Jim and Mary the next day and were hoping that they would also be at home when they arrived.

After finishing their breakfast the next day, they broke camp preparing for their departure. Gwendolyn remarked that it was amazing to her that Dreki could find the small cabins and homesteads of the people that they wanted to visit in such a vast wilderness as they were traveling through. Dreki said that he just kept his general direction by landmarks in the far distance and as they got closer to a destination he kept looking for familiar landmarks closer by adjusting his direction accordingly. He also said that the more times trips were made over the same route the more familiar it became.

Gwendolyn thought about visiting her cousins back home. The first time her dad drove them there the route seemed strange and unfamiliar, but on later trips she was able to recognize landmarks they were passing and knew where they needed to turn and about how much further it was to their destination. She realized it must be the same for Dreki, but for her it was very different flying through the air than driving on roads.

Traveling on westward towards Jim and Mary's place Dreki pointed out certain landmarks to Gwendolyn as they got nearer and he was making slight course adjustments. She said that since he was mentioning them as they flew she could feel them and see the slight changes, but when they had occurred previously since she had not been thinking about it she had not really noticed them. They were all thankful for the beautiful flying weather they had experienced so far, and it seemed that they were at Jim and Mary's in a very short time.

They found it a little disappointing to find both Jim and Mary away from home, but since the open area surrounding their cottage was spacious they set up camp and after exploring the area a bit had their noonday meal. While discussing the fact that they should be in Glyka the next day they heard the sound of cartwheels coming along the narrow lane behind the cottage. They were delighted to see Jim and Mary appear with a load of supplies on their cart. They warmly greeted each other, made introductions, and with the added help the supplies were quickly unloaded and put away.

The afternoon was spent in enjoyable conversation as news and updates were exchanged. Both parties shared that things were peaceful and quiet in their surrounding areas and that no troubling news or rumors had been heard. Jim shared that the devastated homesteads nearby had been rebuilt and the owners were living there again. When news of their return was passed along people from nearby homesteads had helped them to rebuild so it had not taken too long or been too burdensome for those returning. Gwen said that she was glad to hear that and shared about how the Pacem restoration was going as well.

Enjoying supper and further conversation that evening made it very pleasant for everyone, and Gwendolyn said she was excited to know that they would be in Glyka the next day. She had only been in the remote areas and was looking forward to seeing what the city was like and meeting some of the people she had read about in Gwen's book. Mary shared that she and Jim had never been as far as Glyka but made trips to Sweet Glade often to get supplies. They always made sure to get a room for the night in the inn planning on spending that evening around the fireplace exchanging news with the townsfolk. She said it was so much nicer now with all the smiling faces and laughter than when they had made their first trip with all the doom and gloom tidings when Nequitia was ruling Mortem.

4

GLYKA AND VITA

THE next morning the travelers were on their way north-west towards Glyka. They were thankful that there was no rain to slow them down this time and only made one quick lunch stop before continuing their journey. Reaching Glyka before sundown they were able to enter through the open city gates. They were respectfully greeted by everyone they met as they were proceeding down the streets to the palace in the center of town. Word of their arrival must have passed fairly quickly as Royal Advisor Jenny was there to meet them when they arrived at the palace. Gwen and Jenny hugged each other and then Gwen made the introductions. Jenny said that their timing was excellent as supper was to be served within the hour. Jenny invited them all to join her in the medium-sized dining room. She said that as soon as word of their arrival came she had told the proper people to have that room prepared with a spot for the dragons as well as the people.

Leisurely making their way to the dining chamber they sat down to have a pleasant time of conversation followed by a lovely lavish meal. Jenny said she knew they would appreciate it after the trail food they had been eating along the way. Gwendolyn remarked that she had never eaten a nicer or fancier meal in her life and asked if every supper there was like this. Laughing Jenny told her that meals were usually nice, but nowhere near as elaborate as this one. Finishing their desserts Gwen asked if perchance Abigail had baked the pie. She said it was excellent reminding her very much of the one she and Dreki had on their trip back to his cave before she went back to her old world. Jenny said that she had, that Abigail seemed very gifted at baking, and she was now apprenticed to the royal baker. The royal baker had confided to Jenny that even he could not make a pie crust as good as Abigail's.

Staying and talking for a while after the remains of the supper had been cleared from the table King Firinne joined them there. When Gwendolyn stood and bowed to him addressing him as "Your Majesty" he waved her to her seat again. "We do not stand upon ceremony here as far as the royal house of Pacem is concerned. You may address me as Firinne. And how does Your Highness wish to be addressed?" This last question was addressed to her with a wink.

She told him that her preference was Gwendolyn, but like Gwen before her it was hard for her to get used to being a princess. He said he could understand Gwen's surprise, but surely being a direct descendant of Queen Gwen of Pacem, she would have known all her life that she was a princess. She said that in her old world this world was completely unknown and to claim to be royalty in her world made no sense. Since she had spent her whole life up to this point as a common everyday person the idea of being royalty would still take some getting used to.

Gwen then asked King Firinne if perhaps "Princess" Gwendolyn (this with a smile and twinkle in her eye) could obtain some nicer clothes from the royal clothier while they were there. He said that was no trouble at all and she should go at her convenience and pick out whatever she would like or get measured and order it if she did not find something suitable. Gwendolyn thanked him and then the conversation became more friendly and informal. When it got to be later in the evening Jenny said she needed to let them know which rooms would be theirs for their stay in Glyka. They could then continue talking until they were ready for bed; at which time they could head to their rooms. She told Gwen and Dreki that they would be in the same rooms they had the first night they were there, that Gwendolyn would have a slightly smaller room next to Gwen, and Dreki's room was large enough for both dragons to share. Everyone agreed that this was great and continued talking a while longer before finally heading to bed.

Enjoying a good breakfast the next day the travelers were discussing what they were planning to do. The dragons said they would enjoy a few days of just relaxing to recuperate from the long trip and the ladies decided on exploring the town and visiting some of the shops. Bidding the dragons farewell the ladies were off on their expedition. Gwen made sure the route they took out of the palace went through the main hall so she could show Gwendolyn the stained dress displayed there. Gwendolyn thought it was very appropriate to remind people that sometimes items that seemed insignificant could play an important role in the overall scheme of things. They then passed through the main courtyard pausing to admire the statues there.

Soon they were slowly walking through the streets of the town and Gwendolyn was asking questions and remarking how nice the shops and other buildings looked. Gwen made sure that they stopped in the shop where she had obtained Dreki's collar and her beautiful necklace. When Gwen introduced Princess Gwendolyn to the shopkeeper and he noticed her looking wide eyed at all the jewelry he pointed out a case of nicer items for her to look at. She thanked him heading over to the case and closely inspecting several items. The shopkeeper asked if Gwendolyn was from Pacem and if she was related to Gwen since the names were so similar and the resemblance remarkable. Gwen then explained that Gwendolyn was related, recently arriving from the world that Gwen came from. Winking at Gwen the shopkeeper then headed over to where Gwendolyn was admiring the pieces on display.

He offered to get something out of the case if Gwendolyn wanted to examine it more closely. She pointed to a necklace that was like the one Gwen had except this one had a gold heart shaped locket instead of the filigree heart. It did have the rubies and emeralds around the outside and a heart shaped, cut diamond in the center. She asked Gwen to come take a look at it and Gwen said that it was very nice looking. Gwendolyn asked the shopkeeper if it was fashioned after the necklaces that Gwen and Royal Advisor Jenny wore. Removing it from the case and handing it to Gwendolyn for closer inspection he remarked that it was a very popular style now to have a heart shape, rubies and emeralds around the edge, and the heart shaped diamond in the center. Pins brooches and even bracelets could be seen in Glyka in that motif.

The shopkeeper then said that he was sorry Gwendolyn had not been present for the victory celebration but did not want her to miss out on part of the fun. She was looking at him with a puzzled expression as she tried giving the necklace back to him. He said that it was hers to keep, as she was the lucky number today for receiving a free gift. When she said it seemed too nice of an item to be a gift he told her to just make sure she mentioned to people where she got it if anyone asked or complimented her on it.

She indeed got several comments about how nice it looked and how closely it resembled the one Queen Gwen wore. Gwendolyn always remembered to mention which shop it came from. Gwen told her that she had felt a little guilty receiving items from the same shop, but that the shopkeeper had always more than made up for it in new business. She was expecting the same thing would happen in the case of Gwendolyn's locket.

Continuing their stroll, they noticed small groups of children playing several times along their walk. The children appeared to have stick swords and were heading off as a group together. One of the groups was close by so Gwendolyn asked what they were doing. "We are going to defeat Nequitia's spies that hide in the woods," they said proudly as they were hurrying off. Gwen said that after the victory that had become a fun make believe pastime for many of the children here.

A little later they saw another group of slightly older children apparently playing the same game, but this group was laughing at a younger girl that was wanting to join in. They said she was too young to keep up with them and that her bow did not work anyway. She was looking very sad and had one small tear running down her cheek as she watched the other children head off without her.

Gwen went up to her and asked to see her bow. Noticing how nicely the ladies were dressed the girl was surprised that someone from the palace would bother to talk to her. She began showing Gwen the bow saying the older children were right it did not work. She had tried to get one of them to help her make a better one, but they were all too busy with their own equipment to bother with her. Gwen asked her what her name was and the girl said it was Fidem. Gwen said it was a pretty name and asked her if she had ever been to the palace. Fidem said no and she was afraid the guards would not grant her entrance in any case. Gwen offered to take her and she said, "Really?.. I would love that!"

Fidem was surprised when the guards did not stop them at the entrance bowing deeply to them instead. As they turned left after a little way heading towards one of the buildings Fidem asked Gwen where they were headed. When Gwen said they were going to the archery range Fidem responded, "Ooh!" Arriving at the range Fidem's eyes widened as she saw several archers practicing. Gwen then noticed a younger archer just finishing her practice and called her over. Gwen asked her if there were any spare small bows appropriate for someone Fidem's size to try. The girl then ran off quickly returning with several bows a quiver and a collection of arrows of different lengths. Gwen thanked her and then took Fidem and the equipment to one of the shortest lanes. The girl remained there watching standing a little behind them as she was curious to see how a person as young as Fidem would do.

Fidem stood there wide eyed as Gwen explained the rudiments of archery to her and had her pick out the bow that was best for her. Choosing the correct length arrows, they put them in the quiver. The target was then moved closer so it would be easier for Fidem who had never held a real bow before. Gwen patiently spent the next hour instructing and encouraging Fidem with her archery. By the end of the lesson Fidem was able to hit the target every time even when the target had been moved a little farther away.

Fidem thanked Gwen for her help and allowing her to use a real bow for once in her life but said it was time for her to get back home. As they were about to depart from the range the young archer approached stopping them introducing herself as Chari and asking if Fidem lived in the palace. Fidem said she wished she did but lived on a farm at the edge of town. Gwen asked why Chari wanted to know. Chari said she had been watching Fidem, was impressed with how well she did in so little time and was hoping that she and Fidem could have started practicing together.

Gwen asked Fidem if she would be able to come every day to practice with Chari and Fidem said she couldn't because she did not have a bow of her own. "You do now," Gwen said as she handed the bow and quiver of arrows to Fidem.

Thanking her and smiling warmly Fidem hugged the bow and quiver of arrows before slinging them onto her back and saying, "I would love to be able to practice every day but will have to check with my mother first."

Leaving the palace grounds Gwen told the guards on duty that Fidem was to be admitted there whenever she wanted to practice her archery. The guards bowed and replied, "Of course, Your Majesty."

As they started walking back towards Fidem's farmhouse Fidem asked in an awed voice, "Who are you ladies and why did the guards address you as 'Your Majesty'?"

Gwendolyn replied with a smile, "Because she is Queen Gwen of the kingdom of Pacem. I am only Princess Gwendolyn and usually only rate the title 'Your Highness'." Fidem immediately stopped dead in her tracks and bowing deeply said, "Oh Your Majesty! Please forgive me! I did not know!" Gwen told her to rise and said that as long as they were not in public she preferred that Fidem just address her as Gwen. Gwendolyn said that she preferred just Gwendolyn as well. Fidem said that if they were sure that was what they wanted she would comply with their request. As they were approaching the farmhouse a woman came out of the door. When the woman saw how the two ladies were dressed she bowed waiting for them to speak. She was afraid that Fidem might have done something to upset them and was trembling a little. Gwen asked Fidem to introduce them.

Fidem said, "This is my mother. Mom this is Queen Gwen and Princess Gwendolyn of Pacem, but they said I should call them Gwen and Gwendolyn if we were not in public."

The woman very nervously replied, "Your Majesties! Please forgive my daughter she must have misunderstood." Speaking quickly to Fidem she said, "Fidem! Bow down! Don't you know that Queen Gwen is the one who defeated Nequitia and freed our entire world?"

Gwen quickly spoke as she saw Fidem getting a frightened expression and bowing instantly, "Fidem I wish for both you and your mother to rise. Madam your daughter did not misunderstand me. It is indeed as she has told you. The three of us have spent a pleasant afternoon at the archery range on the palace grounds."

Explaining that the bow and quiver of arrows now belonged to Fidem Gwen stated that she was allowed to go to the archery range daily to practice with another young archer named Chari. Gwen and Gwendolyn said their goodbyes heading back to town while Fidem began filling her mother in on the details of her incredible day. When Fidem told her mother that it all started with the older kids teasing her about her pretend bow her mother said it had all worked out for the best. She told Fidem with a twinkle in her eye that she bet the other kids would sing a different tune when they saw her going to the royal archery range with a real bow and arrows now!

Fidem's mother then got a wistful expression on her face and remarked, "Fidem you do not realize what we have been granted. Anyone in the kingdom would consider it an honor and privilege to just receive a smile and wave as Queen Gwen passed by, but to have her speak personally to us as well as taking the time to give you an archery lesson is unbelievable! Being on a first name basis with a queen is not something that usually happens to commoners either. And having that queen be Queen Gwen herself is truly a wonder!"

Walking back towards the palace Gwen and Gwendolyn were discussing how long they wanted to spend in Glyka before heading to Vita for a visit there. They planned on stopping back in Glyka before heading back to Pacem in any event so they figured a couple more days right now would be good enough. They spent them wandering about Glyka, exploring a little in the woods outside the city, and just visiting some of the people Gwen had gotten to know on her previous visits.

The day after receiving her bow and quiver of arrows Fidem was heading off to the archery range right after her chores were finished. As she was passing through the streets of town on her way to the palace grounds the group that had teased her the day before was about to start in on her again. Hesitating when they saw the real bow and quiver of arrows she was carrying they started looking at each other with puzzled expressions on their faces. The oldest boy there said incredulously, "Where in the world did she get a real bow and arrows! I wonder where she is heading with them?" They decided to follow her and see what she was up to.

When they got to the entrance of the palace they watched wide eyed as the guards raised their spears and let her through with a nod. Approaching the entrance themselves the guards blocked their way. The oldest boy then asked why Fidem got to go in and they could not. When they heard that Fidem was to be admitted and allowed to practice on the royal archery range by order of Queen Gwen herself they could hardly believe their ears. Since there was nothing else they could do they turned around and slowly headed back to town. As they walked along one of the girls said, "Yesterday she had a pretend bow that wouldn't even work and today she has the real thing. And now Queen Gwen herself gives her permission to practice on the royal archery range! Maybe we made a mistake in thinking her too small."

On their last day in Glyka before heading on to Vita Gwen said she was curious how Fidem and Chari were doing on their practice and was going to the archery range to check. Gwendolyn decided she wanted to come along as well.

Arriving at the range they noticed that there was quite a commotion there with several soldiers running back and forth and quite a bit of shouting going on. One of the soldiers came up to them and told them the danger was over now and that they had nothing to fear. Gwen asked what the trouble had been and the soldier told them that a pack of rabid wolves had burst out of the woods running through the city gates toward the palace. When they arrived there they had attacked the guards at the palace entrance.

"The guards were able to defend the gate killing all but one of the wolves with their spears. One wolf managed to slip through coming here to the archery range." The soldier said he was on duty on the grounds but was on the far side at that time. He said he came over as quickly as he could, but that the wolf had gotten here first. He told them that most of the archers had panicked either running off or just standing frozen on the spot. He said that he was amazed at one very young archer though and was not sure he could have done the same thing himself.

"Walking straight towards the wolf she calmly fitted an arrow on her string, got down on one knee pulling the arrow back to her cheek, and just stayed there waiting. Running straight towards her the wolf jumped. She waited for him to get airborne and then shot him right through the heart! The wolf fell dead at her feet, and she quickly fitted another arrow looking around to see if there were any more wolves. By that time, I had finally gotten to where she was standing, and she told me to watch out in case there were more wolves about. I told her that only the one had gotten through. She then sat down on the ground and started trembling. That's her over there in the yellow dress."

Going over to check on the girl Gwen and Gwendolyn recognized her as Fidem with Gwen greeting her warmly and asking if she was alright. Fidem said she was fine, but now that the wolf was dead she realized how much danger she had been in. "Your Majesty, I wasn't thinking about it then, but now I can't stop shaking."

"That was a very brave thing you did! I felt the same way after meeting Nequitia, but because of the trouble in the dungeon I kept going and was able to get over the feeling more gradually. Just sit still for a while longer and it will eventually pass."

At this point King Firinne came up to the group and spoke, "The guards just reported the incident to me explaining that they killed all the wolves but one. When they came here they saw he was dead and immediately came and gave me their report." Turning to the soldier standing there he said, "I see that neither Queen Gwen nor Princess Gwendolyn has their bow with them, so I guess I have you to thank for killing the wolf. Excellent job soldier! Who knows how many people would have been killed or maimed if you had not acted so quickly?"

The soldier began pointing at Fidem. "It wasn't me Your Majesty! It was this young lady here and a braver or truer shot I have never seen in my life!" The soldier then described what Fidem had done and that everyone else had either panicked or frozen even though they were older and more experienced archers than she was.

Gwendolyn noticed a large soldier rapidly approaching, mentioning it to King Firinne. When King Firinne saw that it was General Hapsom he greeted him ardently. General Hapsom began excitedly, "Where is the archer who shot the wolf? I have been looking for the longest time for one to be part of the elite palace guard corps. The brave archers can't hit the target, and the accurate ones freeze under pressure. This one sounds ideal to me! When I heard what a witness to the event told me I said to myself, 'I need that archer!' "

Speaking up with a smile on her face Gwen said, "I am afraid I have some bad news for you general. It appears that the witness failed to mention the archer's age." Gwen then introduced Fidem to General Hapsom.

General Hapsom said that it was indeed unfortunate for his present need that Fidem was so young, but he asked if she could be transferred from whatever her present position was to the elite palace guard corps anyway. He did not want to lose the opportunity of having her join the elite palace guard corps when she was older. The general was afraid she would be sought out by someone else before then and the opportunity would be lost. He said she could be apprenticed to one of his archery instructors and eventually become part of the active guard corps when she was old enough. Explaining that she did not live in the palace Fidem said she only came to practice archery here at the range. Gwen then told how she and Gwendolyn had met Fidem filling the king and general in on her story.

Asking King Firinne if he could speak with him privately for a few minutes General Hapsom was pointing to a nearby building and the two of them stepped inside conversing for a short while. When they came out they asked Fidem if she would be willing to move into the palace to become an elite guard apprentice if her mother approved. Fidem asked if she would be able to visit her home on occasion if she moved into the palace. They assured her she would, so she agreed to the plan excitedly picking up her bow and arrows. One of the palace officials then approached Fidem and bowed to her presenting her with the arrow she had shot the wolf with. Accepting it reverently, she thanked him. King Firinne then departed while General Hapsom and Fidem exchanged questions and answers about her new position. The general then asked her to accompany him to the armory for a few minutes and told her that they would be coming right back.

Returning a short while later Fidem was wearing the uniform of the elite palace guards and General Hapsom said that he had remembered having several smaller uniforms that were used for an anniversary of the guards' ceremony a few years ago. The children whose parents were guards were given uniforms as well and there was a huge parade through the town at that time. One of the uniforms had fit Fidem perfectly.

When a trumpet sounded near the palace entrance General Hapsom bid farewell to Gwen and Gwendolyn leading Fidem out to the gate. The royal carriage was waiting for them with King Firinne already inside. General Hapsom and Fidem joined him and the general helped Fidem into the carriage and seated her next to the king. He then sat on the other side of Fidem with the carriage slowly making its way through the town and out to Fidem's farmhouse. Fidem felt very nervous being seated right next to the king, so she just sat quietly looking straight ahead.

As the carriage was pulling up in front of the farmhouse and the trumpet was sounded again Fidem's mother came out bowing deeply. She asked what she could do to be of service to the king. King Firinne asked if she would be gracious enough to allow Fidem to move into the palace and become one of the elite palace guards. Her eyes widened as she recognized that the young guard seated next to the king was actually her daughter! She said of course she would, but could not understand why Fidem, who was so young and a mere farm girl, would be asked to fill such an exalted position. When King Firinne himself explained about Fidem's bravery in protecting all the people at the archery range her mother said she certainly had a daughter she could be proud of but would miss having her around. When she was told Fidem would be allowed to visit at times she thanked him graciously. The royal carriage and party then headed back to the palace while Fidem and her mother were entering the farmhouse.

Fidem then filled her mother in with all the details of her exciting day.

Fidem's mother slowly shook her head saying, "A few days ago Queen Gwen stops by our farmhouse and speaks kindly to us and now you show up in the royal carriage sitting next to King Firinne himself! He then asks if you can join the elite palace guards and explains that you killed a wolf to protect a whole group of people. I truly wonder what the future holds for you!"

Meeting the dragons at dinner time Gwen and Gwendolyn asked what they had been up to. They said that they had relaxed and visited with a few people Dreki knew over the last couple of days, but that they had been busy for most of today. Explaining that when they heard about the wolf attack they started checking with animals in the woods nearby to see if there were any more around. The animals told them no and that the wolf pack had come from the north. Dreki and Hratt then flew quite a way in that direction checking with animals now and then along the route. They found out that the wolf pack had originally come from a small range of mountains farther to the north, but that they were the only wolves around and no other animals had been infected with rabies. Reporting their findings to King Firinne they had made their way here just in time for supper. The rest of the meal was enjoyed with conversation mostly concerning their trip to Vita on the following day.

Enjoying a leisurely breakfast, they said goodbye to several of their friends before departing. Since they would be stopping back again in Glyka the goodbyes were not of a lengthy nature. Because they were riding dragons and not hiking on foot the trip was accomplished in a very short time rather than the two-day hike. Arriving late in the morning they were heartily greeted as they crossed the draw bridge and headed into the castle grounds. News of their arrival apparently passed on fairly quickly as they had not proceeded very far before they were met by King Kelan and Queen Rachel. After introductions and hugs all around the travelers were invited to join the king and queen for lunch.

Finishing their lunch the king and queen asked if the travelers would like a tour. They realized that Gwen and Dreki would not see much that was new, but they knew Gwendolyn and Hratt had never been to Vita before. All of them said they would like the tour and Gwen and Dreki said they might be able to answer questions relating to the battle. Gwendolyn asked if they could possibly go to the clearing in the woods to the north and then trace Gwen's battle route from there. They all thought this was a good plan but explained to Hratt that the dragons would miss the part where Gwen went through the beginning passages through the castle as they were too narrow for the dragons to fit in them.

Arriving in the clearing, Gwendolyn and Hratt admired the commemoration plaque that was set up there before starting towards the castle. Gwen reminded them that the path they were on was not there on the day of the battle and that she had to make her way through the trees. They stopped in the clearing next to the moat looking at that plaque also. Gwen pointed out the spot where she crossed the moat and scaled the wall before proceeding with them to the front of the castle. Crossing the drawbridge and entering the castle proper, they proceeded down the main corridor towards the throne room stopping when they reached the intersecting passage Gwen had come on. The dragons waited there while the rest of the party headed backwards the way Gwen had entered until they were on the inside of the wall Gwen had scaled. Here they began tracing her route through the passages with Gwen narrating what happened along the way. Gwen also pointed out a crack in the outer wall as they were traversing the first passage. Explaining that all the rest of the walls had been repaired she said that since this was where the mouse had entered for his spying mission it had been left as a memorial reminder. She did mention that the crack was sealed on the outside of the wall to prevent drafts or the entrance of any unwanted pests. They met up with the dragons finishing the rest of the battle route with them.

They then allowed King Kelan and Queen Rachel to guide them for the rest of the tour.

Leaving the orphanage, which was the last stop on their tour, they heard the cry of an eagle above them. At least it sounded like a cry to Gwen and Gwendolyn, but it was clearly a greeting to King Kelan and Queen Rachel who called out to him. He slowly glided down landing in the courtyard. After bowing and addressing the king and queen the three of them continued conversing for several minutes before the eagle bowed again and then flew off.

King Kelan then spoke to Gwen, Gwendolyn and the dragons telling them that the eagle had brought some rather disturbing news. Apparently there was trouble in the lands much further to the west. Unfortunately, since the eagle was unable to understand regular human speech he was not able to supply any specific details. He was able to inform them that there was a group of forest dwellers living between here and where the trouble was located. He said that they might be able to tell them what the trouble was. If not there was a small country about another day westward that was much closer to where the trouble was. They would almost certainly have details. Discussing this further it was decided that the best plan was to have the travelers head further west and try to find out more from the forest dwellers. Since the trip there and back could possibly take several weeks the travelers thought it was best to head back to Glyka for supplies before making the journey.

Arriving in Glyka in the late afternoon they met with King Firinne giving him a quick update. He suggested that they make use of the medium dining chamber for supper and to discuss plans. Eating their dinner, they talked about what they might need for their trip and King Firinne said he would have all the needed supplies gathered the following day. They spent the rest of the evening in more pleasant conversation. The following day all the supplies were packed and ready for departure early the next day with the travelers heading to bed a little earlier than they had been doing so they would be fresh for an early start in the morning.

5

Westward Journey

AFTER a hearty breakfast the travelers were on their way again. Since the speed the dragons were flying was close to that of the eagle they had a fair idea of how far it would be to the forest dwellers and then on to the trouble as they continued westward. After their usual one day stop in Vita the travelers continued their journey once more. They knew they could not get to the forest dwellers in a day but just kept flying steadily westward at a good pace. As they were traveling Gwendolyn remarked that it was too bad they were on a mission rather than just sight-seeing, as they were passing some low mountains to their left that were particularly beautiful. The mountains had a little snow on the peaks with many pines from where the tree line started down to the base. At the base there were several types of deciduous trees and a few grassy meadows with wildflowers growing in them. There was a mountain stream that started high enough up the mountain that it was in the snowy portion at the top. This stream went a short way before falling in a cascade straight down a sheer face of the mountain for several hundred feet. It ended in a bubbling pool at the base of the mountain and from there emerged as a gentle stream again flowing on through the meadows. Sighing, Gwendolyn said it was interesting how different things were beautiful in different ways. The volcano's beauty had been exciting and invigorating while this waterfall and stream were peaceful and relaxing.

Since it was nearing noon they decided on stopping for lunch where they could at least enjoy the waterfall's beauty while they ate. Finishing lunch, Gwen suggested that they get going before the relaxing sound of the waterfall put her to sleep. They all agreed and were soon on their way again but were a little sad to have to leave the peaceful spot behind. Passing over some grassy plains that were not near as extensive as the ones to the east of Dartan they were not lulled into tiredness by seeing the same terrain for hours. After the plains came an area of mixed woodlands, grassy pastures and rolling hills with rivers and streams running through them occasionally. By the time the sun was setting, and it was time to set up camp for the night and have their supper, the terrain had changed to almost entirely woodlands. Climbing slightly so they could spot a clearing large enough to camp in for the night they saw several not-too-distant ones, but these were a way to their left and right. Seeing one farther away, but directly in front of them they started making their way to that one landing in the dim dusky light shortly after sundown.

Setting up camp quickly before the light was entirely gone they then sat around the campfire enjoying their supper and talking over the interesting things they had seen so far on their trip. From the eagle's description they expected to reach the forest dwellers' area in a few more days. They might get there in the early afternoon of the third day, but certainly not before then. They decided that they would have to start actively looking after their noon meal on that day. After the evening meal they talked for a short while but soon were settling down for the night.

Breaking camp after breakfast they were on their way again. Crossing a small range of low mountains about midmorning they stopped around noon in a meadow on some hilly ground on the far side. Resuming their journey after their meal was over they varied their altitude throughout their afternoon flight in the hopes of being able to more easily locate one of the forest dwellers' camps. Seeing what appeared to be smoke from several fires ahead and a little to their left about mid-afternoon they adjusted their course accordingly.

Reaching the source of the smoke fairly quickly they found it to be coming from the chimneys of several huts. The huts were nestled in the woods and there were no clearings to land in nearby. Climbing slightly higher they circled the area checking it out. Noticing a path heading away from the huts that was wide enough for the dragons to walk on Dreki remarked that it was not wide enough for them to land.

They decided to follow the path for a while to see where it led. The path appeared to be a lengthy one, but only a short way down it there was a fairly large clearing with several gardens in it and with sufficient open space to land as well as to set up a camp for the night. Making their landing in the clearing they then started heading back down the path towards the huts they had seen. Nearing the huts they could hear the sound of children playing. Once they got close enough to see the huts and the children playing nearby Gwen called out her usual greeting waiting there for someone to answer. The children stopped playing, entering the nearest hut. A woman then emerged and stated that they were the first visitors they had seen at that group of huts wondering why they had come to such a remote area.

Explaining that they were from far to the east Gwen told her that they had heard of trouble in the Western lands. They were hoping to find out more about the trouble and if there was anything they could do to help. The woman said she was not aware of the trouble, but being so isolated she never got news from elsewhere in any case.

Gwen then asked if the woman knew where there was a larger settlement of forest dwellers that may have received news. Explaining that there was a very large group of forest dwellers almost due west of them the woman said she was not sure how far it was. A few years ago, several of the men in the group had decided the settlement there was too large for their liking and had taken their families and moved away.

Dividing into groups of three or four families each the smaller groups had headed off in different directions. The group she was part of had finally settled here after wandering about and camping in a few nearby areas for a while. This one was finally chosen because it had good hunting and a clear stream not too far away.

Thanking her Gwen and her fellow travelers then headed back down the path to the clearing. By the time they reached it evening was approaching and they decided to set up camp for the night in the clearing and then start heading westward again in the morning. They knew that with the gardens there a source of water must be pretty close. Locating it fairly quickly they soon had their supper cooking while they were planning the next day's travels. Since they were looking for a larger settlement they figured a higher altitude would be better for spotting it. They were now in an area comprised almost entirely of dense woods so they had no idea if they would be finding any suitable landing areas before they reached the forest dweller settlement.

This was a very dangerous situation to be in. If they could not find a clearing and got too tired to fly further they would be forced to make a crash landing in the thick woods. Even if they escaped major injury they would be unable to get back into the air until they found a large enough clearing for the dragons to be able to take off from. It was unlikely that one would be found without extreme difficulty and much lost time. Also, there was the very real danger of running out of food. As they were flying they would have to be constantly searching for landing sites. They would have to remember how far back it was to the last one at all times. If they started getting fatigued or too much time had passed they would have to backtrack to the last landing site rather than take a chance they might find one ahead of them.

They got an early start the next day to allow them the maximum hours of daylight for flying. Flying over dense woods all morning and even a little into the afternoon they finally found a clearing to land in. They stopped there eating a late lunch. Heading off westward again they were hoping to find another landing site before it got too late. Flying for about half the time between when they ate lunch and sundown they had seen nothing but the dense woods below them. Dreki told them he was going to try flying higher to see if anything could be spotted and if not they would have to head back to where they ate lunch. Unfortunately, nothing was visible, even flying at a higher altitude, so they headed back with disappointment to their last landing spot. Getting there just around sundown and making up their camp for the night it was a gloomy group sitting around the campfire that evening. They were all hoping that if they got a fresh start at sunup in the morning they would be able to reach another clearing before noon. If not they would again try climbing higher to get a better view.

Eating a hurried breakfast and breaking camp quickly they got started a little before sunup. The early start gave them hope that they would have better luck that day. When noon arrived without any clearing being sighted even after climbing higher, they ended up turning back once again to the last clearing. By the time they got there it was a little after sundown, and they were then kept busy setting up camp once again in the dim dusky light.

During the meal different ideas were suggested and discussed since the normal plans had not worked for them. Dreki suggested that he could try going alone that way more distance could be covered before being forced to retreat again. If there was a clearing slightly farther that they had not gotten to, he might be able to see it going a longer distance.

Another suggestion was that the dragons go alone with one heading west-northwest and the other west-southwest. If something was found they may be able to set a course like a sailing vessel tacking back and forth into the wind. A final suggestion came up when Gwendolyn commented on how beautiful the moonrise was as they were sitting around the fire talking. Dreki then said that since it was a bright full moon and the sky was clear there would be enough light for them to travel at night. If they got a few hours of sleep and left at midnight they would get about three extra hours of flight time added before they had to be turning back. The other advantage of leaving at night would be that the part of the trip during the night had already been carefully checked. They would not be getting to the new territory until well after sunrise. They all agreed that this last plan was what they should try and if it failed they could try the tacking option. Since the dragons needed sleep more than the riders Gwen and Gwendolyn traded off keeping watch while the dragons slept. Gwendolyn woke everyone at midnight, and they broke camp heading west once more. Gwen had suggested that if she and Gwendolyn tied themselves to the saddles they could possibly get a little sleep during the night portion of the flight. Everybody thought this was a good idea and so it was implemented as well. Both of the ladies got a few hours of sleep this way. It was not as refreshing as uninterrupted normal sleep, but it did help some. After passing the farthest spot they had reached so far everyone started looking more carefully for a landing spot.

The time was approaching when they would have to turn back again if they had not found something. They had been skipping all meals that day so that the time was spent searching rather than on the ground. When they had gotten as far as they dared still not seeing anything the dragons started making their usual climb.

Suddenly Gwen said, "Oh! What is that ahead and slightly to the right? That patch of ground looks much lighter than the rest."

Dreki replied, "It is not much farther, and I think we should check it out."

Getting closer they could all see that it was indeed a clearing large enough to land in and set up camp for the night. They were congratulating each other as they were gliding in for the landing and Gwendolyn remarked that this was a great spot as there was even a stream at the edge of it. Quickly setting up camp they had a large meal even though it was in the middle of the day. They figured on having a lighter meal that evening. They were all tired and decided not to try and get any farther that day, but just to get well rested and start heading out again the following day.

They did a little exploring that afternoon and were rewarded by finding a bunch of puffballs. They broke one open discovering that the inside was still moist and white. Gathering enough to sauté for their evening meal the travelers continued looking around for a short while but did not discover anything else of interest. They spent a relaxing afternoon heading to bed early after their supper of delicious, sautéed puffballs.

Rising early after a good night's sleep and eating a substantial breakfast, the camping gear was packed up, and they were on their way again. Finding another clearing just after noon they stopped there for lunch. After continuing for a few more hours, they noticed several smoke columns ahead and off to their right. Altering their course they started heading for the smoke columns. They were still a fair distance away but could see evidence of a large clearing slightly to the left of the smoke columns. Approaching the clearing they noticed several separate garden plots in the cleared area. This gave them hope that they had either found the main group of forest dwellers or at least a large secondary group.

Noting which path led from the clearing to the smoke columns they then made their landing in the clearing. Assuming that the smoke columns came from the homes of the forest dwellers they started heading down the path in that direction. They could hear children playing and adults talking before they could see the homes. When the homes came into view they noted that they were fair sized cabins and much nicer than the huts they had seen earlier. Also, these cabins seemed to have a cleared area around them like a yard rather than being nestled right amongst the trees.

Emerging from the path into an open area they saw a group of several people conversing. One of the men noticed them calling out to them in greeting. They went over introducing themselves and telling them where they had come from. One of the men introduced himself as Rogan and told them he was the leader of the settlement. He said he was amazed that they had been able to make the long journey as he knew there were few places a dragon could make a landing along the way. Dreki then related the difficulties they had encountered and that it had taken them longer than they had been hoping to get there. Rogan said he was surprised they had persevered and was wondering why they went through so much trouble as there was nothing in the forest dwellers' location of particular value or interest to attract people from so far away. Dreki then explained what the eagle had told him asking if Rogan had any details to add.

Rogan said that the forest dwellers were not worried about their settlement as there was nothing there of interest to outsiders. He said he did not think there was much danger for Dreki's kingdom either being located so far away, but that he would give whatever information he had in any case. Dreki thanked him with Rogan proceeding to fill the travelers in with the information he had. He said that a little further west was the small peaceful land of Socair and beyond that across a deep gorge with a river at the bottom was the kingdom of Relitto. Relitto was ruled by a man named Sordibus who was very cruel and despotic. Rogan could not give him any details, but he said that the inhabitants of Socair should know more being much closer to Relitto. He remarked that the forest ended with the landscape changing dramatically not much further to the west. At that point there was a wide highway going all the way through Socair from the forest to the capital city on the other side. The capital city of Maith was just this side of the gorge. Maith was the only city in the country with the rest of the people living either in smaller villages or on single farmsteads.

Thanking Rogan for the information Dreki and the rest of the travelers headed back down the path to the clearing they had landed in. Here they set up camp for the evening and began preparing their supper. While eating they were discussing the following day's plans. They figured that they would be able to reach the capital of Socair around noon if they got a normal start in the morning. Even if they didn't it would not be a problem as they would be out of the dense forest and have the wide road to land in if they did not find a clearing or open ground. They were able to enjoy conversation later into the evening than they had been able to do lately, but eventually all were sleeping soundly.

Finishing up a leisurely breakfast they proceeded to break camp heading westward towards Socair. It was not long before the landscape underwent the dramatic change Rogan had spoken to them about. At this point they started climbing higher to be able to have a better chance to see the highway passing through the country from east to west spotting it immediately about a mile to their south. Adjusting their direction slightly they would be intersecting it within about an hour rather than heading straight south to get to it immediately.

The landscape they were flying over looked particularly beautiful to them especially after seeing nothing but dense woods for so long. They could see a fairly wide river to their left which seemed to end abruptly a few miles away. Where it ended there was a large amount of mist in the air, and they were guessing that there was a good sized waterfall at that point. They were sorry they did not have the time to check it out but decided that it would be worth looking at if they were not on an important mission. On their right they could see a few grassy rolling hills covered with wildflowers of several different hues. Ahead of them they could see some forests, but these were broken up by meadows, lakes and even some marshy areas.

They were commenting to each other as they noticed different things of beauty as they continued their westward journey. It was not long before they were flying directly above the east-west road through the country. There were plenty of open spaces to land in, so they picked a nice grassy meadow

with some shade trees in it for their lunch stop. Enjoying a
leisurely lunch, they were on their way again in the afternoon.

After about another hour of flying they could see the city
of Maith ahead of them. Landing in the road just this side
of the eastern gate, a few minutes later they began leisurely
walking into the city. It was very similar to Glyka in that there
were several shops along the streets, and the people seemed
to be going about their daily routines in a normal manner.
Gwen asked a lady that they were passing where news about
the trouble in the West could be obtained. The lady told her
there was an inn a little further down the main road near the
center of town called the Traveler's Rest. There was always
a friendly group gathered in the large common room in the
evening discussing the latest events. Thanking her Gwen and
the rest of the travelers headed down the street towards the
inn.

6

What was Learned in Maith

————————

Arriving at the Traveler's Rest Gwen and Gwendolyn went inside to see about getting a room for the night and if anything could be done for the dragons. The ladies' room was easily taken care of, but when the proprietor was asked about dragon accommodations he said there had never been dragons in that area, so he had no rooms for dragons. Asking about a stable or barn the man told Gwen that there was a stable for guest's horses, and he had a large barn of his own further back on the property. Asking him to accompany her outside to meet the dragons Gwen led the way and as soon as he saw them he said that the stables would be way too small. Offering the barn, he said it would just be a layer of hay on the ground and that the dragons needed to promise him they would not set the barn on fire.

Dreki assured him that the accommodations would both be acceptable and remain intact. The travelers then went to the barn and began unpacking their traveling gear leaving it there while they explored the town. Finding a restaurant with outdoor seating they noticed a couple of tables off by themselves with open spaces next to them. Dinner was ordered and they enjoyed it while waiting for the evening to arrive. Heading back to the inn once night fell Dreki and Hratt went to the barn and waited as Gwen and Gwendolyn said they would come to tell them what they found out that evening in the common room.

Making their way to the common room Gwen and Gwendolyn joined the discussion there. The townsfolk were surprised to find out how far the travelers had come and were curious why they made the effort. Gwen spoke up and told them they had heard reports of trouble further west in Relitto and were hoping to get as much information as possible in that regard. Several people made comments which prompted questions and after getting answers to those and some other questions that came up Gwen and Gwendolyn ended up learning quite a bit about what was going on in Relitto. Thanking the townsfolk they headed off to the barn. The dragons were waiting for them asking if they had been able to get some useful information or not. Gwen assured them that due to Socair being so close they were able to get a fair amount of detail about the situation. Several of the people in the common room had known some of those individuals who had been in Relitto before it had gotten to its present evil state. They were able to provide rough details about the layout of the Island Citadel as it was called as well as general information about the rest of the kingdom west of the river. Once Sordibus' rule was well established, changing things drastically there, the people were no longer free to come and go as they pleased.

Explaining that other than the Island Citadel the rest of the kingdom was entirely west of the river and gorge Gwen continued updating the dragons. It was pretty much like Socair in that it had villages and farmsteads but was despotically ruled by Sordibus. The Island Citadel was named for the fact that the deep gorge with the river running at the bottom split into two gorges for about a quarter of a mile and then converged back into one. This left an almost round "island" of land about a quarter of a mile in diameter. In the center there was a large castle which Sordibus used as his headquarters. He had a substantial armed force there and both lived and ruled from there.

Like Nequitia he had guards pacing the fortress walls day and night as well. Unlike Nequitia he also had guards continually walking around the outside perimeter of the fortress. There were watchtowers on the four corners of the citadel, two facing east and two facing west, that were always manned. Lookouts were posted there to make sure there was no attempt at rebellion from his own kingdom or threat of attack from the east. There were two suspension bridges spanning the wide gorge beside the citadel one going east towards Socair and one going west into Relitto. Each of these had a guard always posted in a small shack on the citadel side of the bridge about halfway between the gorge and the citadel. There was no way of approaching the citadel from either direction without being seen.

Gwen had also discovered that Sordibus was the much older brother of Nequitia. Unlike Nequitia Sordibus was content as dictator of his own lands and had no ambition for conquest. His armed force was strictly to ensure his rule was unchallenged. He did not have a scepter to enslave people, so he had to use other means of safeguarding the loyalty of his forces. This was accomplished by imprisoning the soldiers' families in the dungeon. Unlike Nequitia's dungeons where the prisoners were barely fed and the conditions deplorable Sordibus was employing a different tactic. He had the prisoners housed in a very large room so there were quite a few people there. They were well fed clothed and had access to bathing and sanitary facilities. The catch was that there was a special cage with an iron grid with spikes beneath it held up on the top with chains. If a soldier displeased Sordibus he would move that soldier's family into the cage slowly lowering the grid until the spikes impaled the prisoners below. This cage was in the courtyard of the citadel, and all the soldiers had to watch and listen to the screams. The grid was then raised and the process repeated with the offending soldier in the cage. Sordibus had only done this once and had not had any loyalty problems after that.

If you are wondering why the soldiers did not just turn on Sordibus, he had a squad of bodyguards with him constantly. They had come with him when he had originally taken over the citadel at the age of sixteen. They were the ones who would put the family and afterwards the soldier into the cage.

They also had orders to slaughter the dungeon prisoners at the first sign of rebellion. The soldiers knew there were enough of them to outnumber and defeat the bodyguards, but not before some of the bodyguards had killed many if not all the prisoners in the dungeon. The soldiers were not willing to take the chance of losing their families in a revolt.

The travelers all agreed that the situation in Relitto was bad; the discussion then turning to what could be done about it. It did not seem possible to get any sized military force to Socair and even then an attack on Relitto would be hard to accomplish knowing Sordibus' defenses. They realized that if a large force came from Socair all Sordibus had to do was to cut the bridge loose and there would be no way of approaching him no matter how large or strong the force was. The width of the gorge was sufficient to prevent either arrows or projectiles from catapults reaching the fortress.

Getting an idea Gwen excused herself to go back to the common room for a minute to get some more information. Saying it would be quicker to just go get it; she did not take the time explaining it first. She was back in a very short time smiling broadly at them all. She said it would be good to get as close a look at the fortress as they could so she began by asking if there was anything right next to the gorge that would give a person a reason to be there. Someone told her there was a purple wildflower growing there this time of year and it was not unusual for people to be gathering bunches of them to put in their houses. They were quite pretty and had an unusually soothing fragrance. Gwen suggested that she and Gwendolyn go and pick some around mid-morning the following day. At that time the sunlight should be optimal for viewing from the east giving them the best conditions to observe the Island Citadel. All agreed that this was a good idea and would probably be best before trying to figure anything out. Deciding to head to bed the ladies said they would come get the dragons in the morning so they could get breakfast at the restaurant with the outdoor tables.

Finishing breakfast, the ladies went to do some window shopping before picking flowers with the dragons deciding to fly a few miles upstream and check out the gorge there. Gwendolyn noticed a pair of binoculars in one of the shops and bought them to get a better view of things on the opposite side of the gorge.

Dreki and Hratt discovered that the sides of the gorge were almost straight up and down with virtually no slope to them at all. The gorge was wide and appeared to be several hundred feet in depth. At the bottom the river was running in the center of the gorge and was about a third of the width leaving a nice bank on both sides. Due to the depth of the gorge and the wall's steepness they knew that the bottom of the gorge would not be visible from the top unless someone was standing right on the edge. This meant that as long as they were flying close to the Island Citadel side of the gorge by the island they would not be seen by Sordibus' scouts no matter what altitude they were flying at.

Gwen and Gwendolyn found many bushes with purple flowers to choose from. By getting down behind a large bush right on the edge of the gorge to do their picking they were able to observe the entire opposite side of the gorge through the binoculars but concentrated on the island and citadel. Trading off the jobs of picking and viewing between them they had a nice bunch of flowers picked as well as valuable information gathered in about 20 minutes.

Meeting the dragons for lunch each group shared what they had found out. It appeared that a scouting flight of the island was possible if desired as long as the flight was made close to the wall of the gorge on the island side. Gwen had noticed what looked like it might be a cave opening not too far north of the bridge and about a quarter of the way down the side of the gorge. She thought it might be worth checking out; she and Dreki deciding to give it a try that afternoon.

Flying far enough north that they would not be seen entering the gorge they made their way from there back towards the Island Citadel flying close to the bottom of the gorge. Getting to the island they were hugging the side of it in the gorge nearest Socair flying at a height about a quarter of the way down from the top. Decreasing their speed to the slowest possible rate they would now be able to get the best view of the suspected cave. The opening was larger than Gwen had thought it would be from her observation and there was plenty of room for them to land. Landing easily in the large space available they discovered that the opening only went back for about 30 feet and then stopped. The floor was nice and flat, and the cave appeared to be just one large almost round chamber very similar to Dreki's cave.

On further inspection Gwen found a passage leading from this large chamber further into the side of the island and heading roughly in the direction of the citadel on top. The passage was large enough for Gwen to stand up in, but far too small for Dreki to enter. Deciding that Dreki would remain in the large chamber Gwen would start exploring the passage further. Lighting the torch they had brought along she started down the passage. The passage made several very slight bends, but the overall direction was towards the citadel. The passage was dry with a fairly flat floor remaining large enough for Gwen to walk down it easily. The air smelled fresh, so Gwen was guessing that there was an exit at the other end of the passage rather than it just coming to a dead end.

After a few minutes Gwen could dimly see something across the passage a little way ahead stopping where she was to listen for a bit. She could hear nothing from where she was, so she started walking slowly forwards. As she got closer she noticed what looked like bars similar to a jail cell blocking the passage. Reaching the bars she again stopped to listen. She thought she could barely hear some very faint sounds coming from further down the passage so apparently the passage continued for quite a way past the bars. Seeing a slight movement on the floor just within the dim light where her torch was barely illuminating it she remained quiet and motionless waiting to see if she would get a better view. Suddenly she saw a rat coming towards her scooting along the edge of the wall. He did not get far; a cat quickly pouncing on him. The rat squealed loudly just before being killed by the cat. Gwen realized that a mouse would not last long as a spy here.

Taking her torch, she began carefully examining the bars. They appeared to be attached to one side of the passage by hinges allowing the bars to be swung open like a gate or door. Unfortunately, the gate was locked on the other side of the passage and not by what looked like a jail cell door lock. There was a long metal bar going back down the side of the passage towards the citadel for about six feet. The end of this bar was then padlocked to a ring in the wall of the passage. There was no way of Gwen reaching the padlock from the side of the gate she was on so it could not be opened from her side even if she had a key.

The passage was not a true rectangle like a normal door frame leaving irregular gaps around the edges. Gwen checked to see if squeezing through any of them was possible. Most were way too small, but there was one between the gate and wall on the hinge side that looked like a possibility. After trying for several minutes Gwen came to the disappointing realization that the gap was too narrow for her to squeeze through no matter how she manipulated herself in trying. It would require someone much smaller than herself to be able to get past the gate. She headed back to the cave chamber to tell Dreki about her findings. She and Dreki then flew back to Socair reuniting with the other two travelers.

Discussing their findings over dinner it was felt by all that there was nothing further they could do presently. Since Sordibus was not planning a conquest there was no threat to either Socair or the regions further east. The travelers still wanted to do something to help free the people of Relitto from Sordibus' despotic rule but felt it best to get council first.

Deciding to make the long trip back to Glyka and see if they could obtain council from them as well as those from Vita they were hoping to come up with a plan for coming to the aid of the people of Relitto.

Knowing the return route and how to deal with the difficult parts the return trip was made in less than a week with a stop in Vita first. Conferring with King Kelan and Queen Rachel they asked them if they would be able to send a delegation of counselors to Glyka to help find a solution to the problem. The travelers were assured that the Vita group would be in Glyka within two days. The travelers then flew on to Glyka informing King Firinne of the need for the council. The council was planned for three days from then, so the travelers spent the remainder of the day by resting that afternoon having a good dinner and retiring early.

The next two days were spent resting from the journey and visiting with friends in Glyka. By the evening of the second day all the counselors had arrived from Vita and been given rooms in the palace. The travelers were well rested from their trip and everyone was ready for the council meeting to be held in the morning.

7

Council in Glyka

ENTERING the council chamber with the rest of the travelers Gwen was surprised to see Fidem posted beside the door as a messenger guard if needed. Greeting her warmly Gwen congratulated her on her position. Telling Gwen that since she was not part of a normal guard squad with regular assigned duties Fidem was explaining that she had asked if she could be given assignments as special needs arose if she was considered qualified for them. Gwen and Fidem spent some time conversing for a while as the other council members were arriving and Gwen then made her way to her seat at the table with Fidem posting herself next to the door in case she was needed as a messenger.

When the council was convened it was a much more cheerful group than when they had to deal with Nequitia. Since there was no direct threat or prophecy to be fulfilled there was not the pressure that they had all felt the last time. They started by having Gwen give a full report of the situation in Relitto with the counselors then asking questions of the travelers so that all those present had a clear idea of the situation and would be better able to suggest solutions to the problem at hand. The entire council agreed that to make any decision, conditions beyond the locked gate would have to be known. General Hapsom said that the smallest soldiers in the army were larger than Gwen and he was at a loss to know what to do. None of the other counselors had any suggestions either with everyone's face taking on a gloomy expression.

Suddenly they heard a voice by the door say, "If I am small enough I would be glad to volunteer and I offer my service to the kingdom." Looking over towards the door they all saw that Fidem had stepped from her position beside the door and was now kneeling directly in front of it holding her sword out to the king with both her hands.

General Hapsom called Fidem over to the council table speaking to her as she was approaching, "Corporal Fidem we thank you for the offer of your service. We are not sure you fully understand the dangers involved so we wish you to join the council. Questions will be asked and answered by both you and the council until we all come to a complete understanding of what is involved and the possible risks. At that time, you will be asked if you still wish to volunteer and the choice will be entirely up to you."

The questions and answers went back and forth for some time, but in the end General Hapsom said he had no objection as head of the armed forces. None of the other counselors had any objections so they were just waiting for Fidem to make her decision. She said without hesitation that she considered it an honor to be able to serve in this way and was ready to depart immediately if necessary.

Fidem was then asked to have a seat with the other counselors so the objectives of her mission could be ironed out. There was some debate about whether she should go alone or be accompanied. It was felt that having an accomplice would probably be an advantage with Gwen volunteering and being accepted for that role. They decided the first thing Fidem needed to do was to get past the gate. After that there was some discussion as to whether she should attempt finding a key and unlocking the gate for Gwen or just keep exploring further on her own. Someone suggested that she could make a quick search for the key and if it was not found nearby then proceed on her own. This plan was agreed to by all.

The trip itself was then brought up and Gwen said that checking with Dreki would be necessary to find out if he could carry both passengers and their supplies or if a second dragon was needed. Some flight training for Fidem would be needed in either case, but less if Dreki was carrying both passengers. Gwen said she would check with Dreki and be getting back to the council with a report. The council was then dismissed until the afternoon with Gwen and Fidem heading off to find Dreki.

Walking along Gwen asked Fidem if she still practiced her archery. Fidem said that her responsibilities as an elite palace guard did not give her the opportunity for daily practice with Chari like she did before. They were able to practice together on Saturday afternoons, but not during the week. General Hapsom had been busy with other responsibilities and had not gotten around to assigning an instructor to her yet. Fidem said that she needed daily practice to keep improving her skills, so she had been getting up early to get in about 30 minutes of practice every workday before her duties started. She also said that she was making use of evening time off and moonlit nights to do practice as well. Gwen remarked that she was impressed with Fidem's dedication and resourcefulness in figuring out how to get practice time into her schedule. Gwen said that as part of the training for the trip she would make sure that Fidem got archery practice time as well.

They soon found Dreki and he said that carrying two passengers and supplies for them all would not be a problem. He pointed out the fact that the craftsmen would have to make a special saddle for two riders with the three of them heading to the craftsmen's workshop. Once they got there the craftsmen made some measurements on the riders and spoke with Dreki for a few minutes. They said they would have a saddle ready for the trip in two days. Dreki thanked the craftsmen with the three of them heading off to the dining area for lunch.

Enjoying a leisurely meal Dreki explained some of the aspects of dragon riding to Fidem and that she would need at least minimal flight training to get her body used to the movements of them flying through the air. Fidem asked that since the double saddle would not be ready for two days could she not use the regular saddle during that time to get used to some of the more basic movements. She realized that the regular saddle might be a little large for her but felt that the experience gained would be worth dealing with the awkwardness of the size.

Gwen and Dreki both thought this was an excellent suggestion as the time she would be spending in the saddle during the initial flights would be minimal anyway. By the time she was ready for longer flights and maneuvers she would be using the double saddle. Fidem was excited about the opportunity to see new places as she had never been away from Glyka before. Gwen promised to point out things of special interest to her as they were journeying along.

Finishing their lunch with about an hour to spare before the council reconvened Gwen asked Fidem if she wanted to use the time for archery practice. Fidem replied in the affirmative with a huge smile on her face. Gwen and Fidem then proceeded to the archery range after picking up Gwen's bow and quiver of arrows. Fidem went and gathered her bow and arrows joining Gwen at the shooting line of the range. When Fidem joined Gwen she noticed that Gwen had already removed all the closer targets from her lane leaving only the farthest target in place. Seeing her wide-eyed expression Gwen remarked that it took her months of daily practice for a good part of the day before she was ready for the longer distance target. Gwen said that if Fidem kept up her practice she would eventually be removing the closer targets as well. Fidem then replied that she did not think she would ever be good enough for the farthest target but asked if she could remove the two closest ones in her lane. Gwen was not sure how well Fidem would do at that distance, but not wanting to discourage her went and removed the first two targets.

Fidem asked if Gwen would go first so that she could be observing her and see if there was anything Gwen did differently that she could adopt for her own shooting. Gwen shot six arrows into the bullseye with Fidem watching wide eyed. Gwen then said she wanted to observe Fidem and for Fidem not to worry about how well she did, but to just concentrate on using proper technique. Fidem then shot her six arrows and did as Gwen suggested concentrating on her technique as she shot. Fidem remarked that she only got three bullseyes, but at least the rest of her arrows were in the next ring.

Gwen then surprised Fidem by saying that her shooting was exceptional for the short length of time she had been an archer. Continuing their practice, they kept it up until the hour was almost over. Gwen then asked Fidem if she would be willing to try something very hard that might not work but could possibly be a help to her as she was progressing with her archery. When Fidem agreed Gwen removed the next target from Fidem's lane meaning that the distance was now twice what it had been. When Gwen returned Fidem said she did not think she could even hit the target at all from that range but was willing to try. Gwen then told her to shoot ten arrows, but to be watching carefully where each arrow hit. She was told to adjust her aim on the next shot to make up for how far off the previous shot had been.

Fidem stepped up to the shooting line aiming at the target like she always did, but because she knew the arrow would hit lower adjusting her point of aim up several inches. Gwen was watching her carefully and was pleased to see her make the compensation. Fidem's shot hit the ground just below the target. Aiming at the top of the target for her next shot Fidem saw that the arrow was still about a foot below the bullseye when it hit. Aiming the rest of the arrows about a foot above the target she adjusted slightly between shots. All the rest of her shots were within the four center rings with one actually hitting the bullseye. Gwen congratulated her on a job well done as they put Fidem's equipment away and headed back to the council chamber. As the council members were making their way to their seats and greeting each other

Gwen motioned for General Hapsom to come over to her on the side. Asking him if he had been able to observe Fidem's archery progress the general replied that it was something he had wanted to do, but other responsibilities had taken priority so far. The general then mentioned that Chari and several of the other archers had been telling him that Fidem seemed to be doing very well. He said he either needed to observe her himself or have one of his seasoned instructors do an evaluation to make sure the assessment was accurate.

Gwen then informed him of the practice session she and Fidem had just completed, her test at the end, and Fidem's exceptional performance. She also mentioned Fidem's dedication in fitting daily practice time into her schedule. The general said that he trusted Gwen's evaluation even more than his own and was very impressed with both Fidem's progress and her dedication. He said he would make sure to include archery practice time in her normal duties from now on and that he would be getting her apprenticed to one of his better archery instructors as soon as possible. Once the meeting commenced, Gwen started filling the council in with what Dreki had said mentioning the need for Fidem to have some flight training and that the double saddle would be finished in two days. Discussing what had been learned up to that point it was decided that the council had served its purpose and could be disbanded. All the council members said that they would be available if future needs came up and King Firinne dismissed everyone.

The Vita contingent remained the night heading back the following day. Those from Glyka merely went back to their normal duties. General Hapsom told Fidem that she was assigned to Gwen and Dreki until her mission to Relitto was completed. She would still use her normal quarters, but the schedule of events was up to Gwen and Dreki. He told her that she would be attending a palace guard ceremony at 3:00 PM in the main palace courtyard the following afternoon, but the rest of her time would be spent with Gwen and Dreki. She was told to be sure and be in uniform for the ceremony, but she could dress casually for her time with Gwen and Dreki.

There were still a couple of hours free before dinner, so Fidem got to try a little basic beginning flight training during that time. Like Gwen's first few flights Fidem felt a little queasiness with slight disorientation afterwards. She did not actually feel sick and got in several short easy flights before dinner. Fidem said she enjoyed them and was looking forward to higher and longer flights as she got used to flying. After dinner they were joined by Gwendolyn and Hratt enjoying a nice time of friendly conversation. Fidem was not saying much and when Gwen asked her about it she said a little shyly that she was still not used to talking with royalty and felt honored to be included. She remarked that she had no problem with communications dealing with guard assignments, but talking to a queen and princess like a friend was awkward. She did say it was not as bad as when she first moved to the palace, but she was still not used to it.

Explaining to her about first coming to Glyka Gwen told her how she felt finding out she was a princess. She then told her about meeting Jenny and how they had become friends. Gwen mentioned that Jenny was now Royal Advisor Jenny in Glyka and how it all started with needing a dirty dress. Fidem said she was amazed that a scullery maid was now the royal advisor. Gwen smiling at her said, "I don't find it any more amazing than a farm girl being an elite palace guard; and that started with a pretend bow that didn't work." Fidem smiled back at her, and they both shared a laugh which made Fidem relax. Fidem then joined in the rest of the conversation, and everyone spent an enjoyable relaxing evening. Fidem finally said she needed to be getting to her quarters and left the rest of the group while they conversed a while longer.

After breakfast the following day Fidem did some flight training heading to the archery range afterwards for some practice. When she had gathered her things and was approaching the shooting line she saw an older archer whom she did not recognize standing there. Coming closer he introduced himself as Colonel Veren and said he had been waiting for her. He told her that she was to be his apprentice and that he would be working around her schedule until she departed on her mission. Once she returned and was back on normal guard duty a regular schedule would need to be set up. He asked her to take six shots when she was ready so he could make an evaluation. He was surprised to see her removing the first two targets going to the shooting line and confidently putting all six arrows in the two inner rings with half of them in the bullseye. He asked to look at her bow quickly testing the draw weight. He then asked Fidem if she had tried any other bows besides that one. She said that Queen Gwen had helped her pick this one out of three choices when she first started archery, but she had not really been thinking about the need to change it. Veren went and got six more bows for Fidem to test. He told her that they were too large for her and were going to feel awkward, but that they were needed to help determine how strong Fidem's pull was.

Fidem was told to try all the bows, but not to worry if she was not able to get them to the anchor point. She was to use one of her normal arrows holding the bow as best she could, drawing the arrow to her normal anchor point and holding it there until Veren told her to release it. She was then to slowly release the tension without shooting the arrow. She was not quite able to draw three of the bows to the anchor point. Fidem got one bow to the anchor point but could not hold it until Veren told her to release the tension. Trying the two last bows she was able to perform the test completely on both of them without difficulty.

Taking those two bows Veren asked her to follow him. They went through the archery storage area and down a short hallway entering a room at the end. There were several tables there with people working at them. Quite a number of different bows were there in various stages of completion. Veren spoke to one of the bow crafters handing her the two bows mentioning Fidem's name as he did so. The craftswoman then introduced herself as Shauna asking Fidem to follow her. They went over to a shelf that had hundreds of different sized grips and Shauna pointed to a set of ten for Fidem to try. Fidem found two that she said felt good to her, but it was hard for her to say for sure which of the two was the best. Shauna said that the larger one would allow her to grow some and still feel comfortable with the grip, so she was going to use that one. Shauna then measured Fidem's draw length as well as her height. Taking the two bows and putting them one at a time into a device that measured the tension Shauna pulled each of them to Fidem's draw length writing the figures down. She said that she would be using the stronger tension for Fidem.

Shauna said she would check the stock of bows they had to see if she could find one that matched Fidem's specifications. She said there were not many in Fidem's size range, but she would see what there was. Fidem went to get the bow she had been using for Shauna to compare with. When Fidem returned Shauna said it was as she feared and an exact match could not be found. They would be making a bow specifically for Fidem, but it would not be ready for a few weeks. Shauna said that she was able to find a close substitute. Shauna was successful in locating a slightly longer bow that had the correct grip size, but with a tension that was a little too high. Shauna explained that the longer bow was built for a longer arrow and the tension should be less at Fidem's draw length. Testing it in the tension measuring device it was as Shauna surmised it was indeed less. It was just a little less than Fidem's ideal draw tension and Shauna was pleased with it as a good substitute bow. Handing it to Fidem she said goodbye and went back to her work.

Taking her substitute bow Fidem followed Veren back to the archery range. Veren asked Fidem to practice a bit with the new bow explaining that the aiming would be slightly different but should be more consistent when she got used to it. He also said her arms might be a little more tired and sore than usual at the end of the practice session. Watching her carefully as she started he saw that her first shot was high, but that she compensated well on the next one. She continued shooting and making adjustments and was back to a consistent pattern in a fairly short time.

Veren then said he would like her to try the next target and see how well she did with it and Fidem mentioned Queen Gwen having her do that yesterday with her old bow and what the results had been. Removing the next target Veren watched as Fidem aimed about a foot above the target the way she had done yesterday. This time her arrow missed the target but was just above it. Lowering her aim to the top of the target she noticed her arrow was still slightly high when it hit. She continued shooting and making minor adjustments. Once she got her aiming settled in she could consistently keep all the arrows within the three center rings and even had several in the bullseye. She told Veren she liked the new bow much better but could feel that her muscles were straining more than before.

Veren then said that even though the farthest target was well beyond the normal range of the bow she had he wanted her to see what it was like to be forced to be shooting beyond the bow's capabilities. He then went and removed the target she had been using so that only the farthest target was left. He told her that the arrow might not even be able to reach the target her aim would have to be very high and to try her best with ten arrows and see how close to the target she was able to get. Standing at the shooting line she aimed her first arrow well above the target and released it. She could not help sighing when it fell quite a way in front of the target. Not realizing she was using almost the same technique Gwen had done she raised her aim to 45 degrees releasing the arrow. It missed the target, but she was pleased to see that it had gone beyond it. Lowering her aim slightly she saw that the arrow was still high, but much closer to the target. She kept adjusting her aim and was able to put the last three arrows into the target, but none were in the three center rings.

Looking at Veren with a disappointed expression on her face she said, "Not a very good score, but at least I hit the target with a few."

Replying slowly, he said, "Corporal Fidem, *I* would be hard pressed to do as well using that bow and your arrows! It will not be long before you are an expert archer. You should now be using all the targets except the farthest one. You will need to be able to shoot consistently no matter what the distance is. Once you are consistent with the closer targets the way they are we will be moving them to different positions within the range so you can learn to adjust for any distance. Once you have worked your way up to a much stronger bow the farthest target can be added to your routine."

Excusing herself, Fidem said she needed to get another flight or two in before lunch and said she would have her schedule passed on to him so he would not have to waste his time waiting for her. Thanking her he told her he would inform General Hapsom that a bow had been ordered for her and let him know she had done well with the temporary one. He then headed off to perform the rest of his duties with Fidem going to find Dreki. She was able to get in several flights which allowed her to get more used to mounting and dismounting as well as becoming more accustomed to the actual flying.

She and Dreki then met the others enjoying a nice lunch. Finishing lunch, Gwen and Dreki worked with Fidem on teaching her some survival skills that would be helpful for their upcoming trip. After that a few more flights were made, but Fidem eventually said she needed to go put on her uniform and get to the courtyard for the palace guard ceremony. She asked if Gwen and Dreki were invited to attend and was told that they would be there as would Gwendolyn, Hratt and most of the Glyka palace officials. Fidem said goodbye heading off to get dressed and then making her way to the courtyard.

Arriving on time Fidem was greeted by General Hapsom with him showing her where to stand in the group of guards.

You might have thought it looked a little strange seeing all those guards lined up with one noticeably much shorter than all the rest, but with all of them in matching uniforms the visual effect was of a unified body rather than a group of individuals and the size difference did not seem to stand out as much. A few minutes later King Firinne opened the ceremony turning the platform over to General Hapsom.

General Hapsom then gave a short speech thanking the palace guards for their service and complimenting them on a job well done. He then called out the names of three of the guards and had them all come forward. He said that they were up for promotion presenting each of them individually with a new rank patch for their uniform. There was clapping and cheering for each guard as they were receiving their patch.

He then said that he had one more award to present. He stated that normally for awards of this type to be earned the candidate must first go through a series of tests to prove their skill. Secondly they would proceed through several ranks receiving an award for each rank as they progressed. He said that one of the guards under his command had shown exceptional progress in their skill. In fact, the progress was so impressive that by recommendation of several trusted experts the initial ranks of Novice earning the black pin and Marksman earning the bronze pin were being skipped.

Turning to the group of guards standing at attention he then said, "Corporal Fidem, please come forward." Fidem then walked up to General Hapsom waiting for him to speak. "Corporal Fidem, though you are the youngest member of the elite palace guard corps and not yet old enough to hold a position of formal rank we do not want to be remiss in failing to give recognition where it is due. You have only been with us for a short time yet in that time have shown exceptional dedication in not only performing all assigned duties but even taking your own time to perfect your archery skill. It is therefore my great pleasure to bestow upon you this silver

Sharpshooter pin for excellence in archery." General Hapsom ended his speech while pinning the award to her uniform.

As she was going back to her place amid clapping and cheering she heard General Hapsom saying that if anyone had concerns about Fidem's ability as an archer they could take it up with his top archery instructor Colonel Veren or Queen Gwen herself. General Hapsom then dismissed the assembly.

Several people came up to congratulate the promoted guards and Fidem was surprised at the number of people who were coming up to her as well. Those she knew she had expected, but there were quite a number she had never met before. After all the strangers had finished congratulating her, her friends, fellow guards and the other palace people took their turn. She was finally able to leave to change out of her uniform for more flight training followed by supper.

Within a week the training was completed, and the needed supplies had been gathered. Gwen, Dreki and Fidem left the following morning right after breakfast stopping for the day in Vita. All three were welcomed warmly and were shown to their rooms. They quickly stowed their belongings and as they were coming out of their rooms Fidem asked if she could get a tour of the castle and grounds. Dreki suggested that Gwen take her and that he would meet up with them at lunch.

Heading out of the castle gate and across the drawbridge Gwen led Fidem to the clearings and then along the route she had taken on the Day of Deliverance. Fidem said she was very impressed but remarked that the dungeons did not look anything like the horrid scene her mind had conjured up from the descriptions she had heard. Gwen told her that they had been totally renovated and now more resembled a city jail than a castle dungeon. Gwen told her that they were indeed hideous when she first saw them but was glad they had been made over.

Fidem was extremely pleased with the orphanage and said it was very homelike and looked even nicer than she had thought it would. Gwen then introduced Fidem to Angela who was now in charge. The three chatted over coffee for a bit while the few children that were still there finished up their chores. Gwen and Fidem then went through the rest of the grounds and admired the statues in the courtyard a bit before meeting Dreki for lunch.

Finishing lunch, they spent an enjoyable afternoon chatting with their friends and answering any questions Fidem brought up. Fidem said she was very glad to have the opportunity to finally see the places in Vita she had only heard about. She said when she heard the account of Gwen's encounter with Nequitia she was wondering how Gwen could have hit the small ball at the end of the scepter. Now that she had actually seen Gwen shoot at the archery range it did not seem as fantastic a shot, but Fidem said she still marveled at Gwen's bravery in facing Nequitia. King Kelan said that he still gets goose bumps remembering turning around after killing Stultus and seeing Nequitia's absolute rage as he attacked Gwen. He said it still amazes him how she did not run or freeze, but held her dagger resolutely in front of her as he charged.

Gwen said that even though several years had passed for her since then she would rather they were discussing something else. Fidem then asked about the swamp and if it was still there. King Kelan smiled telling her that it is now reduced to a small boggy area next to the lake. The streams now run clear, and the lake is entirely healed as well. He said there had been talk of filling in the boggy area so that it was dry land again, but when they had gone to investigate they found many cranberries growing there. Since it was a clean bog now and the cranberries a wanted commodity it was left intact for that reason. Enjoying a leisurely supper with more conversation afterwards they finally headed off to bed.

8

The Journey to Relitto

WAKING refreshed and ready to start their journey, Gwen, Dreki and Fidem had a good breakfast bidding farewell to their friends from Vita. Gwen and Dreki were pointing things out to Fidem as they were making their westward journey to Maith in Socair. Fidem was thrilled to be able to see so far remarking how beautiful some of the country they passed over was. She particularly liked having lunch by the waterfall. Gwen said she remembered her first long distance flights and how enjoyable it was for her as well. Explaining to Fidem about the long leg flight after a hearty early breakfast one day the travelers were again on their way. Stopping a little before sundown they all enjoyed a large supper after setting up camp. Gwen said she was hopeful that they would be repeating what they had enjoyed on the first trip westward as an after-dinner treat. Finishing their meal they all went puffball hunting in the area where they had been found in the past. Searching for about 20 minutes with no success they were ready to head back to camp, but they all said they would be missing the puffballs.

On the way back Fidem was pointing out a low area a short way over to their left that looked shady and damp. Suggesting that they give that area a quick check she said there was a similar spot not far from her farmhouse that often had puffballs growing in it. It turned out to be a good thing they had decided on checking as there were a good many puffballs growing in the damp gully there. Gathering quite a few and continuing back to camp they all had smiles on their faces. They all enjoyed the puffballs thanking Fidem for helping them find them. Eating and talking during their after-meal treat Gwen let out a laugh saying it was ironic that the one person in the group who had never been that way before was the one to point out the location of the puffballs.

The following day they made it to the forest dwellers' location and were lodging in Maith the day after that. They were again staying at the Traveler's Rest inn eating at the same restaurant as the last time while discussing the plans for the following day over supper. Dreki would be flying them to the main cave chamber waiting for them there. Gwen and Fidem would proceed down the passage until they reached the barred gate. Fidem would then try squeezing through the narrow gap between the gate and the wall. If successful, she would start looking around nearby for a key to unlock the gate. If she found one she would let Gwen through the gate and they would both start proceeding carefully down the passage; if not, she would be making the exploratory trip herself.

The plan was to get as far as possible down the passage without being seen gaining as much information about what was at the end of the passage as they could. Depending on what they found out they could possibly explore further gathering more information or return to Dreki to discuss what they discovered. They would then decide on what to do or possibly return to Glyka for more council input. Further conversation occurred in the barn later that evening, but they ended up deciding that an initial report of what was beyond the gate was needed before any additions to the plans could be made. The rest of the conversation that evening was just reminiscences of events along the trip route and friendly small talk.

Rising early and partaking of a good breakfast the three were on their way. It was not long before Dreki was dropping Gwen and Fidem off waiting for them in the cave chamber.

Gwen and Fidem each took a torch proceeding quietly down the passage until they reached the barred gate. Pausing here for a while they both stood listening carefully. Like the last time only very faint sounds could be heard coming from further down the passage. Since Gwen and Fidem could hear sounds from farther down they assumed if someone was there that they could possibly hear sounds made by them. Gwen and Fidem were very careful to move quietly only talking in very low whispers.

Handing her bow, quiver of arrows and torch to Gwen, Fidem approached the barred gate. She managed to squeeze through the gap between the gate and wall without much trouble retrieving her items from Gwen once she was on the other side. Smiling at Gwen, Fidem said she would take a quick look around for the key. Quietly searching the nearby area, she returned to Gwen in a few minutes. She whispered that she had seen a hook on the wall of the passage just beyond the padlock for the gate, but there was no key hanging on the hook. She then turned around heading slowly and quietly down the passage pausing periodically to listen for a bit. The further she went the more noticeable the noises became. They were still very quiet and indistinct, but she could tell that she was gradually getting closer to the source.

Continuing stealthily down the passage she noticed unlit torches in brackets periodically along the wall. These torches were all the same, but very different from the one she was carrying. Deciding that if she happened to be seen it would be better to be carrying a Relitto torch than a strange one and not wanting to take the chance of waiting until she reached the next one, Fidem turned herself around backtracking to the place where she had last spotted one of the torches. Lighting that one and extinguishing hers she then took the lit one out of the wall bracket putting her unlit one on the floor beneath the empty bracket. On her return trip she would be exchanging the torches once again leaving only unlit Relitto torches in their brackets.

Moving a little more rapidly until she got to the next unlit torch Fidem then paused listening for a moment proceeding once again from there in a stealthy manner down the passage. After a bit, she could see dim light ahead, so she stood waiting there and listening for a little longer than she usually did. The sounds were still indistinct enough to tell her that the source of them was well beyond the dimly lit section of the passage. She then removed the nearest torch from its bracket laying it on the floor putting her lit one into the bracket in its place. She continued down the passage very slowly into the dimly lit section listening carefully as she went.

The dim light was very gradually becoming brighter and the sounds progressively louder, but the sounds were still too indistinct to identify. She noticed that not much further ahead the passage seemed to end. She could not yet tell if it ended at an intersection with another passage, if there was a room there, or she had reached the end of the tunnel and it emerged into the open. She did not think this last option very likely as the light was way too dim to be daylight. Perhaps there was another cave-like chamber at this end. The only way to find out was to get to the end and see for herself.

Making her way to the passage end she carefully peeked beyond it. What she saw was a good sized round room with three more passages leading away from it. The room and the three other passages were not like the natural cave tunnel she had just traversed but were definitely man-made structures.

Entering the room, she started looking around at her sur-roundings. There was light coming from a type of chandelier hanging from the ceiling. It was not a fancy beautiful one like you might see in a formal dining room, but a rather utilitarian variety consisting of six wooden arms extending from a central hub. At the end of each arm was what looked like an oil lamp. There was a fair-sized reservoir on the hub of the chandelier with pipes leading to the lamps. She had no idea how long the reservoir would last before it needed to be refilled, but from the size of it and the relatively small flames on the lamps she was guessing it would probably last several weeks. She did not know how often people came here but figured that someone had to refill the reservoir periodically. The only thing in the room besides the chandelier was a table in the middle of the room so she surmised that it was merely an intersection of the four passages. Since there were no chairs she wondered what the table was for.

She then went to each of the exits looking down every passage and listening carefully for any sounds coming from them. The two passages going left and right from where she entered the room were totally dark and absolutely quiet. The one on the opposite side was dimly lit and was where the sounds were coming from. The dark passages also had a very slight musty smell whereas the lit one smelled more like fresh air. Wanting to give the dark passages a quick check she found she could not quite reach the chandelier with an unlit torch to light it even standing on the table. She realized she would have to backtrack to get the lit torch from the bracket where she had left it. Sighing quietly to herself she started making the return trip.

Retrieving the lit torch, she went back to the round room pausing again to listen before entering. Since there was no apparent change in the noise level she carefully entered the room then proceeded down the passage to the left. It was not a long passage and ended at a closed door. Putting her ear to the door and hearing nothing coming from beyond it she looked at the gap between the bottom of the door and the floor. Seeing no light there she carefully opened the door a crack and peeked inside seeing nothing but complete darkness. She then entered and took a look at what was on the other side of the door. It appeared to be a fair-sized wine cellar with many bottles in racks both along the walls and in the central area of the room, but no other exit. Closing the door, she headed to the opposite passage again stopping to listen in the round room.

This passage seemed the same as the other one, so she listened at the door again opening it like she did the first one when nothing was heard beyond it and no light was seen under it. It was not another wine cellar but appeared to be a storage room of some sort. There were several boxes and crates either on the floor or on shelves against the walls. Like the wine cellar there was no other exit, so she headed back to the round room after closing the door. She was now guessing that the table in the round room was merely there to facilitate sorting items either going into or being removed from the wine cellar or storage room. She returned her lit torch to the bracket again making her way back to the round room. After another pause to listen in the round room she continued slowly heading on down the dimly lit passage.

It was not long before she came to the end of this shorter passage. Peeking beyond the passage end she saw what appeared to be a large dimly lit open area. This portion seemed to be a kind of central section with several other areas attached to it. The other areas appeared to be spacious as well, but they were not well lit, and it was difficult to tell as her perspective was limited by her position. She could now definitely hear indistinct voices and faint sounds of movement, but as yet had not seen any people. There were a few large barrels and crates just outside the passage she was in, and she was guessing that either they were too large to put in the storeroom or contained items that were used more often and kept there to avoid longer trips all the way to the storeroom.

Creeping out of the passage she ducked behind one of the crates. Peering out from behind the crate, first around one side and then the other, she was able to get a better view of the attached areas. One appeared to be part of the dungeon as she could clearly see bars and beyond them more bars. Beyond the further bars she could barely discern some movement, but the light was dim, and it was hard to make out any details. The other area appeared to go further into the citadel with passages beyond it. She could detect no movement in that area, and all the sounds appeared to be coming from the dungeon section. Looking back towards the passage she came in by she saw that there was a ring with three keys on it hanging just to the side of the passage. Since the only locks down the passage were on the two storeroom doors and the padlock on the barred gate she was guessing that one of the keys would open the padlock.

Heading back to the passage entrance she closely examined the ring of keys. Noticing that they were covered in a thick coating of dust she was thinking that they were not used any more but just kept there in case they were ever needed. She was about to take them off the hook but then thought that if someone happened to come that way the missing keys might be noticed. A further inspection of the keys showed her that two were almost identical looking very similar to the one used to lock the attic door in her grandmother's old house, but the third was of a different style altogether. Guessing that the matching keys probably went to the storeroom doors and the unique one was for the barred gate she decided on removing the suspected gate key leaving the ring with the other two keys hanging on the hook. She figured the ring with the two keys would not look that much different than the ring with three keys in the dim light.

Taking the key with her, she started making her way back to where Gwen was anxiously waiting for her and found that the key did unlock the padlock. Fidem said she had a lot to tell Gwen, but Gwen said they should probably wait until they were with Dreki so Fidem would only have to tell her story and answer questions once. It did not take them long to get back to Dreki. After letting Gwen and Dreki know what she found and answering their questions they discussed what to do next while eating the lunch they had brought with them. They ended up deciding that the best plan for the time being would be to let Gwen through the barred gate but then close it again with the padlock in place. The padlock would not actually be locked though at a quick glance it would appear to be so. Gwen and Fidem would then go back to the area next to the dungeon returning the third key to the ring. From there they would have to see if they could get closer to the dungeon without being seen by a Relitto guard. Depending on what they found they would act accordingly.

Finishing their lunch, Gwen and Fidem proceeded to carry out the plan. Gwen was let through the barred gate, and the unlocked padlock was put back into place. Taking only one torch with them and making their way quickly but carefully to the round room, they paused to listen and then went to the open area putting the third key back onto the ring. They then dragged the keys through a dusty spot on the floor before returning them to their hook, so they were all coated in dust again. Ducking behind the crates they both checked the area heading back towards the citadel. Since it was clear they made their way over to the closer bars of the dungeon area and began looking around. This set of bars was very large. It went all the way from the ceiling to the floor for its entire length and went from one wall of the open area to the other. There was one locked barred door in the entire set of bars, and it was very near to where they were standing. Taking a closer look at the door, they noticed that the key was still in the lock! Turning it, Gwen remarked that it was very dusty like the three other keys and probably not used any more either.

Hesitating before opening the door Gwen paused and thought about it first. Mentioning to Fidem that since it was not used now it would probably squeak horribly when they opened it. Fidem asked if they found the oil used in the chandelier could they put some on the hinges of the door to keep it from squeaking. Gwen said that was an excellent idea, so they went back to the barrels and crates looking around them. After a bit they found a large jug of oil and a ladder next to it. They were guessing these were used to fill the chandelier reservoir as well as the few lamps here and there in the larger areas near them. Taking the jug over to the door they began oiling the hinges well. They returned the jug to its normal location heading back to the door. Very slowly pulling the door both Gwen and Fidem smiled at each other as it swung almost silently open. They closed it behind them moving over to the wall on their right, which was the farthest distance from the citadel passage. Gwen and Fidem crept closer to the next set of bars staying against the wall where the light was very dim.

Getting to the bars they could clearly see people moving about on the other side. The people seemed to be doing household jobs or just talking to each other in normal conversation. There was no sign of a guard anywhere, so Gwen made a hissing sound putting her finger to her lips as a woman not too far away turned towards her at the sound. The woman's eyes grew wide and the woman began slowly walking over to where Gwen and Fidem were standing. Reaching them the woman asked in a low voice, "Who are you and how did you get out of the dungeon?"

Gwen quickly asked her about the guards and the woman said there were no guards at this time of day. Gwen then told her about how she and Fidem had come to try and help free the people of Relitto from Sordibus' evil rule. Conversation then went back and forth for a while with Gwen and Fidem trying to learn as much as they could about the layout of the dungeon and how they might possibly get to Sordibus. Gladly sharing all she knew the woman said she was not sure what two girls could do against Sordibus' entire armed forces but found it incredible that they had gotten through the citadel and down to the dungeon without being seen.

Explaining how they had come through the cave passage and not through the citadel Gwen enlightened the woman. Gwen then asked for details about how and when meals were delivered, when guards made rounds, where the locked doors in the bars were located, how many people were in the dungeon and several other questions of a more general nature.

Gwen and Fidem found out that there were about 300 people in the dungeon and the guards only made trips for meal deliveries at sunrise, noon and sunset picking up the dirty dishes from the previous meal at those times. There were only two locked doors in the bars surrounding the dungeon. One of the doors was just to the left of where they were standing and was never used. The other was in the bars on the opposite side of the dungeon area and was the one used for delivering meals or adding new prisoners.

Since it would be several hours before the next meal delivery Gwen went back to the door in the first set of bars removing the key. Then taking it to the second door she began trying it in that lock. She and Fidem were smiling at each other when it worked perfectly. Asking Fidem to go get the jug of oil she stayed talking further with the woman. As Fidem was heading over to get the jug Gwen told the woman that they would try to come up with a plan for rescuing the prisoners and freeing Relitto from Sordibus' rule. Returning with the jug, Fidem and Gwen started giving these hinges the same treatment as the others and were pleased by the same results.

Gwen then asked if there were ever any times that the prisoners were allowed visits from family members serving in Sordibus' army. The woman said yes, they were allowed visits once a week. These visits were always on Friday. About a fourth of the soldiers at a time were allowed into the dungeon. Once they were admitted the door was again locked. Each soldier would go to his family separating from the others so there were a lot of small groups scattered throughout the dungeon. They would have about two hours together. That group would be replaced by the next and so on until all four groups had spent two hours with their families. Other than the once-a-week meeting there was no other time together and the meetings were always concluded before the supper meal was delivered.

Gwen said that she and Fidem needed to check some things out before making further plans promising to return in about an hour to let her know what was decided. Gwen then re-locked the door to the dungeon. She and Fidem then passed back through the first barred door shutting it and leaving it unlocked with the key in the lock for the return trip.

They then made their way back to Dreki informing him of what they had discovered.

Discussing what was found out in the dungeon they tried coming up with some sort of plan. After talking over the options, it did not seem likely that wandering through the citadel looking for Sordibus to confront him would be successful. It was also felt that trying to spy out where his location was for a sneak attack later would also end in failure. Gwen suggested that if they could successfully rescue all the prisoners the soldiers would have no reason to follow Sordibus any longer. If they knew their families were safe they could overpower Sordibus and free the kingdom.

How to go about getting 300 people out of Sordibus' dungeon and safely to Socair was the next discussion. It was decided that the best time to get them out would be after the evening meal since the guards would not return until breakfast at sunrise. Getting from the dungeon to the round room would be easy, but beyond that the darkness could be a hindrance. If some of the torches in the brackets were lit on the trip in there would not be darkness to worry about on the way out so that issue was solved.

What if someone came from the citadel to get a bottle of wine or other supplies while they were escaping? This had the potential of ruining the entire plan, so they had to come up with a way to handle the situation. Knocking the person out or locking them up seemed a possibility until they realized that the person would be missed long before the escape was completed. Fidem suggested that a lookout could be stationed where the passage from the citadel entered the open area. If someone came down the passage the lookout could warn them. Dreki said that was a good idea, but he was not sure that everyone would have time to get to a hiding place once the group started filing out of the dungeon into the passage since 300 people is a pretty long line. Gwen asked if it might be better to send the people in groups of ten. Once ten got all the way from the dungeon into the natural cave passage the next group of ten could go. All agreed that this was a good idea.

Discussing the cave entrance was the next topic. The chamber was large, but not large enough for 300 people. How could you get 300 people out once they were there? The people would have to be removed in smaller groups as there was no way to transport 300 at one time. The double saddle would only hold two and that was not practical either. Dreki then mentioned how the craftsmen had devised the ladder carrier for the Day of Deliverance and was thinking that the craftsmen could devise a way for the people to be carried. He said for that short of a trip he could easily manage eight and that if there were two dragons instead of one the people could be moved twice as fast. He also said they would have to have a way for the cave entrance to be plainly seen in the dark so they would know where to land. Fidem then began pointing to the south side of the chamber right by the entrance suggesting that they could build a campfire there. She said it would be out of the way of transporting the people, easier to see as the dragons were approaching from the north and not visible by anyone on the Relitto side of the gorge.

Gwen then suggested a bonfire on the Socair side a little farther north than the cave entrance and right near the edge of the gorge. The dragons would be able to easily see it when leaving the cave and they would then know where the edge of the gorge was as well as its height for the landing. Gwen said that she had promised to get back to the woman in the dungeon in about an hour so they needed to finish up the rough plan so she could do that. Since the family meetings were held every Friday it was decided that when the time was right for the operation it would be held on a Friday night. The rescuers would let the woman know on the Thursday before so word could be passed to the others in the dungeon and then on to their soldier relatives the following day during the meetings. Any other details could be worked out later.

Returning to the dungeon to inform the woman of the rough plans Gwen and Fidem told her that it would take at least three to four weeks before the rescue could be attempted. They told her it might be longer if they were delayed somehow, but not to give up hope and that they would eventually be getting there. They also asked the woman to not say anything to anyone else before the Thursday that the rescuers returned. That way people would be less likely to arouse any suspicion by behaving differently than normal. Gwen and Fidem then said goodbye locking the second barred door after going through it and leaving the key in the lock.

Heading back to Dreki they made sure things looked normal as they were passing them. The jug of oil was back by the ladder, and the three dusty keys were on the ring next to the passage entrance in the large open area. All the torches in the brackets were of the Relitto variety, and all were unlit. Reaching the barred gate Fidem handed her equipment to Gwen opening the gate for her. When Gwen was past the gate Fidem shut it putting the padlock in place, so the gate appeared to be locked, but she did not close the padlock all the way. Fidem then squeezed through the gap retrieving her equipment from Gwen. She and Gwen then made their way back to Dreki by the light of the torch they had originally brought with them. All three then headed back to Socair for supper and then to the Traveler's Rest for a good night's sleep. Within a week they were back in Vita and made the usual one night stay there giving King Kelan and Queen Rachel an update on the rescue plans while they were there. The following day they were all back in Glyka where they reunited with Gwendolyn and Hratt updating them as well. Hratt said he would be glad to be the second transport dragon and Gwendolyn said she did not know what she could do but was wanting to help as well.

Mentioning that there would be a need to have several people monitoring those rescued and keeping the evacuation orderly Gwen smiled at Gwendolyn. Gwendolyn then said she was happy to be able to finally participate in an adventure although she was glad it would not be as harrowing as the encounter with Nequitia. The need for both Dreki and Hratt to meet with the craftsmen was brought up and they both agreed to go right after the discussion was finished to explain what was wanted and to get measured for the transport harnesses. Fidem said she wanted to check and see if her bow was ready and if it was finished before they left try getting in some practice to get used to it. She said she had really missed being able to practice while she had been away from Glyka. Suggesting that while the dragons met with the craftsmen and Fidem checked on her bow Gwen said that she and Gwendolyn could give King Firinne and General Hapsom an update. All agreed to meet at lunch with updates for the rest of the group and everyone went their separate ways to take care of what was needed.

Meeting with the craftsmen did not take long. Once the craftsmen knew what was wanted they made various measurements of both dragons and said they would have the transport harnesses ready in three days. They said they could easily construct them in a day, but it would take them two days to get enough leather to do the job.

Making her way to the bow crafters building Fidem knocked on the door. When the closest crafter saw her he greeted her warmly asking her to come on in. He then called out to Shauna telling her that Fidem was here. Smiling broadly at Fidem, Shauna approached telling her that her bow had just been finished the night before. Leading Fidem over to a rack with several bows on it she handed Fidem's new bow to her. Shauna said she had made Fidem's bow a priority not knowing when she would be back from her trip. Shauna wanted to make sure that Fidem was happy with the bow asking if they could go to the shooting line so Fidem could check it out. Fidem said she was not sure how well she would do with both a new bow and lack of practice for so long, but that she was also anxious to try it out. Grabbing a quiver with the right length arrows they headed out of the building towards the shooting line.

Arriving at the shooting line Shauna told Fidem to go ahead and give it a try. Shauna was surprised that Fidem did not step up to the line immediately and start shooting. While Fidem was setting her bow down Shauna asked if anything was wrong. Fidem said no, but that she was going to be removing the first three targets. When Fidem returned Shauna asked if she was sure she wanted to try a target that was that far away. Fidem said that it might take a few tries to get used to the new bow but was hoping she would do alright after that. Shauna had heard that Fidem was doing well and making rapid progress but knowing how short a time Fidem had been an archer was not too hopeful at this distance. Letting Fidem try anyway she saw that Fidem's first few shots were off but was amazed that after that she was able to keep them all in the center three rings with most in the center two rings and about a third of them in the bullseye.

Turning to Shauna with a huge smile Fidem said, "I really like this new bow! It feels much better than the one I borrowed. By the way I will return the borrowed one the next time I come to the range. Heading back to the bow crafters' building to put the quiver of arrows away, just as they reached the doorway a young boy several years older than Fidem came out.

When he saw Fidem he said with a smirk, "So this is the famous archer we keep hearing about. She doesn't look like much to me!"

Shauna told him that he would be wiser to keep comments like that to himself. He then bragged that he could shoot better than anyone else his age and that Fidem did not stand a chance against him.

Shauna then asked Fidem if she would be willing to shoot against Prale. Fidem said she had never competed before but would be willing to give it a try. The three headed back to the shooting line with Prale stepping up to a lane with the first two targets removed and asking Fidem if she could even hit the target in that lane. Fidem then said that if he was as good as he claimed why not use the next lane. Prale had never tried shooting with the first three targets removed but figuring that even if he only hit the target a few times Fidem would not even be close he agreed. Suggesting that he go first Fidem stood waiting for him, so he stepped up shooting ten arrows. Three of them hit the target, but two were in the outer ring and the last just outside of it. When he started going to get them Fidem said not to bother they were not in the way. She then took her turn putting all but two in the inner two rings with three in the bullseye. Prale just stood there staring unbelievingly at the target.

Shauna then asked Fidem if she would mind retrieving the arrows while she had a word with Prale. Shauna did not start speaking until Fidem had reached the target, so Fidem did not hear what she said. Returning and handing Prale his arrows Fidem noticed his face was very red. First thanking her for retrieving them he then gulped apologizing for being such a fool. He asked her if she had ever tried to hit the farthest target. She told him not with the nice bow she had now, but that she had been able to put three arrows out of ten into it with a borrowed bow on her first attempt.

Slumping slowly away Prale headed off to put his equipment back. Shauna turned to Fidem thanking her for helping to put Prale in his place. She said that he was too quick to brag about his abilities but would probably be a little more careful now. She also asked Fidem to please not tell anyone about the contest. She felt that Prale had been humiliated enough and if the word got out his peers would be constantly teasing him. Fidem promised to keep quiet about it and Shauna thanked her. Heading their separate ways each of them left the archery range, Shauna to the bow crafters' building and Fidem going to check in with General Hapsom.

The general told Fidem that since it would not be long before she headed off again she was free to do whatever she needed to do according to the schedule Gwen and Dreki came up with. She said she was not aware of anything specific and wanted to get in as much archery practice as she could manage. Asking the general if he could let her know Colonel Veren's schedule Fidem said she could work some time in with him without messing up anything he already had planned.

The general said he would check with him and let her know at lunch. Thanking him she headed off to find the rest of the group.

Meeting for lunch Dreki updated the group on the transport harnesses and Fidem said she now had her new bow and that it was much better than the borrowed one. She also said she was hoping to get in as much archery practice as possible mentioning her conversation with General Hapsom. Everyone thought that archery practice would be the best use of Fidem's time as no more flight or survival skill training was needed. When General Hapsom joined them part way through the meal Fidem told him she would be able to work around whatever schedule Veren already had. The general then told her Veren's schedule for the rest of the week had him busy in the mornings and later in the afternoons, but he was free every afternoon at 1:00 PM for a couple of hours. Thanking the general for the information Fidem said she would plan on meeting Veren at the archery range every day at 1:00 PM until she had to leave.

Gathering supplies for the trip did not take too long so the group of rescuers was able to spend some time visiting friends, relaxing and conversing with each other. Fidem was spending most of her time at the archery range but enjoyed the relaxing conversation time with the rest of the rescuers as well. With the completion of the transport harnesses, they were ready to make the journey to Relitto once again planning to leave the next day. They made their usual one day stop in Vita enjoying their visit there and were on their way further westward the next morning.

9

Disaster Strikes

PREPARING to leave Vita the following morning after a nice breakfast the rescuers were saying goodbye to all their friends. Soon they were on their way and were enjoying the beautiful scenery again. Lunch by the waterfall was especially nice with the larger group making plenty of friendly conversation. Setting up camp in the clearing by the gardens they made sure they went to say hello to the forest dwellers living in the huts. Nothing out of the ordinary happened the following day and they ended it making camp in the clearing in the dense woods.

Heading to bed a little early because they knew the long leg of their journey was next they were wanting to make sure they were rested up and ready for it. Rising early, they broke camp after a hearty breakfast. Although it was a long way to the next clearing they had all made the trip before knowing they should get there just before sundown. They would then be setting up camp and having a large supper since they would be skipping lunch.

Making their way steadily westward as the day progressed they flew on until mid-afternoon without seeing anything unusual. As the afternoon progressed, however, dark clouds started forming and they could see some flashes of lightning farther westward. Slowing slightly, Dreki allowed Hratt to catch up with him and begin flying next to him so everyone could talk to each other.

"This could be bad, but we have no choice but to go on. There is no way we could make it back to the last campsite and could not outrun this storm even if we could make it," Dreki said.

They continued their westward journey with conditions worsening the farther they got. Mentioning that they were getting close Gwen remarked that hopefully they would get to the clearing before the storm reached them. Picking up their speed in hopes of beating the storm they continued pressing on, but the sky was very dark now and the lightning strikes were getting far too close for comfort. Flying slightly higher than normal to be able to see the clearing in the dim light the dragons were putting forth their best effort. Spotting the clearing almost directly ahead Gwen said it looked like it was less than two miles away. She had just finished shouting her findings to Gwendolyn and Hratt when the unthinkable happened. A bolt of lightning struck Dreki on his left wing and he went down into the dense forest carrying Gwen and Fidem with him!

Gwendolyn and Hratt knew there was nothing they could do as there was no place to land anywhere near there, so heading on to the clearing they began setting up a quick camp. Gwendolyn said she would go and look for them once the weather cleared and it was light enough to see. They were both worried about their friends but knew they were unable to do anything in the rain and darkness.

Dreki knew flying was no longer possible as soon as he was hit and did his best gliding into the trees despite the intense pain. He could not steer very well but managed to glide for a pretty long way before spotting a slightly less dense section. Shouting as he was about to crash land he told Gwen and Fidem to jump just before he hit. Seeing a thick bush of some sort just to the left Fidem jumped into it sustaining a few minor scratches but cushioning her fall somewhat. Gwen was not so fortunate spraining her ankle when she landed. Dreki knew he could not fit between the trees as his wingspan was too great and began tilting his body so that his right wing just cleared the nearest tree on that side. His already injured left wing struck a tree on the left side causing him to spin slightly skidding into the forest. Fortunately, most of the foliage there was bushy and softened his landing a bit and the only other trees encountered were very small saplings that did not cause any major damage.

All three were somewhat dazed by their impacts, but since Fidem's landing was the softest she was the first to recover. Heading over to Gwen who was closest, she quickly learned that although Gwen's ankle was sprained and painful she had sustained no further injuries. Fidem said she was going to check on Dreki and let him know that both she and Gwen were not seriously injured. Dreki was pretty groggy when she reached him but anxiously asked her about Gwen. Fidem told him that Gwen was in good shape other than the sprained ankle and that she herself only had a few minor scratches from the bush she landed in. Checking Dreki for injuries Fidem proceeded carefully as Dreki said he was aching all over from the impact and that his muscles felt tingly due to the lightning strike. After thoroughly inspecting him she informed him that his left wing was the only thing visibly injured, but that it looked serious. There were some burn marks from the lightning strike about midway down the leading edge, but what was more concerning to her, one of the main wing bones appeared to be broken. Fortunately, there was no major bleeding from any of the injuries and Fidem told him she was hoping there were not any serious internal injuries that she could not see.

Suggesting she quickly set up a tent for Gwen then help her to get inside Fidem said she would then try to come up with some sort of splint for Dreki's wing. Dreki said he also thought the plan was a good one and Fidem began hurriedly setting up the tent in the first clear spot close to Dreki. Gwen had managed to get the tent unstrapped from Dreki but had not been able to drag it to a clear spot and start setting it up. It was the larger tent intended for the dragons, but Fidem was setting it up as a smaller version. It looked somewhat rumpled and sloppy but was adequate for Gwen and most importantly quickly erected. Heading back, she helped get Gwen to the tent explaining the situation as they slowly made their way over to the makeshift camp. Settling Gwen inside with her ankle wrapped Fidem then went to see what she could do to help Dreki. She had Dreki lay on his left side with his wing close to his body and the wing tip next to his tail. Using some of the longer tent poles as a splint Fidem began binding them to Dreki's wing above and below the broken section.

Thanking her Dreki told her he would be fine now. Checking on Gwen Fidem helped her out of her wet clothes and into her pajamas then began erecting a sort of porch just outside the tent with some leftover tent material. After a lot of effort, she finally succeeded in getting a small campfire going under the porch. Rigging up a drying rack using some of the branches broken off in the crash landing and after changing out of her wet things she placed them as well as Gwen's clothes on the rack near the fire. Wearing her poncho and retrieving some food she began making supper for the three of them.

Giving Gwen hers first Fidem then went and gave Dreki his. She was not sure if she would have to feed him herself, but he said he could manage on his own once she handed him his plate. Fidem got her own supper last and then joined Gwen in the tent; all were soon fast asleep. Waking in the middle of the night and rather than just dropping back off to sleep Fidem first went into the porch building up the fire so the clothes would dry better. She then went back into the tent and fell asleep again in a few minutes.

Waking the next morning Fidem was surprised how stiff and sore she felt, but after moving around a bit and getting dressed most of the stiffness had worn off. It was still raining lightly, but there was no thunder or lightning and not much wind blowing so Fidem was guessing that they had encountered the storm front as it had blown through. Building up the fire to finish drying the clothes Fidem was warming her hands at the same time. Putting on her poncho again she went to check on Dreki. He was awake so she told him she would get them some breakfast as soon as Gwen was up. Checking his wing she said the break was not swollen and should heal alright. She then started checking the burns now that it was light enough to see them properly and said that in addition to the damaged flesh where the lightning had struck there was some redness and swelling. Telling him she needed to clean and dress the wounds so infection would not set in she went and got the first aid kit. Fidem asked Dreki how he was feeling in general as she was working on the burns and he said he that the feeling of being achy all over was lessening and that the tingling sensation had gone away completely. As she was finishing, Gwen was poking her head out of the tent to check on them. Gwen told them she felt very stiff and sore, but other than the dull ache in her ankle had no other complaints.

Fidem then got them breakfast, and they began discussing what was to be done next as they were eating. They all felt that they should remain where they were until the rain stopped, but after that they should try to meet up with Gwendolyn and Hratt. It would be best if all of them had a single camp in the clearing until everyone was well enough to travel again. Once the single camp was set up they would be staying there for quite some time while Dreki's wing healed. Water was available from the stream in the clearing, but they had not brought along enough food for an extended camping time. Someone would have to try to obtain some from the forest dwellers, further west in Maith, or it would require hunting to supply their food requirements.

Fidem said she would start heading towards the clearing once the weather improved to try meeting up with Gwendolyn and make sure she and Hratt were alright. They could then figure out the best way of getting everyone to the clearing and setting up a single camp there. The rain continued steadily for the rest of the day finally stopping after sundown. Fidem said she would try heading out after breakfast the next day if it was not raining and try to meet up with Gwendolyn.

Coming to pretty much the same conclusions that the others had regarding the weather conditions Gwendolyn and Hratt were anxious about checking on the others hoping that the rain would stop so Gwendolyn could try to find where they were forced down and see how they were doing. She was also planning to head out after breakfast the following morning if the weather had cleared.

Finishing their breakfasts both Fidem and Gwendolyn headed out to see if they could make contact. They were each heading in pretty much the correct general direction but knew they could be off by quite a bit by the time they had gone the proper distance. There was a much better chance they would be passing each other by rather than meeting up. Also, there was the worry of how to get back to their camps once contact was made or if they did not make contact. Each of them being resourceful individuals had come up with the same plan putting it into action as they proceeded. What they did was to find a brightly colored piece of cloth tearing it into narrow strips. Getting to where their camp was still just visible they tied a cloth strip to a tree or bush branch at about eye level. Then proceeding as far as they could get while still being able to clearly see the strip they tied last they would then tie the next one. Continually repeating this process, they were periodically calling out each other's names.

After what seemed like hours, but was actually less than one, Fidem thought she heard something off to her left. Stopping and remaining perfectly silent she stood listening for a few moments. She did not hear anything else, but turning in the direction she thought the sound had come from she tried loudly calling out Gwendolyn's name. Listening again silently this time she thought she heard a voice coming from the direction she was facing, but it was very faint. Immediately tying a strip of cloth on the nearest branch Fidem started walking towards the faint voice sound. Calling out again about every 30 seconds she kept moving in the direction she was now headed. She was careful to remember to tie a strip before she got too far from the last one. In a couple of minutes, she was sure she could hear Gwendolyn's voice shouting that she was coming that way. Gwendolyn had also altered course heading towards Fidem now placing her strips at intervals as well.

Catching sight of each other they both waved tying a strip nearby before running and giving each other a big hug. Gwendolyn said that she and Hratt were fine and camp was set up in the clearing they had been heading to when the storm hit. She said they had been worried but could not set out any earlier to check on their friends.

Fidem then began telling Gwendolyn what the situation was in her camp. Gwendolyn said she was surprised, but also very glad that Fidem had been able to handle the situation so well. She said it was bad that Gwen had sprained her ankle and Dreki's wing was broken, but glad the injuries were not worse.

Sitting down and discussing what was going to be the best option for them now they spent a few minutes conversing. They were trying to figure out how to get the three crash victims to the clearing camp as soon as possible without aggravating existing injuries or causing any further ones. Suggesting that they head back to Fidem's camp Gwendolyn thought they should be talking it over with Gwen and Dreki as well. Fidem agreed and they began following the strips back without any difficulty and at a much faster pace.

Arriving back at Fidem's makeshift camp Gwen and Dreki both warmly greeted them. The discussion of how to get everyone to the clearing camp went on for a bit continuing as they ate a slightly early lunch together. Gwen said she could try hopping the distance or try leaning on Gwendolyn to get there. Helping Gwen to her feet the two of them tried walking slowly around the makeshift camp for a bit. Gwen said that walking with Gwendolyn for support was very doable and that she would be able to get to the clearing camp with her help. Suggesting that they go ahead and start that way Fidem said she would be staying with Dreki. She and Dreki would try to figure out how to get the both of them to the clearing camp while Gwen and Gwendolyn made their way there. Gwen and Gwendolyn agreed, and Gwendolyn said that Hratt would probably be getting worried if they took too much longer. Waving goodbye, Gwen and Gwendolyn started heading to the clearing while Fidem went over and began discussing their own situation with Dreki.

Dreki said that he would probably be able to walk through the woods weaving between the trees and picking the larger openings to pass through. He said there would be a couple of difficulties to overcome for him to be able to do this. One was keeping him on course. With him having to concentrate on finding the gaps between the trees large enough for him to pass through there was no way he would be able to keep track of his general direction at the same time. If they could not find a way to keep him heading in the right general direction with all the weaving he would be hopelessly lost in a very short time. The second had to do with the injured wing. He could not just let it drag on the ground. The bumps and pulls would be painful and would most likely cause further injury to the break site. If he tried lifting it using his wing muscles it was extremely painful and would also probably cause further injury. Some way of binding the wing to his body would have to be found.

Coming up with an idea for the wing Fidem went off to see about getting some rope. Returning with the rope she asked Dreki if it was possible for him to stand. He tried rolling over onto his feet but said that with his wing dropping the pain was too much. Fidem then took the rope tying it to the part of his wing that was about two-thirds of the way back from the shoulder joint. Tossing the loosened end of the rope over his body to the other side Fidem went around Dreki retrieving it. Now tying the rope to the transport harness on the right side of Dreki's body she had Dreki roll as far as he could to the left without hurting his injured wing stuffing the rest of the rope as far as she could under him. Now he was asked to try rolling over as far as he could the other way without pain. When he did this Fidem was able to retrieve the rope from Dreki's left side and tie it to his splinted wing on that side.

This time Dreki was able to roll over getting onto his feet without the wing dropping. Thanking Fidem profusely for figuring out a solution to their problem Dreki got a huge smile on his face. Fidem then asked if he could try walking through the trees a short way to see if any unforeseen issues occurred. He had no trouble getting through the first few turns, but then one of the pieces of luggage still strapped to his side got caught on a tree forcing him to back up. He said that he was afraid that he would not be able to do the necessary weaving with the luggage on. Deciding to just leave all the baggage at the makeshift camp they would worry about figuring out how to retrieve it later.

Fidem asked Dreki if he could see the cloth strip while weaving between the trees. Giving it a quick try he said no because once he started weaving the strip became blocked from view. He then said, but I could see or hear you if you were standing by the next strip. I could then be weaving heading in your direction as best I could. When I got close enough you could start moving to the next strip and I could just keep following you. Fidem said it was a great idea and that they should try it at once. If it didn't work they could just return to the makeshift camp until they could figure out something else.

Heading off with Fidem by the strips and Dreki weaving amongst the trees in her general direction they continued making their way. It was taking longer to get to the clearing than if there had been a path, but the progress was steady with Dreki being able to both pick a good weaving path and knowing where to head by watching and listening to Fidem where she was waiting. In about an hour they started hearing the voices of Gwen, Gwendolyn and Hratt, spotting them a short time later through the trees. Entering the clearing a few minutes later with the others eagerly welcoming them all were glad to be together once again.

Since it was mid-afternoon they began discussing whether there was a way to get any of the supplies from the makeshift camp moved to the clearing camp. With no path to follow getting through the woods would be much more difficult. Gwendolyn and Fidem would have no trouble managing the smaller and lighter items, but it would take a number of trips to get them all. That would still leave the bulky larger and heavier items stranded. Asking about a travois, Gwen mentioned the one used to get Daniel and his supplies home. Dreki said it was hard enough for him to be weaving through the trees by himself and did not think a travois was practical without a path. Gwendolyn said, "We could sure use a helicopter here!"

Gwen then said, "Wait a second! Dreki do you remember when you hovered so I could jump into the stream to help Daniel? If Hratt had a long rope would he be able to keep hovering above the temporary campsite long enough for us to tie the rope to a large bundle with everything in it?"

"If the rope were long enough that a bunch could lie on the ground while the end was being tied ,yes, it would work!"

"Gwendolyn and Fidem, do you think you could lay the tent flat putting all the stuff in the middle and tying the four corners together?"

"Sure, we could easily do that!" they replied.

"Why don't you two get Hratt the long rope from the third pack over there and then go get the stuff ready at the other camp. How long do you think it will take to get there and pack up?"

Gwendolyn said that she and Fidem should be able to have it done in an hour and a half and Fidem ran quickly getting the rope out of the pack and giving it to Hratt. Taking off for the makeshift camp following the cloth strips they were back at the crash site in a short time. Making sure everything had been collected they began laying it in the middle of the flat tent. Bringing the four corners together at the top they securely tied the corners to each other. Standing on opposite sides of the tent and a few feet away from it they were awaiting

Hratt's arrival. They had placed some damp green branches on a small campfire ensuring that the fire was making a lot of smoke. Hratt would have no trouble spotting the smoke column thereby finding the location easily.

It was not long before Hratt showed up lowering the rope until there was a fair amount lying on the ground. This allowed Hratt to be able to be rising and falling somewhat as he hovered without hindering the rope tying process. Firmly attaching the rope to the bundle Gwendolyn and Fidem began shouting to Hratt that it was ready. Easily lifting it and flying it to the clearing camp Hratt quickly set it down there. In the meantime, Gwendolyn and Fidem had extinguished the campfire and were making their way to the clearing camp as well following and then removing the cloth strips as they went along. Untying the bundle the gear was quickly stowed away. Now they were all together in the same camp again!

The next day was spent relaxing and planning what needed to be done next. There were several things to work out. Since it would take about six weeks for Dreki's wing to heal to the point where he could fly again they were going to have to camp out for quite a while. There was plenty of good water in the stream nearby so that was not an issue, but more food would be needed. This would mean a two-day trip getting to the forest dwellers and back or a four-day trip getting to Maith and back. Hratt would be able to carry about a two-week food supply, so several trips were going to be needed during their extended stay. Another option would be hunting for food, but this could not be relied on for the main food source. They also felt they were needing to tell the woman in the dungeon what the situation was. She was told there may be a delay, but six weeks more than what she had originally been told was much longer than what she would be expecting.

Discussing who should make the trip next did not take too long. Agreeing that Hratt had to go and that Fidem was a must to get past the barred gate in the passage was the first item. Dreki was obviously staying in the camp. Since it was a long walk in either location from where they would be landing to where the supplies could be obtained they felt it was best for Gwendolyn to go and for Gwen to stay with Dreki and let her ankle heal. With only Gwen and Dreki in the camp there was enough food for well over a week, so the plan was for Gwendolyn, Fidem and Hratt to be the ones flying to Maith and getting supplies. While they were there they could also be passing the word on to the woman in the dungeon that the delay was going to be much longer than anticipated, but that they were still planning to eventually make the rescue. They all got a good night's sleep and Gwen and Dreki were waving goodbye to their three friends as they were flying off after breakfast the next day.

Gwen was able to get around well enough that she took care of preparing meals and checking and redressing Dreki's burns. In a few days her ankle had healed to the point where she no longer felt any pain, and she was able to move around normally. Dreki's burn injuries were also healing nicely. Setting up the large tent and cutting poles to replace the ones used for Dreki's splint Gwen proceeded in setting up a somewhat permanent campsite. She found herself going into the woods and cutting quite a few straight branches. Cutting these further into different lengths she began tying them together in such a way as to make several sets of shelves. Moving the shelves into the large tent she was arranging them across the back wall. She spent some time going through the supplies and organizing them for an extended camping time rather than for ease of transport. Placing the items on the shelves at the back of the large tent they were now easily accessible when needed. There were also a couple of empty shelves waiting for the food to arrive from Maith.

Returning with the food Gwendolyn, Fidem and Hratt were surprised to see the large tent set up. Greeting them cheerfully Gwen told Gwendolyn and Fidem to start bringing the food into the large tent. Entering the tent Gwen took the bundle she was carrying to the back asking Gwendolyn and Fidem to bring their bundles to the back as well. Unwrapping their bundles they began stacking the items neatly on the shelves. Repeating the process, unpacking all the bundles and neatly placing the items on the shelves did not take them long at all. Heading back outside both Gwen and Dreki enjoyed hearing about the journey and Gwendolyn, Fidem and Hratt were being brought up to date about camp conditions.

Mentioning that the markets in Maith were well stocked Gwendolyn said that when further supplies were needed it would probably be best to take the extra time to shop there rather than hoping the forest dwellers had sufficient surplus. She also said if any non-food items were needed Maith would be the place they would have to go as well. Fidem then began filling them in on how the trip to the dungeon had worked out. She told them it was easier than the first time as they knew what to expect. Fortunately, they had not encountered anyone in the passages although they had been using caution in case someone had been sent for either wine or supplies. It was disappointing to the woman to learn of a further delay, but she was glad the injuries to the rescuers had not been worse.

Hratt mentioned that while they were there they had gone back to the cave entrance at dusk lighting the campfire by the south wall. Then flying back to Socair they lit a small bonfire by the edge of the gorge once it got a little darker. Making a practice run to the cave they found Fidem's suggestion of the campfire in that location was excellent allowing them to approach and land without difficulty. The cave entrance was also lit well enough to facilitate easily getting people into the transport harnesses. Extinguishing the fire, they left a stack of wood sufficient to be used for the fire on the night of the rescue. Finding that the bonfire in Socair worked equally well to guide them to a safe landing there they sat around the fire talking for a while as they felt that it would seem odd to be lighting a fire and then putting it out too soon. A good supply of wood had been left in that location as well.

Noticing some fish in the stream on one of her exploratory hikes Gwen thought they would make a good addition to their diet as well as adding some variety to their meal choices.

She had also noticed some deer tracks down by the stream and said that some venison would be good too. The three ladies said they could possibly try some hunting over the next few days seeing if they had any luck. Everyone knew that the fishing would have to wait until after the next trip to Maith when some fishing poles and tackle could be purchased. Fidem asked Hratt if carrying a couple of hay bales in addition to the food would be a problem. He said it would not be a problem at all but was wondering what Fidem wanted them for. She said as long as they were stuck there for quite a while she wanted to set up an archery range to practice on.

Over the next few days additional work was being done around the campsite to make it more permanent rather than just an overnight stay type of camp. Gathering some larger rocks from near the stream and placing them in a circle around the fire pit stacking them upon each other to form a ring or wall about a foot high was one of the main improvements. This way a roasting fish would not have to be held over the fire on a stick but could be skewered on a stick long enough to rest on the stone walls just turning it as needed. If larger game were obtained the stone walls would make cooking much easier as well. The next shopping trip would include looking for some type of metal grate or grill as well as a frying pan for the fish. Since there was no good way of cooking venison at the present time the deer hunting was put off until after the next shopping expedition. The ladies did do some scouting in preparation for actual hunting, later discovering when and where the deer usually came to the stream for water.

Some exploring of the general area was done, but nothing new of particular interest was discovered on these expeditions. They were not worried about getting lost as all they had to keep track of was the location of the stream. Before heading out they would note where the stream was and if they needed to be turning left or right when they got back to it after exploring. The stream would then lead them back to camp. They did find more puffballs a few times and were glad to add them to their meal as a nice treat.

By the time the second shopping trip had been completed things were in pretty good shape at the camp. Dreki's burns had finished healing, Gwen's ankle was well again, and all the minor scrapes and bruises were a thing of the past. Waiting on Dreki's wing break to heal was the only thing left now. At this point the splint had been removed since Dreki was not yet putting pressure on the wing by flying. He was now holding it next to his body without pain while walking around the campsite. Also, if anyone checked his wing by squeezing down where the break had been Dreki said that he did not feel pain there anymore. This was good news as all were anxious to resume the rescue operation and were hoping to be on their way in about two more weeks.

A hunting expedition was successful in getting a small deer early in the morning the day after the shoppers returned and they spent the rest of the day butchering the meat, grilling some steaks for that day, and preparing strips of meat for drying into a type of jerky. Preparing some steaks for the following day by putting them in a burlap bag and keeping them in the cool water of the stream was also done. It was nice to have the fresh meat for two days, but they did not want to take a chance on trying to keep meat fresh any longer than that. Having some of their dried provisions the following day they caught enough fish the day after that to have a nice fish fry.

Fidem had been diligent in her archery practice especially since there was so much time on their hands. Gwen and Gwendolyn had also been making use of Fidem's range quite a few times, but several times when Gwen and Gwendolyn had gone walking in the woods Fidem had opted for using her time for archery practice. After a couple of weeks of spending most of her day practicing she was becoming quite good. Gwen said that when they got back to Glyka she would make sure General Hapsom had her go through the qualifying test for the next level as she was sure Fidem was now good enough.

Testing his wing was the priority for Dreki when it was time for another shopping trip to be made to see if they were all able to leave together or more time was required for healing. Right after breakfast, going to the central open area of the clearing Dreki just tried flapping his wings feeling how it felt as the pressure on his bones and joints increased. This test seemed to be going well so he tried a couple of short easy flights right above the clearing. Landing after the third flight and smiling broadly at everyone he said that other than some stiffness from not using the wing so long it felt fine. Next, Gwen tried putting on the double saddle and he made a few more easy flights. Now came the transport harness along with the saddle. Adding Gwen to the load next, and finally Fidem as well, allowed Dreki to be testing under more actual conditions. All these trials were showing that the wing had healed to the point where it was strong enough for travel and Dreki did not have any balance or maneuvering issues, but did Dreki have the stamina for a long flight after being idle for so long?

Needing to find out the answer to this question they began discussing what the best way was to check this out. One suggestion was for Dreki to try flying towards the next clearing for an hour and then turn around and come back; then try flying for two hours and returning. The danger with this plan was that if Dreki got too tired he would be making another crash landing. Maybe they could try shorter trips and gradually lengthen them. This would end up being more time consuming and there still might be a point where Dreki became fatigued and yet was too far from a safe landing spot. Dreki finally said that if he was fairly high when he got tired he could start gliding at that point and be able to cover a good distance. Suggesting that instead of flying directly away and then directly back Dreki said he could make large high circles around the campsite until he got tired or proved he could fly longer than necessary to get to the next clearing.

Everyone agreed that this was by far the best suggestion as Dreki would not be too far away from the clearing to make a safe landing at any time during the test.

Here is what they finally did. Adding enough rocks from the stream to the transportation harness to make up for the weight of the supplies Dreki would carry Gwen and Fidem both got into the double saddle. Taking off easily and climbing to a decent height Dreki began making wide circles around the campsite. Meanwhile Gwendolyn and Hratt stood watching for a while eventually getting lunch going for them all. When enough time had passed for them to have easily gotten to the next clearing Gwendolyn and Hratt waved for them to land. Making a nice smooth landing Dreki exclaimed happily that he was not tired at all. He said his wing muscles were a little stiff at first and were now a little sore, but not enough to worry about.

Enjoying their lunch they all started packing their supplies for travel again rather than for the extended camping time. They decided on just leaving the metal grate, frying pan and the fishing poles and tackle at the campsite for the return trip. Putting the shelves Gwen had made under some trees to keep them out of the weather a little they left them stored there planning to use them as firewood on the return trip.

10

THE RESCUE

LEAVING camp directly after breakfast the following morning they were getting settled in Maith by the evening of the following day. Since it was Tuesday and the rescue was planned for Friday night they had some free time to make sure all was ready in preparation for the event. The next day Dreki, Gwen and Fidem made sure the firewood was still piled by the gorge in Socair then flew to the cave entrance. Checking the firewood in the cave first Fidem then made a trip down the passage verifying the padlock was still in place but not actually locked. Returning with the news that it was just as they had left it they all returned to Maith meeting up with the others. They spent the rest of the day relaxing and enjoying the freedom of being able to wander about without being confined to a clearing.

Thursday morning was also spent relaxing and wandering about town. About an hour after lunch Gwen, Fidem and Dreki made their way to the entrance of the cave. Traversing the passages to the open area Gwen and Fidem paused checking it out then heading on from there to the dungeon. Speaking to the woman they had talked to before they told her all was ready for the rescue the following night. Only if the weather turned bad or something else of a drastic nature occurred would there be another postponement. Heading back the way they had come Gwen and Fidem met up with Dreki a short time later in the cave entrance. All three then flew back to Maith and met up with Gwendolyn and Hratt. A bit more wandering, a leisurely meal and evening conversation rounded out their day. Since they had spent time getting to know several people in Maith during their evenings in the common room they had no trouble getting some to volunteer to remain sitting around the bonfire keeping it going on the night of the rescue.

Dawning bright and clear Friday looked good weatherwise for the rescue that night. Nothing unusual was done during the day, but it seemed to be dragging somewhat as all were anxious to complete the rescue freeing Relitto from Sordibus' tyranny. Gathering at the bonfire site by the edge of the gorge after dinner they remained waiting there until well after sundown. It was now dusk, and the light was almost gone. They could still barely see the cave entrance, but if they had not been so familiar with its location from their several previous visits missing it would have been easy. Lighting the bonfire, they stayed sitting around talking for a few minutes with the volunteers. They then went some distance further north so they would not be seen flying into the gorge heading from there to the cave entrance.

Landing easily in the dim light they soon had the small campfire started. Since they were sure by that time that the guards had finished delivering the prisoners' dinner they went ahead with the rescue as planned. They would just be cautious listening carefully before entering each new section. Heading down the passage with a lit torch Gwen, Gwendolyn and Fidem made their first listening pause at the barred gate. Only the expected very faint sounds were heard, so squeezing through the gap Fidem went to check the padlock. It looked just the way she had left it, so she removed it opening the gate. After lighting and exchanging the first torch they came to the three ladies continued heading on down the passage periodically lighting torches along the way but not lighting them all. This left some places where the light was very dim, but they did not want to have to be extinguishing a lot of torches while trying to crowd people further into the passage if trouble arose.

Arriving at the spot where the light from the round room was just visible they exchanged the lit torch for the one in the nearest bracket leaving the unlit one on the floor like the last time. Fidem left the other two ladies there creeping quietly up to the entrance into the round room. After pausing and hearing nothing unexpected she made the usual listening and light under the door checks at the wine cellar and storeroom. Determining that the coast was clear she was soon heading back to join Gwen and Gwendolyn.

Entering the round room Gwendolyn posted herself next to the passage entrance they had just emerged from. She would be guiding the escapees down the correct passage to the entrance of the cave from where she was now standing reminding them to continue quietly. Proceeding down the dimly lit short passage towards the open area ahead Gwen and Fidem continued on their way. Once again the listening pause was made before entering the open area. Entering the open area Fidem was removing her shoes and tying them to her belt before proceeding further. She was now in her stockinged feet and could be running if need be without her shoes making noise which someone could possibly hear. Walking over to the entrance to the passage heading towards the citadel Fidem posted herself there as lookout.

Knowing the way was now clear Gwen began crossing the open area unlocking and opening the first barred door. Taking the key with her, she then unlocked and opened the second door. The woman she had spoken with was waiting there with the rest of the prisoners waiting behind her. Gwen was telling the woman to let ten at a time go and remain waiting until all ten were inside the passage out before letting the next ten go. If an alarm was raised by Fidem she was to close this barred door lying down on the floor with all the other prisoners keeping silent until Gwen gave them the okay to continue the escape. Accompanying the first ten escapees to the natural passage entrance and letting Gwendolyn usher them on Gwen returned to the entrance by the open area and remained waiting there to signal for the next group of ten escapees.

Making good progress in getting out the escapees were steadily moving along. Since there was so much time before the next scheduled meal delivery nobody felt the need to rush. Making their way into the passage the group of ten could then see it was not a long one. Emerging from this passage into the round room they were crossing it and heading down the final passage to the cave entrance in a matter of seconds. By the time the first group of ten had arrived at the cave entrance there were several groups of ten proceeding along the passages at various points. Volunteering as loading helpers two of the men in the first group remained in the cave entrance. They were assisting the rest of their group by lifting the smaller ones into their seats in the transport harness. The seats were very similar to the bucket style child swing seats you might see at your neighborhood park, but deeper and with no opening at the front and once a person was in they could not accidentally fall out.

Dreki was loaded and heading off to the bonfire fairly quickly. The two men said they would be remaining until the end and would keep assisting people into their seats. They finished loading Hratt with his eight and he was taking off for the bonfire in a short time. Landing past the bonfire so he would not be seen if one of Sordibus' guards happened to look that way Dreki told the people to just head over to the fire and that there were people waiting there to tell them what to do. Heading back to the cave he passed Hratt as he did so. Hratt had a couple of men that were helping unload once they landed and like the ones in the cave were staying by the landing area assisting further groups. Hratt was passing Dreki on his way back to the cave with the process continuing in a very efficient manner until about half the escapees had been transported.

Fidem had been watching the escape progress and was pleased to see how smoothly the operation was going. Suddenly, she heard noises coming from down the passage to the citadel. Since they had plenty of time she figured it would be better having a false alarm than to be taking a chance and getting caught. Running quickly towards Gwen and giving her a warning Fidem went and closed the first barred door warning the woman in the dungeon. Quickly closing her door the woman was soon lying down with the remaining prisoners. Running over to Gwen, Fidem began helping her and the two of them started herding the escapees in the passage forward at a much faster pace. Getting them quickly through the round room the three ladies were rapidly guiding them into the final passage on the other side. Hurrying them all past the first lit torch they took it with them further down the passage. They continued leading them until they were all past the second lit torch.

Passing the word as she passed them that they were to remain still and silent, Gwen quickly made her way to the cave entrance telling each of the groups of ten that they were just waiting for the danger to pass. She had no idea how far down the passage noise from the cave entrance would travel so having everyone remain still and quiet was the safest.

Creeping back until she was almost in the round room, but just far enough in the passage where she would not be seen, Fidem remained listening. Waiting for about a minute she then clearly heard someone coming into the round room. Holding her breath and carefully listening she could tell that there was only one person and that they were going into the wine cellar. She figured they had been sent for a bottle of wine and would soon be coming out with it and heading back to the citadel. She was surprised that the person did not come back out. She was puzzled by this and was thinking to herself, "Surely they don't plan to sleep in there!"

After a few minutes, to her relief, she heard the door opening and the person coming out. When the person got to the round room Fidem discovered the reason for the delay.

Hearing a loud belch followed by a satisfied "Ahh" and the sound of smacking lips being wiped on a sleeve Fidem was enlightened. The person then headed back towards the open area down the short passage. Following at a discreet distance Fidem made sure she could still hear the departing footsteps. Peering out into the open area she saw the person continuing over to the passage into the citadel. Hurrying over and waiting she stayed listening just outside the passage. When she could no longer hear any sound of his retreat she waited listening for about a minute more to make sure the person did not return for something forgotten. She then began heading back to where Gwendolyn and the escapees were silently waiting. Due to the time spent by the person sampling the wine Gwen was able to make the journey to the cave entrance and back to rejoin Gwendolyn again outside the round room.

Telling Gwen and Gwendolyn what happened they were sharing a low chuckle about the belch before Fidem said the dragons could start the transport operation again. She then told Gwen and Gwendolyn to get the escapees back into their groups of ten again putting the torch back in its bracket and letting the woman know to restart the escape by more groups of ten from the dungeon when the last group closest to the round room started moving again properly. Fidem then headed back to re-post herself as lookout by the citadel passage.

Once the escape process was operating normally again it continued smoothly until all the prisoners were evacuated. When the woman from the dungeon was coming up to Gwen with the last of the escapees Gwen sent them on down the passage going back and shutting and locking the door in the bars at the dungeon. Closing the door in the bars by the open area she left the key in the locked door as they had found it. That way if someone else was sent on an errand and happened to be glancing at the dungeon they would not become suspicious seeing an open door. Joining Fidem and Gwendolyn at this time the three of them were following the escapees extinguishing torches as they passed them. Reaching the barred gate Fidem remained behind until everyone else passed. She then closed the gate locking it shut with the padlock. Squeezing through the gap she then joined the rest of the party. It was not too long until all the escapees were in Socair. Dreki made a final trip to the cave to retrieve Gwen, Gwendolyn and Fidem. They then extinguished the fire there and all of them made their way back to Socair.

Once all the rescuers and escapees were in Socair the escapees were all following Dreki as they had been instructed. He was leading them through the town stopping at various locations where townsfolk had offered their barns and other large buildings as overnight sleeping accommodations for the escapees. It was not as comfortable as their usual beds but knowing they were now free more than made up for it. Most of the people did not sleep well that night. It was not because of poor accommodations, but because they were anxious to see the signal the following morning indicating that Sordibus had been overcome. The arranged signal was that the soldiers in the citadel would be lowering Sordibus' flag and raising one of a different color. The flag would clearly be visible from the west side of Maith.

Rising early Saturday morning the escapees and rescuers were all up and finished dressing without delay. Finishing a quick breakfast, they were all making their way to the west side of the city and were soon watching the flag above the citadel. They were not sure how long they would be waiting, but they knew it would be after sunrise. Time seemed to be dragging on them as they anxiously waited.

Making the breakfast delivery the soldiers were glad at finding the dungeon entirely empty. Even though they knew that was what they were to expect it was still amazing to them that so many prisoners could be rescued without anyone in the citadel even being aware of it. Leaving the food there they were carrying the empty plates back just like they always did passing the word on to the other soldiers and guards they met along the way. Within a very short time all the soldiers and guards other than the ones loyal to Sordibus were aware of the successful rescue.

Since Saturday morning was when Sordibus would be doing his weekly review of the soldiers and dispensing praise or discipline to the troops at that time this was when the soldiers were planning the overthrow. As Sordibus was stepping forward in front of the troops instead of remaining at attention like they always did they made their move. Running around behind Sordibus and the bodyguards that surrounded him, the ones on the far sides began taking up a position in the rear, the ones on the near sides moving to his sides and the ones directly in front remaining there. Demanding that Sordibus and his bodyguards surrender the soldiers all drew their swords.

Shouting to the few remaining bodyguards not surrounding him to slaughter the prisoners Sordibus was surprised when the soldiers surrounding him totally ignored them. He had been expecting that most would have gone after the other bodyguards to try and save their families. Had they done this about half of his close bodyguards could then have easily attacked them from behind killing them as they ran off. Since none of the close bodyguards were making an attempt to attack a few of the outlying soldiers left the main group standing on either side of the passage the assassin bodyguards had just gone down. Returning, those bodyguards were so dumbfounded that there were no prisoners at all in the dungeon that they did not see the soldiers beside the passage entrance as they were emerging and shouting at Sordibus that there was nobody there. Being quickly surrounded those bodyguards surrendered immediately.

Seeing the others surrender the bodyguards surrounding Sordibus also began laying down their arms and surrendering as well. Sordibus was furious, but helpless at this point. The soldiers took him to the courtyard locking him in the cage. Taking the bodyguards to a large jail cell nearby they quickly locked them all in. Lowering Sordibus' orange flag and replacing it with a bright green one they began raising this up the flagpole atop the pinnacle of the citadel. They then went to the citadel gate facing Socair waiting for visitors to arrive.

When those waiting in Maith saw the flags change they let out a tremendous cheer hurrying out of town and beginning to cross the bridge over the gorge. The rescuers did not bother with the bridge simply flying over the gorge instead. Landing on the other side they were waiting for the escapees to join them. They were going to follow the escapees into the citadel, but arriving at the end of the bridge the escapees said that the honor of entering the citadel first should go to the rescuers. The two dragons with their riders then entered amidst many hurrahs followed by the cheering crowd behind them.

Hugging each other and shedding tears of happiness soldiers and family members were reunited. After the tumult had subsided one of the soldiers said they needed to decide what to do with Sordibus and his bodyguards. Several suggestions were shouted out including the cage treatment especially for Sordibus, shoving them off the cliff of the gorge one by one, hanging and by a firing squad of archers. Gwen asked to speak and being one of the rescuers everyone became silent listening to her intently.

Beginning by saying that each of the suggestions seemed justified she paused for a moment. This was accompanied by several shouts of agreement. Next stating that although just none was showing mercy. This was accompanied by a little soft grumbling. Explaining that by mercy she did not mean setting them free without punishment for their deeds again she paused. Some murmured agreement was heard now. Asking if anyone knew how the kingdom was governed before Sordibus took over and if there was any record of the laws of the land from that time period she stood silently waiting for any answer. Hearing none she suggested that before anything was done it might be good to try and find out what the original law of the land stated for dealing with the situation.

Everyone seemed to agree with this but nobody there was familiar with what the actual laws of the land had been before Sordibus. Dreki said there might be a citadel library with old records in it like what was in Vita. Asking about Vita and the laws there and how that applied to their situation the people waited for Gwen's reply. Mentioning that when she was in Vita they had been looking things up in the annals and the blue book of laws when they wanted to know what the original laws were and that both these volumes had been found in the library there. She also mentioned that she had found similar volumes in the castle library in Pacem where she was now queen and would refer to them when questions of law came up there.

The people seemed somewhat awed when they found out Gwen was a queen and asked if she would be willing to look at the library there and see if any books of laws could be found. Agreeing to do so the three ladies went with a group of people to start looking for the library. Dreki and Hratt were remaining in the courtyard as most of the citadel passages were too narrow for them to travel through. Passing through several corridors and looking into several rooms they finally discovered the library.

Spending the rest of the day there searching, by the end of the day they had not found anything useful in the volumes located in the library. They then decided to look for a second library in case there was more than one. They did not have any success in locating any other libraries in the entire citadel. Becoming a little discouraged and not sure how best to proceed someone suggested that they could take a vote on the best punishment with someone else suggesting that they could use the laws from Pacem or Vita. Another person then asked that if the laws were different in Pacem and Vita how would they know which one to use? Since no definitive answer was found they all decided to sleep on it and see what they could come up with on the following day.

Needing to come up with living quarters for the soldiers and their families was brought up. They did not wish to continue living with the soldiers all in barracks and the families in the dungeon. Agreeing that keeping Sordibus and his bodyguards locked up for the time being was best they also agreed that it was more humane to move Sordibus from the cage to a small cell near the larger one the bodyguards were in so that is what they did with him.

Heading back to Maith for dinner and to spend the night the rescuers said they would return to continue helping the following day. Leaving the citadel and flying across the gorge the restaurant was their next stop, and they enjoyed a hearty dinner. Since they had eaten a quick breakfast and skipped lunch entirely they made up for it at supper. Talking about what they thought should be done about Sordibus and the bodyguards they decided that without documented laws of the land it would be very difficult to know. Getting an idea Gwen asked what they thought of asking in the common room. They were not sure if anyone from Socair would know about laws in Relitto but felt it would not hurt as they were running out of other options at this point.

Finishing supper, they sat relaxing for a bit afterwards finally making their way to the barn. The dragons made themselves comfortable there with the ladies heading off to the common room. Sharing the good news of the overthrow of Sordibus in Relitto they asked if anyone there could give them information about the laws. Mentioning looking in the library but not finding anything they were hoping that maybe one of the people they had talked to before that knew people that had lived in Relitto earlier could help them.

An older woman said that their best chance would probably be to ask old William who was originally from Relitto. She said that he lived in a small cottage at the far south end of town. The cottage had a small stone well in the front yard and a bright blue door. Thanking her the ladies headed back to the barn to update the dragons. The rest of the evening was spent in more enjoyable conversation, but after all that had been done that day they were all tired and headed to bed early.

Rising much refreshed after a sound sleep the ladies met the dragons in the barn and all went to get a good breakfast. Finishing their breakfast the dragons said they wanted to wander a bit but would be waiting for the ladies back in the barn in about an hour. The three ladies then headed south to look for William's cottage. Walking along they were discussing what to ask him and were hoping to find him at home. Continuing down the road they noticed that after a while they no longer saw any more shops or businesses and only houses were beside the road. The further they went the farther apart the houses became and the size of the houses was diminishing as well. They could now see the end of the road ahead of them and only two houses and three cottages between them and the end. Passing the houses they were now looking at the first cottage. Since it had no well in the front yard and the door was red they passed it by. The next cottage appeared to be the one they wanted as it had the stone well and a blue door.

Going up to the door Gwen was about to knock when Fidem grabbed her arm gently pointing at the side yard. There was a man there with snowy white hair and a long silver beard. He was working in a small vegetable garden beside the cottage, so Gwen said, "Excuse me Sir, but is your name William?" Smiling at them the man said yes and asked how he could help them. Explaining to him the situation in Relitto they asked him if he could help them at all. Suggesting that they come sit on the patio and talk there he said he just needed to wash his hands asking them if they would like some cool water to drink. Excusing himself when they said yes he then went into the cottage.

Coming out he was carrying a tray with four glasses of water on it which he set on a small table on the patio. Handing them each a glass of water he took the last one for himself. "Now that we are comfortable let me see if I can help you," he said with a smile. "When I used to live in Relitto it was called Evimeria which is a much better name as far as I am concerned although Relitto was appropriate while Sordibus ruled. There is indeed a book with the laws of the land as well as a copy of the *Annals of the Kingdom of Evimeria* in the library there. I doubt if Sordibus even knew they were there because they are well hidden. The royal family of Evimeria feared that if ever a tyrant conquered them he would destroy the books of the annals and laws, and their history would be lost forever.

There is a secret niche in the library where these books are kept. Gaining access to the niche is very easy if you know the secret and extremely difficult if you don't. What you must do is go to the shelves labeled 'Stories for Children from Ages Past'. The books are in alphabetical order by title. You must find the first book with each letter of the name of the kingdom and pull it out about two inches. You will have two 'E' and two 'I' books side by side and one 'V' 'M' 'R' and 'A' book. Once these are all pulled out go to the middle shelf pressing in on the farthest left and farthest right books at the same time. A section about a foot wide in the middle of that shelf will now pop out. Removing this section will reveal the niche right behind it. When you are ready to hide the niche again push all the books back into place. Sliding the section hiding the niche back in will lock it into place."

Asking him how he knew about the niche if it was a royal family secret Fidem sat waiting with knit brows. William said that he was the personal servant of His Majesty the king when he had lived there as a young man retiring from the position when he injured his ankle and was not able to respond to a summons quickly any longer. At the time it was difficult for him to be in the citadel seeing everyone else going about their normal routines but knowing he was unable to do what he had so loved doing. Moving to Maith so he would not have that reminder constantly throughout the day seemed the best alternative for him. He would sometimes visit the citadel and was always heartily welcomed there and enjoyed visiting with those he knew. This arrangement had worked well for him. He did not have the constant daily reminder of his lost position but had been able to go and enjoy visiting whenever he wished.

Asking him if he wanted to go back to the citadel with them now that Sordibus was no longer there Gwendolyn sat waiting patiently for his reply. He said that he felt no desire to go there at the present time but would like to go there for a visit once the kingdom had a good ruler again.

Thanking him for the information and the good visit they had Gwen said they needed to get back to the citadel so they could retrieve the hidden books. They all said their goodbyes and the ladies went to meet the dragons in the barn. Walking quickly, they made their way back as they were anxious to tell Dreki and Hratt what they had learned. Entering the barn, they saw the dragons waiting for them and quickly began telling them about their visit with William and what they had learned. Leaving Maith, they all crossed the gorge heading to the citadel.

11

Evimeria Once Again

Entering the citadel, they greeted those they met while the dragons waited in the courtyard offering their help if needed for quicker transport back to Maith. Proceeding to the library the three ladies split up as they started searching for the shelves labeled "Stories for Children from Ages Past". After a few minutes Gwendolyn called the others saying she had found it. Gathering in front of the shelves they began pulling the volumes spelling Evimeria out the required two inches. Once all the volumes were pulled out the three ladies stood looking at each other and Fidem suggested that since Gwendolyn had found the shelves she should get the honor of releasing the niche cover. Smiling at each other as Gwendolyn centered herself in front of the shelves pressing the two required volumes they waited in anticipation. Working totally unseen the mechanical linkages all lined up properly thus releasing the center section covering the niche.

Removing the covering section Gwendolyn set it aside; all three ladies breathing a sigh of relief as they clearly saw three volumes in the niche. Asking Gwen to get one to look at since Gwen was the one who had the idea of checking with people in the common room again Gwendolyn stepped out of her way. Taking the volume on the left Gwen set it down on one of the nearby tables. Since the niche had been totally sealed by the shelf section the books inside were not dusty at all and looked pristine.

Retrieving the other two volumes and setting each one down on the same table with the first volume they were now ready to begin examining them. They then resealed the niche leaving the shelves looking like normal. They decided that once there was an official ruler of the kingdom again they would inform them about the secret niche. The volumes were all finely bound but had no titles or other labels on them. Opening each one to the title page they could now see what each volume was.

The three titles were *Annals of the Kingdom of Evimeria, Laws of Evimeria* and *Record of the Royal Bloodline of Evimeria*. Gwen then said, "We should probably get some representatives from the people here before checking these out." Agreeing with her they all went to find someone. Meeting a small group just as they came out of the library they told them what they had discovered suggesting that they get together with the rest of the people of the kingdom choosing some representatives to check out the volumes in the library. The three ladies then went back to the library conversing for a while as they were waiting for the representatives to show up. About an hour later a group of five people entered the library. There was a soldier, a guard, two women and an older man.

Explaining to them that there were three volumes of interest and that they would be learning different types of information from each of the volumes Gwen showed them the books. The group said that they wanted to start by checking the laws first so they could take care of Sordibus and his bodyguards according to those laws. After they were taken care of the next thing they wanted to check was the volume recording the bloodline. They were hoping that there was still someone of royal blood left to rule the land although they were aware that Sordibus had eliminated all the royal family and any of their friends that he was aware of when he took over. Lastly they would try looking over the annals for any other information that might be useful in the history of Evimeria.

Saying that they would now leave the decisions and actions affecting the kingdom in the hands of the representatives the ladies said that they would probably be heading back home the following day. Introducing himself as Vertrieder the older man said that he was spokesperson for the representatives. He asked them to wait for a bit then gathering his group off to the side he consulted with them for a few minutes. Vertrieder then asked if it would be possible for the rescuers to remain a bit longer. Since few people presently in the kingdom had lived under anything but Sordibus' despotic rule there might be questions of interpretation of the laws or external input needed as decisions were being made. Assuring him that they would like to remain longer if their help was still needed the ladies said they would be glad to do that, but they were not sure how much longer they could afford the cost of lodging and food in Maith.

Vertrieder said that arranging both those accommodations for them would not be a problem. He then told them that food and lodging would be provided for them in the citadel and that they could start moving in as soon as they wished. Gwen asked about sleeping quarters for Dreki and Hratt and Vertrieder said they had several larger rooms in the citadel with doors big enough for the dragons to pass through. Agreeing that the arrangements sounded good Gwen asked him to show them their rooms. Once the ladies were shown where they and the dragons would be lodging Gwen asked if they could meet the dragons getting their quarters settled as well. Heading out to the courtyard they escorted the dragons to the rooms they would be occupying. The representatives then went back to the library to begin checking the laws with the rescuers heading to Maith to settle their account at the Traveler's Rest and retrieve all their goods getting them moved to the citadel.

Retrieving the supplies from the barn the dragons then met the ladies outside the Traveler's Rest. Since the ladies had paid the proprietor while the dragons got the supplies they were all ready to go. Walking out of Maith using the west gate they then flew off landing in the citadel courtyard. The supplies needed for their stay in Evimeria were stored in their own rooms and what was needed for the trip back home was stored in the dragons' larger quarters. The transport harnesses and torches used in the rescue were temporarily left in the courtyard. Once everything was packed where it needed to be the ladies headed to the library to see if the representatives were there.

Finding the representatives seated around the table with the three volumes they entered the library and made their presence known. Welcoming them the representatives asked if they wished to be seated. They each took a seat, and Gwen told them that they were all settled in their quarters. She also mentioned that the transport harnesses and torches used for the rescue were in the courtyard in case they were wanted by the citizens of Evimeria for posterity. Thanking them Vertrieder told them that the items would indeed be kept as a memorial of the event. Gwen then asked for an update on the progress with the laws.

Vertrieder told them that they had indeed found references in the laws regarding their situation, but the way the law was written did not give them an immediate solution. Asking if he would explain the law to them and allow them to give suggestions Gwen sat waiting for his answer. He said they would welcome any suggestions proceeding to tell them that the law stated the punishment for a tyrant who had taken the throne by force from the rightful ruler was to be determined by the rightful ruler once that ruler was reinstated. If the original ruler was no longer living the heir to the throne would make the judgment when he was crowned. The punishment for anyone that had aided and abetted the tyrant in his overthrow of the rightful ruler was banishment from the kingdom unless they had killed someone during the overthrow. In that case, the guilty person was to be executed by hanging.

Asking if they knew who killed the royal family Gwen was told they were not sure if it was Sordibus himself or if any of the bodyguards did the killing. Vertrieder said that neither Sordibus nor the bodyguards were saying anything, so they did not know for sure. Wondering if William in Maith might know since he had helped them locate the books Gwen suggested that she go and talk to him again and Vertrieder agreed that it was a good idea. Gwen then went looking for Dreki as a flight to William's cottage would be much faster than walking the whole way.

Finding Dreki in his quarters doing some further arranging of the supplies Gwen asked him if he could fly her to William's cottage. He said that it was not a problem, so she told him that it was almost at the very end of the road going south through town. Climbing on, Gwen and Dreki took off. Rather than landing outside the gate and walking from there Dreki continued flying above the road south landing right outside William's cottage. William was in his yard staring wide eyed as Dreki landed. When Gwen got off and he recognized her he began smiling at her but said that her arrival by dragonback had certainly startled him. Introducing him to Dreki Gwen smiled warmly at William. William apologized for his patio and cottage not being able to accommodate a dragon. Dreki said it was not a problem and that he would just remain waiting in the road until Gwen was finished talking to him.

Inviting Gwen to the patio William asked if she needed a drink. Thanking him for the offer Gwen declined politely saying that the trip was very short and she was not at all thirsty. They went and sat down, and William asked what he could do for her. Explaining the need to dispense justice and what had been found in the books she asked William if he could be of any help in locating an heir to the throne.

Thinking for a bit William said he knew that Sordibus had killed all the royal family that was in the citadel, and none had escaped. Asking him if he knew whether Sordibus had done the actual killing or if any of his bodyguards were involved Gwen was waiting hopefully for his response. Again, he sat thinking for a bit, so Gwen remained waiting patiently not disrupting his thoughts. Finally, he said that it was Sordibus himself and one particular bodyguard. William could not remember the bodyguard's name, but he said it did not matter. Gwen would be able to pick him out easily. He was the only bodyguard to have a scar on his left cheek going all the way from his ear to his chin.

Thanking him for all his help Gwen said she was a little sad that none of the royal family had been spared. She said it was a long shot bet anyway and had not held out much hope. At that William quickly stood up exclaiming, "Wait! When you said 'long shot bet' it reminded me of the horse racing that they used to do here long ago. That in turn reminded me of something that may be helpful. The youngest prince in the royal family had always been extremely fond of horses and was often spending time at the royal stables. When he got a little older he asked if he could go live with his uncle who oversaw one of the royal horse farms far inland from the citadel. Since there were several older princes the king felt there was no chance his youngest son would ever sit on the throne, so he gave permission allowing the boy to go and stay with his uncle. That boy would not have been killed with the rest of the royal family as Sordibus did not even know of his existence! I do not remember the boy's name, and he would be a man by now, but the Record of the Royal Bloodline of Evimeria would have his name recorded."

Smiling broadly at William Gwen said, "Oh, thank you, William! I am so glad you remembered him. I better get back to the citadel and give them the news." Excusing herself and heading back to the road Gwen excitedly gave Dreki an update as they were flying back to the citadel.

Proceeding to the library to join the others she told them that William had told her that only Sordibus and the one bodyguard with a scar on his left cheek were guilty in the slaughter of the royal family. Vertrieder said that at least they knew that all the bodyguards, but the one with the scar were to be banished and the one hanged. He said that if nothing else they could hang Sordibus as well since there was no ruler reigning.

Gwen's mentioning what William had said about the youngest prince caused them to set aside the *Laws of Evimeria*.

Looking at the Record of the *Royal Bloodline of Evimeria* Vertrieder was turning the pages to find the last entries. Seeing all the princes listed with their dates of birth they could see that the youngest was named Lobarat. Suggesting that the dragons and their riders do a search to the west the following day since they had a name and possible location Gwen was hopeful that Lobarat could be found. Vertrieder had a quick consultation with the rest of the representatives saying that they all agreed to the search but felt it would be best to limit the time. They all felt that if Lobarat could not be located within two weeks execution by hanging for Sordibus and the guilty bodyguard and banishment for the rest should be carried out at that time. Agreeing that this was an acceptable plan the rescuers spent the rest of the day preparing for the search on the following day after enjoying a slightly late lunch.

Rising early and partaking of a hearty breakfast the dragons and their riders were soon on their way. They had a rough idea where to look as they found out there were several horse farms in the kingdom west of the gorge and where their approximate locations were. Flying over the gorge on the west side of the citadel and on from there they started their search. Since they were not sure of the exact locations they decided to split up so they could see more area and fly at a fairly high altitude to see farther. Flying in the same direction but only separated to the point where they were still clearly visible to each other they could cover more ground. If either saw an area with horses they would drop altitude as a signal to the others with all landing to investigate.

After flying for about an hour Fidem started pointing to an area off to the right where she thought she had seen movement in a large open field. Veering over in that direction to get a better look Dreki made a quick check but was prepared to veer back quickly so that Hratt and Gwendolyn would not lose sight of them. Finding that the movement was indeed horses Dreki immediately veered back dropping altitude. It was not long before Hratt and Gwendolyn noticed the signal.

Changing direction so they were heading directly towards the other three searchers Hratt and Gwendolyn glided down to their altitude as they approached. Catching up to them they followed Dreki as he turned gliding down towards the field of horses. They noticed stables located on the north side of the field landing near them.

Dismounting from the dragons the riders took the lead approaching the stables and calling out to see if anyone was there. Coming out of the nearest building a stable boy stopped dead in his tracks when he saw the dragons. His eyes widening even further when he noticed the saddles, he stammered at Gwen who was in front, "You... you actually rode those dragons here?"

Smiling at him Gwen replied, "Yes, we have ridden them quite far. It takes about two weeks flight to get back to where we started from. Hoping you might be able to help us find someone in your own kingdom we stopped to check. We are looking for a man named Lobarat who came from the citadel several years ago when he was young to live with his uncle. Do you know where we might find him?"

"I have never heard of him and why would you come here to find him?"

"His uncle was at one of the royal horse farms at the time, so we are just checking any place that has many horses. Could you tell us how far it is to any of the other horse farms and what direction they may be?"

"I have no idea but let me get Donal; he is in charge and has been here a lot longer than I have." Heading back into the building he came out of the stable boy disappeared. A short time later a large man with curly brown hair and a reddish beard came out approaching them.

Introducing himself as Donal he stood waiting as Gwen made the introductions for her party. Donal then said they had never seen anyone arriving by dragonback before and could understand Jack the stable boy's surprise. He said that he had never heard of Lobarat either but could help them in locating the other royal horse farms telling them that there were three more. There were multiple reasons for the separation of the farms. One was so that if wild animals attacked or there was a prairie fire the entire herd would not be wiped out. Preventing a disease outbreak from decimating them all was another reason. Controlling the breeding process was easier with the smaller herds as well. Explaining that the kingdom could be thought of as four quadrants with a horse farm roughly in the center of each quadrant Donal continued. This quadrant was the northeast one. From here they would find one almost due south and another almost due west. The last one would be to the southwest, but obviously in a different direction if they went to one of the other two he mentioned first.

Thanking him for that helpful information Gwen asked about how far apart they were. He asked her how long it had taken them to get here from the citadel and she told him about an hour. Thinking for a moment he then told her it would be roughly two hours to either of the closer ones, but probably more like three hours to the farther one. Thanking him again Gwen waved goodbye as he was heading back to his work.

Discussing the information given to them the searchers decided to make a loop checking the remaining three sites and returning from there to the citadel. Since a counterclockwise loop would be shorter and faster from where they were they were heading due west as they made the next leg of their journey. Since they now had a much smaller "target area" to be searching for as well as a direction to be going they did not feel the need to separate quite as far, but they kept flying high to get a good long view as they continued onward.

Finding this one was a little easier for them than the first one. It looked very much like the first and they only had to make a small course correction after spotting it. Landing near the stables Fidem mentioned that they were on the north edge just like the first one and she wondered if there was any particular reason for that. Making herself a mental note to ask about it she stored the question in her memory for later.

Gwendolyn said she thought there were more white horses in this herd than the last which made sense to her if one of the purposes for separation was for breeding. This time they saw a woman outside the stables as they were approaching, and she smiled at them after her first astonished look at the dragons and their saddles.

Coming up to them and greeting them she introduced herself as Bonnie welcoming them and saying she was curious why they were there. Explaining their mission to her and their progress so far she said she knew a Lobarat but was not sure if he was the one they were looking for. Since she knew they had just made a two-hour flight and it was around noon she asked if they would like to come into the larger barn to rest a bit while talking about it. Offering them food and drink if they wanted some she said she was about to have her lunch. Bonnie said it might be nice to be talking as they all ate. Thanking her profusely Gwen said they could all definitely use a break and the food and drink would be greatly appreciated.

Making their way into the barn Bonnie led them to a large table just to the right as they went in. With the three ladies offering to help the table was set and the food served in no time. The large table worked very well as the dragons each sat on the ground at the ends and the four ladies sat on benches along the sides. The conversation was mostly about Lobarat and anything helpful they could learn from Bonnie about him.

Bonnie said that about a year and a half ago was when they first met. Due to the distance between horse farms, there had never been anyone from another farm to visit hers before.

Lobarat said he was coming to see which breeds of horses were at her farm as he had an idea of crossbreeding one of his breeds that had been bred especially for speed with a breed that was bred for endurance. Since he did not have any high endurance breeds on his farm he was hoping that she might have one on hers. After introducing themselves to each other she showed him a group of horses that had been bred for endurance, and he said that they looked like good candidates for his idea.

After talking at some length, they decided that Lobarat would be taking one of the strongest mares back with him as he said he had an exceptionally fast stallion in his herd he would like to breed with her. He was hoping that after a few years the mare would have foaled both a colt and a filly. He wanted to try starting the new crossbreed with them. The mare had given birth to a beautifully colored filly that appeared to have the desired characteristics, and they were waiting to see what the next foal would be when the time came for it to be born about six months from now.

Bonnie said that at first Lobarat would make a visit about once a month to give her updates and that she looked forward to those visits a lot. As time progressed the visits became more frequent; their talks beginning to extend far beyond the horse updates. The relationship had become quite close. They had become engaged with him visiting her once a week now. They had been making plans for getting married and living in one location together but had not decided which location would be best. Since they were not sure where they would end up each of them had been training a replacement so that no matter where they went the other location would have a qualified horse master. Thinking about the last visit from Lobarat two days ago Bonnie smiled as she told them that the training was now complete and they could get married and move in together soon. Since the farms were laid out almost identically neither location was clearly better than the other. Remembering her mental note at that point and before she forgot Fidem asked Bonnie if there was a particular reason for locating the stables on the north side of the pasture.

Explaining that they were located the way they were for a simple practical reason Bonnie said that with the doors and windows facing south it allowed the sunshine to enter better in the winter months warming the stalls, but they were more shaded from the sun by the roof and nearby trees in the summer and stayed cooler. Bonnie also mentioned that there were vents for fresh air on the western end of the building because that was the direction of the prevailing winds. Fidem said she thought those were really good ideas and imagined the horses really appreciated it.

Thanking Bonnie again the searchers were on their way heading south this time, but with much more hope in their hearts. Approaching the next stop, they were all expecting to see the stables first as they were coming in from the north. Sure enough, they had to fly over them circling back and then making their landing in front of them. Gwendolyn remarked that she was glad the counterclockwise route had been shorter. When she saw a puzzled look or two she said it was because they never had to fly looking into the sun on the entire trip. Everyone agreed that it was indeed an unexpected bonus.

Approaching the stables they saw a man coming out smiling as he greeted them. He said he had always loved riding horses but had no idea dragons could be ridden. He said he expected it to be even more exciting than traveling on horseback. He said his name was Lobarat and asked how he could be of help to them. The searchers were delighted to have found him, but just to make sure there was not more than one Lobarat in the kingdom Gwen finished introducing everyone then asked him why he chose to live way out here so far from the citadel.

Explaining that ever since he was a little boy he had loved horses and that is what brought him there. He said they would probably not believe it, but he was a prince. He said he had so many older brothers that he had asked to come out here to live with his uncle so he could be with the horses he loved. Knowing that there was no chance that he would ever be king it had not been a problem at all. His oldest brother might even have been crowned by now and have produced an heir to the throne. Being so far away he never got news from the citadel and had been thinking of making a trip there one of these days to see how his family was doing.

Asking if there was somewhere they could sit and talk for a bit Gwen followed him as he led them into a large barn like the one that they had enjoyed their lunch with Bonnie in. Asking if they wanted anything to drink they all said some water would be great. Bringing out glasses and a large pitcher of cold water he put them on the table. Once everyone had their water Gwen said that he was who they were looking for.

When he got a puzzled expression on his face asking why Gwen said that she had some very bad news for him.

Slowly explaining about Sordibus, what had transpired in the kingdom and that he and his uncle were the sole surviving heirs to the throne Gwen then paused. Hearing that his entire family had been killed Lobarat wept for a bit and Gwen sat patiently until his initial grief had time to pass. Apologizing to Gwen for his emotional reaction Lobarat thanked her for helping to free the kingdom from Sordibus' rule. Noticing tears on her cheeks he also thanked her for her sympathy. Gwen then mentioned that her situation was similar telling him about the history of Pacem and that the restoration was going well there. She said that at least for him the citadel was intact, and he had subjects to rule.

Needing some time to process what he had been told Lobarat asked if the search party wanted to spend the night there. He remarked that the accommodations would be very humble, but he would appreciate it if they would be willing to give him council the following morning. Replying that they had been used to camping out in the wilderness for extended periods of time and that whatever he had would be more than adequate Gwen thanked him. Lobarat then showed them some bunks in a room at the back of the barn and Gwen told him they would be fine.

The searchers spent the rest of the afternoon just watching the horses and walking in the pasture. They left Lobarat by himself so he could have time to think alone. Coming back to the barn around sundown they found that Lobarat had the table all set and was just setting the platters of food down. Smiling at them he remarked, "Oh good! Now I don't have to ring the dinner bell." They all shared a laugh as they sat down enjoying food and conversation for the next hour.

Lobarat had quite a few questions about conditions in Evimeria with the searchers answering as best they could and asking Lobarat about his life on the horse farm and where his uncle was. Lobarat told them that his uncle had died a few years ago and that he was now running the farm himself. Explaining his uncle's death, he told them that his uncle had been trying to break a particularly spirited animal for riding and had been thrown high into the air off the horse's back. Unfortunately, he landed on his head breaking his neck and killing him when he hit. They said they were sorry to hear that and the subject changed to the more pleasant topic of running the farm.

Helping clean up after supper made the job go quickly and they all sat around the table afterwards and continued talking until bedtime. Lobarat said that he needed to let them know a couple of things of concern to him so that they could be better prepared to give council in the morning. Leaving the horse farm would not be a problem for the horses as he had just finished training a replacement horse master. He then told them about his engagement to Bonnie, and the searchers let him know that she had already explained that part to them. At this point they all decided to get a good night's sleep and save further discussion until after breakfast in the morning.

Resuming their discussion after breakfast Lobarat said that his main concerns would be what Bonnie would think about being queen and how both of them would adjust to royal life in the citadel and being away from the horses they loved. Remarking that she had faced a similar situation in Vita as well as in Pacem as she had previously told him about, Gwen said Vita had been difficult for her at first because like him she had led a normal everyday life up to that point and royalty had been thrust upon her suddenly. She told him that for her having others to help her through the situation was what allowed her to adapt. Confessing that she had no idea how Bonnie would react to the news she suggested that if Lobarat wanted council in that regard it might be best to have both himself and Bonnie together for that.

Mentioning that the Evimeria representatives in the citadel had been very accommodating to their needs and seemed to be working well together as a group Gwendolyn hoped to encourage him. Following the laws of the land and restoring the rightful ruler to the throne seemed to be their main objectives and she was sure they would be able to help and advise Lobarat in his new role as monarch. She also said that the five searchers would be willing to stay for a while at the start to offer their aid if needed.

Fidem had noticed Lobarat glancing at the horses from time to time during the discussion and particularly at the stallion, mare and foal that Lobarat had been hoping to create his new breed with. She asked if she could make a suggestion continuing when everyone answered in the affirmative. Concentrating on relocating and adjusting to royal life in the citadel was of primary importance she said, but the issue of missing the horses had not been addressed yet. Asking if it would be possible to take the stallion, mare and foal along to the citadel Fidem suggested that the new breed could be developed there on a small farm just across the gorge from the citadel. As the herd grew to the point where the limited space would no longer accommodate them the herd could be split. An appropriately sized small herd could remain at the small farm, and the rest could be sent to the various regular royal horse farms further inland.

Getting a huge smile on his face Lobarat said he thought that was an excellent idea and turned the conversation to getting together with Bonnie as a large group to see what her thoughts were. Deciding the easiest way to get together would be to all go to Bonnie's farm and meet with her there the search team all flew off in that direction with Lobarat following them after turning the responsibility of his farm over to the recently trained horse master.

Flying faster than Lobarat was able to travel by horseback the search team arrived there first. Conversing with Bonnie they were able to bring her up to date on the situation saying that Lobarat should arrive shortly to work out the details after finding out what Bonnie's thoughts were. Gwen was able to alleviate some of Bonnie's initial fears by sharing her own experiences and Bonnie was feeling a little less nervous about adapting to the change. The search team felt it would be best if Lobarat was present before discussing any actual plans, so they did not bring up the details of what was discussed earlier with Lobarat that morning.

Finding out from the search team that Lobarat would be arriving soon Bonnie suggested that they prepare lunch for all of them and then begin discussing things while they ate. Everyone agreed that this was an excellent idea and with the extra help Bonnie soon had a substantial lunch ready for them all. They continued conversing for a while, but it was not long before Lobarat joined them.

Finishing tending to the needs of his horse Lobarat then joined the rest of the party for lunch in the barn. Once they were all seated with full plates they began eating and discussing Lobarat and Bonnie's future together. Both Lobarat and Bonnie were excited about getting married and being together but were also apprehensive about Lobarat being king. Since neither of them had grown up at the citadel they were unfamiliar with the laws of the land concerning royalty. Lobarat had left to join his uncle before he had gotten old enough to have been educated in the royal protocols and Bonnie had never been to the citadel but had grown up on the horse farm. They were a little worried that there might be a law stating that the heir to the throne must marry a princess. Bonnie said she was also not sure she could handle being away from the horses she loved. Lobarat then told

Bonnie about Fidem's suggestion of starting the new breed just across the gorge from the citadel and Bonnie smiled warmly at Fidem telling her she thought it was an excellent idea. After finishing their lunch, the table was cleared and the dishes washed and dried. They then sat around the table continuing their discussion for some time.

Deciding that they really could not make any permanent plans until they knew the laws of the land they began discussing the best options for accomplishing this. Since both Lobarat and Bonnie had trained replacement horse masters leaving the horse farms was not an issue. Getting them to the citadel was the next step that needed to be taken. Also, the Evimeria representatives needed to be informed that the search for Lobarat had been successful. Lobarat and Bonnie agreed that they needed to make the journey, but that both needed to officially hand over temporary leadership to the trained horse masters while figuring out their future plans. Packing some clothes for the journey would also have to be done so Lobarat and Bonnie decided to make the journey on the following day.

Bonnie would be packing her clothes and accompanying Lobarat to his farm. After dinner Lobarat would do his packing and he would bunk with the rest of the men while Bonnie made use of the guest quarters. They would both be traveling on to the citadel after breakfast the following day meeting the searchers there. The searchers could introduce them to the Evimeria representatives and plans could be made after meeting with the representatives.

The searchers knew they could make it back to the citadel before it got dark, so they decided on heading back right away. Bidding fond farewells to Lobarat and Bonnie they were soon on their way reaching the citadel around sundown. Informing the representatives of their success in finding Lobarat they said that he and Bonnie would be arriving the following afternoon. The searchers then made their way to the dining area for supper enjoying some relaxing conversation along with their meal.

12

A New King

FINDING Vertrieder shortly after breakfast the searchers suggested that he gather the representatives and meet them in the library to discuss the situation concerning Lobarat and Bonnie. He said that they would be there in a half hour leaving to gather the rest of the representatives while the searchers were making their way to the library. While waiting for the representatives to arrive the searchers took a quick look at the *Laws of Evimeria* to see if they could find any law relating to whom the king was allowed to marry. They had not found any by the time the representatives showed up and suggested that the representatives try and find some. Explaining that this was one of Lobarat's main concerns as he was wishing to marry Bonnie.

Leaving the representatives to peruse the *Laws of Evimeria* the searchers took the *Annals of the Kingdom of Evimeria* over to another table to see if they could find any reference in it regarding marriages out of the ordinary. Since there was no "section" of the book relating to marriages the searchers knew they would just have to start at the beginning and go all the way to the end. They had been at this for several hours when they noticed Vertrieder approaching their table. Stopping when they saw him he suggested that they all break for lunch discussing their findings with each other during the meal. Marking their place in the book the searchers followed him and his group to the dining area.

Sharing what they had found Vertrieder explained that there was a fair-sized section on marriages in general and some specific references to royal marriages. He said they had finished skimming the entire section and the only reference they had found so far stated that a king must marry a princess. They were planning on carefully going over the entire section after lunch to see if anything was missed, but they were not hopeful of finding anything else. Gwen shared that checking the annals required a beginning to end search and that they were more than halfway through. They also planned on finishing after lunch but were also not very hopeful. All the references so far just stated a marriage had occurred but did not give any details indicating it was other than ordinary.

Finishing their meals both groups got back to work and finished after a few more hours with no success. Someone then suggested looking at the *Laws of Evimeria* to see if there were any laws explaining how Bonnie might become a princess. There were references for how a commoner could become a knight or dame by rendering valuable service to the kingdom, but nothing that allowed a commoner to become royalty other than a single reference. This reference was the same as in Vita allowing for a commoner who vanquished a foe in single combat. Since Bonnie had not been involved at all in Sordibus' overthrow and Sordibus had not been vanquished in single combat they knew it could not be applied in her case.

Hearing a slight commotion outside the two groups started heading that way to investigate. They found that the excitement was caused by the arrival of Lobarat and Bonnie. Approaching and ardently welcoming them Vertrieder suggested that they all go back to the library to discuss the situation. Lobarat noticed that all eyes appeared to be on him so he suggested that they all be seated and that Vertrieder as head of the representatives should continue leading the discussion filling him and Bonnie in on what the status of the kingdom was and any actions that had been decided on. Explaining first that Sordibus and his fellow conspirators were locked up awaiting trial and punishment Vertrieder began answering

Lobarat's questions. Lobarat then realized that if he was to be the one to decide Sordibus' fate it would have to be after he was crowned king. Lobarat said he felt hanging was appropriate for Sordibus then asked Vertrieder about the laws regarding whom a king could marry. Vertrieder reluctantly informed Lobarat that the king must marry a princess and that there was no way to make Bonnie a princess.

Looking over at Bonnie Lobarat saw tears in her eyes and told her that he would rather abdicate the throne than live without her. Vertrieder said that if he did that there would be nobody to rule the kingdom and a whole new government would have to be formed. Lobarat asked Vertrieder if he was sure all the marriage laws had been checked. Vertrieder explained that the book was laid out with each section complete and followed directly by the next section and that they had diligently searched the entire marriage section.

Gwendolyn then said she had a question. When Vertrieder asked her what it was she replied, "If a new law is declared or an old one amended does that mean they have to rewrite the whole book so it can be in its section? That seems like a lot of work to me. Is it possible that changes could have been added at the end?"

"We never thought about that, so I have no idea! Janice you are closest. Can you please bring the *Laws of Evimeria* over here so we can check it out?" Opening the book to the last entry Vertrieder started quickly turning the pages backwards. After about twenty pages he came to a blank page and stopped. He read aloud what was at the top of the first page following the blank one "Addendums to the Laws." Beckoning Lobarat and Bonnie to join him at the table he started turning the pages as the three of them were looking on. When they got to the ninth page of the addendums Bonnie suddenly gasped giving Lobarat a huge hug. Vertrieder loudly exclaimed, "Good news! It clearly states that if there is no princess of marriageable age in the kingdom the king may choose whomever he wishes as his bride. Thanks to Gwendolyn our biggest problem is now solved!"

Vertrieder then suggested that the representatives, Lobarat and Bonnie needed to come up with a plan for getting Lobarat crowned as a first step. He said that any comments or suggestions that the searchers had would be more than welcome as well. Vertrieder then stated that since it was getting near dinner time it would probably be best to be heading that way and just have a general discussion during the meal. This could possibly answer some of Lobarat and Bonnie's questions, but actual planning should be done at a formal meeting and not during the meal.

Agreeing that this was a good idea everyone continued making their way to the dining area. Most of the questions had to do with accommodations at the citadel and how Lobarat and Bonnie would be fitting in there before and after the coronation. They also discussed the length of time it would take sending messengers throughout the kingdom and for the subjects to make their way to the citadel. Setting up a small horse farm just over the gorge did not appear to be a problem so that was one less thing to worry about.

Finishing their meal they all headed back to the library to continue the planning. Prioritizing the coming events was the first thing they wanted to do so they started by listing them out. There was a coronation for Lobarat, a wedding for him and Bonnie, dispensing of justice to Sordibus and his accomplices, setting up the small horse farm across the gorge, as well as moving Lobarat and Bonnie into the citadel. All agreed that the most important thing would be to have Lobarat crowned king with the dispensing of justice following that. The wedding and horse farm could fit into the schedule sometime after that. As far as Lobarat and Bonnie moving into the citadel that could be handled immediately with each of them having a room of their own. Once the coronation had taken place Lobarat would relocate to the royal chambers with Bonnie joining him after their marriage.

Realizing that the coronation could not take place for several weeks they decided to go ahead and get the plans in place for that celebration and then see what could be worked out for the intervening time. The coronation was set for three weeks away and would be on a Monday. If the weather was good it would be held in the main courtyard of the citadel and if inclement it would be held in the citadel's main hall. The representatives would check with the general populace and find those best suited to help with decorations, meal preparations, accommodations both in the citadel and in Maith, and in planning the actual ceremony itself. The representatives would also have the soldiers send as many horsemen as they could gather to go throughout the kingdom proclaiming the upcoming coronation.

Moving on to the next item, dispensing of justice to Sordibus and his accomplices was discussed. It was felt that they should be dealt with on the day following the coronation. Since there were only two to be hanged the soldiers would be constructing two gallows for that purpose. The rest of the bodyguards would be divided into three equal groups and each mounted on a horse, but with their hands bound. They would then be accompanied by enough mounted soldiers to ensure that no one could escape. One group would be led to the northernmost boundary of the kingdom, one to the westernmost boundary and the last group to the southernmost boundary. Each group would then be dismounted from their horses have their hands unbound and be freed with the command to never enter the kingdom of Evimeria again on pain of death. The soldiers would then return to the citadel with all the horses.

Having the general populace already gathered and housed for both the coronation and dispensing of justice it was felt that it made sense to have the wedding on the third day. Vertrieder informed Lobarat that after checking with the soldiers he had confirmed that there was plenty of extra room in the citadel stables for the stallion mare foal and any needed supplies. They could be kept there until the small horse farm across the gorge was far enough along to move them there. Some of the soldiers would take a large wagon and make a trip to Lobarat and Bonnie's farms to get any supplies and personal belongings they wanted bringing back the three horses at the same time. Bonnie and Lobarat were then allowed to each pick a room in the citadel to move into and everyone retired for the evening.

Preparations had gone well, and everyone was looking forward to the upcoming ceremonies except for Sordibus and his bodyguards that is. Lobarat and Bonnie were settled in their rooms and were now familiar with the layout of the citadel. The three horses were comfortably lodged in the citadel stables and work was in progress on the small horse farm across the gorge. The rest of the preparations were completed, and all was in readiness for the coronation on the following day.

Dawning bright and clear the day of the coronation began splendidly. After everyone was gathered in the main court-yard Vertrieder opened the ceremony by welcoming all those from Socair as well as Evimeria that had made the journey to be present. The laws were followed as closely as possible, but because of the situation some minor adjustments were necessary. It was still a joyful occasion, and all were happy to have a benevolent ruler on the throne once more. Lobarat made a short speech stating that he promised to uphold the laws of the land to the best of his abilities and follow Evimeria traditions wherever possible.

Lobarat then called the rescuers forward and had them stand with him on the platform with the dragons standing next to the platform due to their size. He then announced that as the first act of his reign he wished to honor those that had taken part in the rescue of the prisoners. The first act he did was naming all of them "Friends of Evimeria" giving them full access to the kingdom including the citadel. They were also given the privilege of being able to have an audience with the king any time they chose. Approaching the dragons one at a time he had each kneel as he knighted them for their service to the kingdom. Climbing back onto the platform he then approached Gwen and Gwendolyn. He stated that they were already queen and princess in their own kingdom of Pacem and that Evimeria would acknowledge and honor those same titles in Evimeria. Lastly approaching Fidem he had her kneel. He then bestowed the title of Dame Fidem on her.

There was much cheering at this point but after a bit, King Lobarat raised his arms and everyone became quiet again. He then called William up onto the platform waiting patiently for him to make his way up there from the back of the crowd. King Lobarat said, "William, we want to honor you for your part in assisting the Evimeria representatives to find the laws of the land and directing them to look for me. We would like you to move into one of the royal chambers here in the citadel as a royal advisor. That way when questions about past events or conditions come up we would not have to summon you from Maith. We will also provide you with a suitable garden plot here in the citadel if that is your wish. Is this acceptable to you?"

"Your Majesty, it is more than acceptable. It is like a dream come true! I very much enjoyed being a personal servant to your father and have missed being able to serve the kingdom very much. This new position will allow me to serve again without having to worry about being too slow. I thank you most heartily for the opportunity!"

"You are most welcome! Is there anything you wish to offer your advice on at this point? Asked the king with a twinkle in his eye.

"Well, since you asked, I was wondering about the archery contest since I have heard no mention of it so far."

"It looks like your service is already of value to the kingdom as I confess I have no idea what you are talking about."

"One of the past traditions of the kingdom was that whenever there was a king's coronation there was an archery contest open to anyone present. If you look in the main hall you will see a target mounted high on the wall. There is a declaration written on the back explaining the event in detail."

King Lobarat asked one of the soldiers if he could bring the target to him so he could read the declaration. While they were waiting the king asked William if he remembered anything else. William said no, but that as future events occurred something might be recalled. After another minute or two they saw the soldier returning with the target. King Lobarat removed the declaration from the back reading it aloud to the assembly. The declaration stated that the contest was to be held on the first Saturday following the coronation, anyone present at the coronation could compete, the target was to be placed at a distance of 75 yards, a single pea was to be placed dead center in the bullseye, each contestant would use a new target and have three shots with the oldest archer going first and the youngest going last. The prize for the archer who had the best shot was five gold pieces and if that archer's arrow managed to touch the pea they would receive a gold arrow and a pouch full of money as well. The king then announced that anyone interested in competing should let Vertrieder know no later than Wednesday evening so that the correct number of targets could be prepared. The assembly was then officially dismissed, but people were encouraged to spend time visiting with each other.

Later that day when Gwen, Gwendolyn and Fidem were telling Vertrieder that they wished to participate in the contest they found out that there were already several of the soldiers who had signed up as well. Vertrieder said that he knew some of them to be very good archers and he was expecting it to be an exciting contest. He said he had been talking to William and that as far as anyone could remember no archer had ever hit the pea although several had come close in past contests.

Gathering the next day, the crowd had much more somber expressions on their faces. The first event was the hanging of Sordibus and the bodyguard with a scar on his cheek. King Lobarat pronounced the sentence and both men were hanged according to the law. The rest of the bodyguards were split into three groups as planned and banished from the kingdom.

The people then went about their normal daily routines just spending time wandering in Maith or visiting with friends.

Wednesday dawned bright and cheery, which matched the mood of the subjects as well. Everyone was joyfully anticipating the wedding and finished up their early morning preparations quickly. The wedding itself was beautifully done with the Prime Minister of Socair officiating since it was not a kingdom and he was the highest official in that land. In Evimeria the law was that when a king or queen got married the spouse was crowned as the ending part of the ceremony and there was much cheering for Queen Bonnie when this was done. There was a lovely reception afterwards and the couple was warmly congratulated by all the attendees.

Only a few people were heading home the following day as most elected to stay until Saturday for the archery contest. Saturday finally arrived and when Gwen, Gwendolyn and Fidem were approaching the range they noticed that there were about 20 soldiers there as well as about two dozen men and women from Maith and Evimeria. They also saw that the three of them would be going last as all the other contestants were older than they were, but a few were not much older than Gwendolyn. King Lobarat officially opened the contest from a platform to the side of the archery range.

As the contest progressed the results were quite varied. It was apparent that some contestants had just entered for the fun of it and were not very good archers, but several of the soldiers had done quite well with one putting all three of his arrows in the bullseye with one only half an inch from the pea. There had been much cheering when this feat was accomplished and the rest of the contestants ahead of the three ladies had not done any better.

It was now Gwendolyn's turn, and she carefully made her three shots, but only one was just in the bullseye and the other two in the next ring. Smiling at Gwen as she was leaving the shooting line she said she had not expected to win but was pleased to have done as well as she did. Stepping up to the shooting line and taking careful aim Gwen put her first arrow in the bullseye about an inch from the pea. Her second shot was a little closer, but concentrating on her last shot she put it so close to the pea that it was almost but not quite touching it. A huge cheer erupted from the crowd at that point.

When the crowd saw Fidem approaching the shooting line a few snickers and some murmuring could be heard about her size, but several gasps were heard when her first shot was about half an inch from the pea. Her second shot was a little closer, but not quite as close as Gwen's was. Preparing to take her last shot the crowd was absolutely silent and some were holding their breath waiting. Noticing the leaves on the trees were moving slightly due to the wind Fidem just stood waiting for a moment or two. When the leaves stopped moving she took a deep breath making her shot as she slowly released her breath. With her arrow hitting the pea dead center the crowd jumped to its feet clapping and cheering with loud hurrahs. Fidem just stood staring at the target until Gwen ran up to her giving her a huge hug.

"Oh Fidem, this is wonderful! It looks like all that practice time you put in definitely paid off."

Quieting the crowd down King Lobarat then called Fidem up onto the platform. He then announced in a loud voice while handing her the gold pieces, the gold arrow and the money pouch, "Dame Fidem, it is not only my pleasure to award you the five gold pieces as winner of the contest, but also to award you the gold arrow and money pouch for touching the pea. As far as it is known from Evimeria history you are the first archer to ever earn the gold arrow. Is there anything you would like to say?"

"Thank you, your Majesty, and I do have a suggestion to make."

"Please tell us what it is!"

"It would seem a shame for me to be taking the gold arrow away from the kingdom of Evimeria even though it was fairly earned. It also seems a shame to make everyone wait for the next coronation for a chance to win one. My suggestion would be to have an annual archery contest. The winner would have the privilege of possessing this gold arrow for the following year. They could display it in a prominent place in their residence. You could keep the original tradition of the coronation contest, and this one could be a separate yearly contest for residents of the kingdom. For my year of possession, the arrow could be hanging under the target in the main hall."

"Dame Fidem, I think that is an excellent idea! We will be displaying the arrow as you suggested and having a yearly contest for the possession of Dame Fidem's Gold Arrow as that is what it will be called henceforth."

The clapping and loud hurrahs erupted from the crowd once more as Fidem was leaving the platform to join her friends. They were all anxious to see the arrow and other prizes she had won. Showing them the arrow first she said she needed to give it to Vertrieder to prepare it to be put on display once they had finished looking at it. They then looked at the contents of the money pouch and were surprised to see that it was filled with gold coins of various sizes and that the contents were worth a sizable amount. Fidem added her five gold pieces to the pouch making it fairly heavy now.

13

Return to Glyka

R EQUESTING an audience the following day the rescuers met with King Lobarat and Vertrieder in the council chamber. Gwen acting as spokesperson for the rescuers told the king and Vertrieder that they felt it was time for them to return home. She said that although they were willing to stay and help if needed there did not appear to be a need with William as royal advisor. She also mentioned that the king should ask William about where the important books they found should be kept.

King Lobarat then thanked them again for all they had done telling them that they were always welcome to visit any time they chose. He also said that it would be good to have official peace treaties between Evimeria and Pacem, Vita and Dartan. He asked Gwen if she would agree to this for Pacem and Vita and asked Fidem if she would be willing to represent Dartan. Gwen agreed immediately to represent Pacem and said as previous Queen of Vita she would sign pending the approval of King Kelan. Fidem said she agreed it would be good for Dartan as well but did not think she had the authority to do so. King Lobarat then suggested that they go ahead and sign the treaties with Dame Fidem signing as a temporary Ambassador to Evimeria from the kingdom of Dartan. Fidem could then take her copy back to Dartan and see if King Firinne would acknowledge it as official. She could then let Lobarat know when she made her next trip to Evimeria.

All thought this was an excellent suggestion and Fidem was officially accepted as temporary ambassador. The treaties were then signed and the rescuers given their copies. The rescuers then made their way to their quarters preparing for their return journey the following day. Once all was in readiness for the journey back they spent the rest of the day saying their farewells to those they had gotten to know in Evimeria.

Making their way back to Glyka was accomplished without any difficulties and they made their usual one day stop in Vita. They gave King Kelan and Queen Rachel an update on the situation and both the king and queen agreed to abide by the peace treaty and were given their copy. The king and queen said they had no problem with Queen Gwen signing the treaty for Vita. The rescuers enjoyed the rest of their short stay in Vita just relaxing and visiting.

Finishing a leisurely breakfast the rescuers made their way back to Glyka by mid-morning. They were asked to go to the council chamber as soon as they entered the palace to give King Firinne a full report of what happened. Fidem was told that she was to go there as well when she asked if she needed to report to General Hapsom's office first. Arriving at the council chamber the rescuers saw that King Firinne, General Hapsom and Royal Advisor Jenny were waiting for them. Jenny had a pen, ink and paper in front of her and was obviously going to be recording the minutes of the meeting so they could be entered into the annals.

Warmly welcoming them all back King Firinne mentioned that he had started to worry a little as so much time had passed since they left. He said he had wondered if Corporal Fidem had not been able to fit through the gap by the gate and if something else had to be figured out instead. Gwen then spoke up, "Your Majesty before we go further I need to make you aware of something." Continuing when King Firinne gave permission, "It seems to me that it is appropriate for

General Hapsom to refer to Corporal Fidem as such since she is under his command, but I think the rest of us should use her proper titles when referring to her in an official manner. She is now Dame Fidem as well as temporary Ambassador to Evimeria from Dartan at King Lobarat's request. She has a copy of a peace treaty for you that she signed on Dartan's behalf pending your approval of course."

King Firinne replied, "It appears that there is much more to Dame Fidem than her age and size would indicate and I am anxious to hear how she earned these titles. Since Queen Gwen was present for the bestowing of the titles and signing of the treaty and I have full confidence in her judgment I approve of the treaty as signed by temporary Ambassador Fidem. Now Gwen, please give us a full report."

It took quite some time to get the report recorded and questions from King Firinne and General Hapsom answered. With the entire group taking breaks for both lunch and dinner, they did not finish until late that evening. King Firinne then dismissed everyone so they could get a good night's sleep telling Fidem that she would have the following day off to recuperate from the journey. He remained talking with General Hapsom for a while and then they both retired for the evening as well.

Gwen and Gwendolyn both spent most of the next day visiting with friends both sharing and getting news of what had been happening. Dreki and Hratt were relaxing in the palace grounds conversing with whoever happened to come up and speak with them. Fidem spent the day with her mother updating her as to all that had happened on the mission to Relitto. Explaining that it was now Evimeria she told her mother about the events that had transpired to bring this about. Her mother could not help shuddering when Fidem mentioned the cruelty of Sordibus and about the person coming for the wine in the middle of the escape. She could hardly believe that her young daughter was not only Corporal Fidem of the Elite Palace Guard Corps but was now

Dame Fidem and the temporary Ambassador to Evimeria from Dartan as well.

The next day at breakfast King Firinne announced to the rescuers that there would be an assembly the next morning at 9:00 AM to honor them for their help in aiding a country that is now their ally. Finishing their breakfast the rescuers agreed with Fidem when she said she needed to report to General Hapsom to find out what her new duties and schedule would be and how to fit the assembly into it. Fidem then departed to report in with the rest of the rescuers spending a relaxing day with nothing special planned.

Approaching General Hapsom Fidem said she was reporting in to get her assignments and see if there was a schedule set up for her yet. She mentioned the fact that since she had been practicing archery the whole time she had been on the mission she was not sure if she would still need the close personal instruction from Colonel Veren.

General Hapsom then spoke, "Corporal Fidem, after hearing Gwen's report yesterday I have been wondering the same thing. I was also hoping you could help me to kill two birds with one stone as Gwen says?"

"How can I do that General?"

"I was hoping you would be willing to demonstrate your archery skill at the assembly tomorrow. That way you can show everyone how you have progressed and I could do an official evaluation of your skill level at the same time. Since you have not practiced your archery while in uniform it would probably be best to dress as you did on the mission. You will be on the platform with the others you traveled with rather than with the rest of the guards in any case."

"I would be glad to do that. What are my assignments and duties to perform for today or tomorrow?"

"Today I would like you to check in with Shauna to see if your bow is still adequate or if a new one needs to be ordered. If you spent as much time practicing as I expect you did a stronger bow may be needed now. After that you can spend the rest of the day as you please. You are free until tomorrow after the ceremony and reception. Report to me then and we will discuss your schedule."

"Thank you General I will check with Shauna at once."

Fidem then began heading towards the bow crafters' building with General Hapsom going to take care of his own business.

Arriving at the bow crafters' building Fidem was greeted graciously as she entered with Shauna giving her a big smile as she came up to her. Fidem told her what General Hapsom had said about checking her present bow which Fidem had thoughtfully brought with her. Shauna then had Fidem hold it and verified that the grip was still the right size. Measuring the draw weight to make sure that it had not changed came next followed by her bringing several bows for Fidem to test. Just like Veren had done before Shauna explained that the test was just to determine Fidem's draw strength and the bows would probably feel awkward. Fidem said she remembered doing this with Veren and the checks were made quickly. Shauna said that Fidem's strength had definitely increased with all her practice and that she would be making a new and stronger bow for Fidem. She said it would be a couple of weeks like last time; and thanking her Fidem headed off to give General Hapsom an update on the bow situation.

Heading to the archery range a little later Fidem spent some time practicing as it was a joy for her to be at an actual range with targets that she could easily move to wherever she wanted rather than her hay bales at the campsite. Approaching the archery range from one of the buildings Veren stopped in the shadows so he would not distract Fidem and just stood watching her for a bit. He was amazed that she did not bother with any of the target positions except the farthest two. She varied the distance between the two keeping the target somewhere between them as she tried adjusting her aim for the different distances. She had no trouble putting all her shots in the bullseye at the closer distance but could only hit the bullseye on about every third shot at the farthest distance.

Coming up to her at that point and greeting her cheerily he said that he would talk to General Hapsom, but he felt that her skills were now beyond his abilities to improve them. He said that in his opinion it was just a matter of her building her strength to be able to get accuracy at the farthest distance and that her technique was fine. When she told him what the general was planning for the ceremony the next day he said that would be great and that he would not mention what he had seen today to anyone. He told her that although nobody had questioned him about her being given the silver Sharpshooter pin he had seen looks on a few faces that showed obvious doubt. Also there had been some talk amongst the guards, particularly the younger ones, about possible favoritism, but again no direct accusations were made. Veren then said he was anxiously awaiting the chance for Fidem to put all the doubts to rest then headed off to his original destination. Fidem then went in search of her friends to enjoy spending a relaxing rest of the day with them.

Dawning bright and clear the next day appeared ideal for a large outdoor ceremony and everyone was looking forward to it. The 9:00 AM time allowed for all the after-breakfast cleanup as well as duties like feeding horses to be completed beforehand. The large outdoor area that had been used for the Day of Deliverance celebration was again put to use as that allowed enough room for everyone that wished to be present to attend. There was a large crowd gathered when King Firinne opened the ceremony.

First, calling the two dragons forward using their titles he presented each of them with a gold medallion on a purple ribbon which he hung around their necks. "Sir Dreki and Sir Hratt the kingdom of Dartan thanks you for your valuable service in freeing a distant kingdom from a tyrannical ruler and securing it as an ally. The titles bestowed on you in Evimeria will also be acknowledged here in Dartan. Please kneel." Here the king knighted both Dreki and Hratt as Sir Dreki and Sir Hratt of Dartan.

Calling Queen Gwen and Princess Gwendolyn up to the platform he presented them with similar medallions. "Queen Gwen and Princess Gwendolyn the kingdom of Dartan also thanks you for your valuable service in freeing a distant kingdom from a tyrannical ruler and securing it as an ally. The titles held by you in Pacem were already acknowledged here in Dartan, but this ceremony now makes it official."

Finally, calling Fidem up onto the platform he presented her with a medallion on a ribbon as well. As he suspected there were quite a few looks of incredulity in the crowd as he used her titles, "Dame Fidem and temporary Ambassador to Evimeria from Dartan the kingdom of Dartan also thanks you for your valuable service in freeing a distant kingdom from a tyrannical ruler and securing it as an ally. The titles bestowed on you in Evimeria will also be acknowledged here in Dartan. You also have never been thanked publicly for the service you rendered the kingdom in killing the wolf at the archery range. It has also come out in the report of the events of the mission that not only were you able to accomplish your intended goal of getting the barred gate open allowing the prisoners to be rescued, but you were also able to render much needed medical assistance to Sir Dreki allowing his wing to heal properly and thus the mission to be completed. Please kneel."

When Fidem knelt down King Firinne drew his sword and proclaimed, "Dame Fidem of Evimeria it is my pleasure to also bestow upon you the titles of Dame Fidem of Dartan as well as *official* Ambassador to Evimeria from Dartan for your services to this kingdom. Arise, Dame Fidem." King Firinne then said, "Let us all thank these worthy individuals!" There was much clapping and loud cheering at this point and when the crowd finally quieted down King Firinne turned the platform over to General Hapsom.

General Hapsom then explained that he wished for Dame Fidem to demonstrate her archery capabilities taking her down from the platform to an archery lane that had been set up there for her. Explaining to the crowd that the target had been placed at the Sharpshooter distance he said Dame Fidem had to put five out of six arrows in the bullseye to qualify. He also explained that if the arrow touched the edge of the bullseye at all it was considered a hit. Fidem was noticing that the target was even closer than where she had been practicing the day before and she had no trouble at all putting all six arrows near the center of the bullseye. A good bit of cheering occurred after her last shot.

General Hapsom then moved the target farther down the lane to a position between the two distances Fidem had practiced at the day before, but nearer the closer distance. Fidem again had no trouble putting all six arrows in the bullseye, but they were not quite as near the center as her first set. Even louder cheering was heard after her last shot this time. General Hapsom said that Dame Fidem had just qualified as Sharpshooter Instructor asking her if she wanted to try the next level. He explained that anything beyond what she had already done was beyond the normal capability of the strength bow she had and would be very difficult. He also said that he had not planned to test beyond the bow's normal capabilities, but seeing how well she had done so far the choice was up to her.

Fidem said she was willing to try, but that she might take a little longer as she would need to concentrate more. General Hapsom then moved the target farther down the lane, but Fidem noticed that it was not as far as the farthest target, but a little closer to that distance than the last position she had shot at. General Hapsom again said that it would take five out of six shots in the bullseye to qualify for this level asking the spectators to please keep silent so Dame Fidem could concentrate.

Fidem had doubts about this distance but was concentrating on the center of the bullseye envisioning a pea placed there like in the Evimeria contest. Though the target was quite a bit farther than in the Evimeria contest she took her time making sure she was relaxed as she loosed her arrows. The first two shots were in the bullseye, but the third shot was just out. The next two shots were just in the bullseye, and she set her bow down shaking her arms out before picking it up again for the final shot. Peering at the target after her final shot she could see that the arrow looked like it was just outside the bullseye. General Hapsom retrieved the target and said as he was bringing it back, "If you look closely the last shot is outside the bullseye, but it did just nick it, so it counts as a hit!"

The entire crowd was now on its feet cheering loudly and clapping. General Hapsom then led Fidem back up onto the platform waiting for the noise of the crowd to subside. He finally had to hold his arms over his head to get the crowd settled back down. "I am now going to address Dame Fidem as her superior as an Elite Palace Guard."

Here he turned to Fidem continuing, "Corporal Fidem, you have achieved much here today. You have easily demonstrated that you had the right to wear your silver Sharpshooter pin that was presented to you earlier. You have also qualified as Sharpshooter Instructor and have earned the gold Expert pin in archery as well. Even though the Sharpshooter Instructor level is not as difficult to achieve as the gold Expert level it also means you have earned a rank promotion. By qualifying as an instructor, you are hereby promoted to the rank of sergeant. You will receive both these awards formally at the next palace guard ceremony. You are too young for your rank to apply to normal guard duties and interactions with other guards on a day-to-day basis, but on the archery range your rank will be fully respected as an instructor."

General Hapsom then turned the platform over to King Firinne who made a few closing remarks and then dismissed the assembly for the reception. Enjoying refreshments and conversation the attendees greeted those that were honored thanking them for their service and congratulating Sir Dreki, Sir Hratt and Dame Fidem for the titles they had earned.

As the reception was winding down Fidem told her friends that she needed to be checking with General Hapsom to find out what her duties and schedule would be. Bidding them all farewell, she went off to find the general. Approaching her quarters Fidem saw that General Hapsom was standing just outside the building. She went up to him saluting saying she was reporting as instructed. He said that after her performance and speaking with Colonel Veren it was evident that she no longer needed his instruction in archery. The general then told her that as her main duty she was assigned to Veren as an apprentice instructor. Veren would show her what she needed to do and once he was confident that she was able to instruct on her own he would have her start with the lower levels working her way up to the Sharpshooter level. He would set her schedule and inform the general what her non-scheduled on-duty times were. The general would then see what other duties could be assigned. If Fidem was wanting to use some of this time for her own practice the general said he did not have a problem with that and she should just let Colonel Veren know. The general then told Fidem she could find him in the bow crafters' building. Fidem then departed to find him heading off in that direction.

14

CHECKING BACK HOME

GWEN, Gwendolyn and the dragons got together and began discussing what they wanted to do next. Gwen and the two dragons felt that a trip back home for them all to check on things there would be good. They could then decide if it would be best to stay home or return fairly soon for more visiting. They asked Gwendolyn if she was ready to go back to her own world or if she wanted to stay in Pacem for a while with them first. Surprising them by saying she had met a young man named Fergal, Gwendolyn said that they both were wanting to get to know each other better. She then asked if it would be possible for the other three to make the journey back to their homes without her. They could spend a few months making sure things were all in order there and then return to Glyka once more. By that time Gwendolyn said she and Fergal would have had enough time to get to know each other and she would be better able to decide what she wanted to do about returning to her own world.

They spent the rest of the morning making plans for the trip and deciding what supplies they would need. They got together with Fidem for lunch all sharing their plans for the immediate future with each other. Since they were planning to be back in a few months Gwen and the dragons made their goodbyes shorter than if their absence was expected to be lengthy.

The usual stops were made at Jim and Mary's and Daniel and Juliette's places on the way and both couples were glad to hear that Evimeria was now free of Sordibus' despotic rule. They were amazed to learn that Fidem had killed the wolf during her first week of archery practice and at such a young age. They were also surprised to hear that she had won the archery contest that was held in Evimeria as they all knew Gwen was an exceptional archer. Explaining that Fidem as well as having a natural aptitude for archery and being extremely dedicated had used every opportunity to improve her skills. Gwen said Fidem was now an apprentice archery instructor.

Both couples had asked if there was anything else new going on in Dartan or Vita with Gwen saying that the only other thing worth mentioning was that Gwendolyn had met a young man named Fergal and was staying in Glyka to get to know him better at this time. Gwen and the dragons were planning another trip to Glyka in a few months, but no set date had been established yet. They were heading back to their homes to make sure things were still alright there. After updates of how things were going for the couples and the couples being given the details of the Evimeria episode the rest of the time was spent with them just enjoying friendly conversation of a more general nature.

Reaching Pacem in the evening the dragons opted to spend the night there before returning to their homes in the morning. Conversing for a while after their dinner they were trying to come up with the best way to coordinate the return trip to Glyka. Since it was several months away there was no need for immediate planning or preparations for the actual trip. They were merely trying to decide the best plan for getting together once the time arrived. Since it was more practical for the dragons to be flying to Pacem than for Gwen to be walking to either of the dragon's homes it was decided that the dragons would be flying to Pacem and all three of them would be leaving for Glyka from there. They had concluded that it would be up to the dragons to decide on the actual day of departure after three months had expired. At the three-month expiration everyone would have all they needed packed and ready for the trip so that all was in readiness no matter what day was finally chosen. After spending a few minutes conversing Dreki and Hratt ended up deciding that whenever one of them was ready they would fly to the other's location with them both heading on to Pacem from there. If neither of them had left before two more weeks had passed they would both be flying to Pacem the following day. Following breakfast early the next morning both dragons were heading back to their homes.

Gwen did not have to bother with any cleanup before she settled back into the castle in Pacem. She knew that those staying with her in the castle to take care of things like that would have continued the castle upkeep whether she was present or not. All she had to do was let them know she was back so meals would be taken care of.

She looked forward to doing some relaxing around the castle and visiting some of her favorite spots in Pacem. Thinking about this for a bit she felt it would be best to check on her subjects first to make sure things were alright with them. The day that Dreki and Hratt had departed after breakfast was clear and the temperature nice for walking so Gwen decided it would be good to go ahead and get started on her checking. She just started wandering from cottage to cottage greeting those who lived there and asking them how they were doing. After a few days she had finished visiting all the occupied cottages in her small kingdom and found out that all her subjects were doing well. They had all expressed their appreciation for her checking on them and wished her a long and prosperous reign. Gwen was then able to visit some of her favorite spots in Pacem as well as spend some time relaxing around the castle reading several of the books found in the library there.

As Hratt was entering the cave that was his home he realized that the first project was going to be giving it a good clean up. Since his cave was merely one large room it did not take him long to accomplish the task. He then sat down with a cup of coffee to decide what he wanted to do next. After thinking things over for a bit, he decided that he would like to spend some time just visiting his favorite spots. There was a tiny waterfall that had a nice small lake at the base with a stream emerging and running through a lush valley that was especially cool and pleasant in the summer. To the east was a very large lake that had some nice sand dunes along one edge. Lastly there was a thermal pool part way up one of the nearby mountains that was great to relax in especially in the fall when the weather turned cooler.

He made several trips to all these places and enjoyed spending time at each of them. As enjoyable as the trips were he also found himself missing the sights he had seen further west. The waterfall reminded him of the one on their trip to Evimeria and the thermal pool reminded him of the volcano in the Mystery Mountains. As much as he was enjoying his visits he often found himself wistfully thinking of his time spent westward.

He was also surprised at how much he was missing the companionship he had enjoyed with the other travelers on their journeys. Finding some puffballs near his cave one day reminded him of the time Fidem had located some on her first trip to Evimeria and caused him to wonder how she was doing as an apprentice archery instructor. He also thought about some of the people they had met at various stages in their journeys and was wondering how they were doing as well.

A couple of times as he was exploring unfamiliar territory and saw something interesting he found himself absentmind- edly saying, "Gwendolyn, look at that!" He began realizing that being able to share his experiences with someone else was probably what he missed the most. He was really looking forward to the next trip to Glyka and decided that as soon as the three months were over he would be heading to Dreki's meadow.

Dreki was not worried about having to clean up his cave. Having made several longer trips in the past he knew that with the door in place the only things needed would be removing a few cobwebs and a quick dusting and sweeping. Being already used to the transitions between traveling and home life he quickly settled into his home routine there. Since he had always appreciated his quiet life there in the meadow he did not feel the same longings as Hratt did. He continued making frequent trips to Pacem and enjoyed visiting with Gwen on these occasions. Since it was less than an hour flight he was able to go for a visit anytime he chose without having to worry about extensive planning or camping out along the way.

After about a month and a half Dreki decided to pay Hratt a visit. Since Dreki could easily make it there and back in a day he was not worried about the possibility of Hratt not being home. As he was gliding in for a landing outside Hratt's cave he noticed there were four dragons there and was wondering what was going on. One of the dragons happened to be Hratt and when he noticed Dreki landing he welcomed him warmly. As Dreki was approaching he recognized one of the other dragons as Slett, but the last two were unfamiliar. Hratt made the introductions and Dreki learned that Vakandi was Slett's mate and that Elskandi was her sister. Slett had asked Hratt to contact him when he returned from the rescue expedition to let him know what transpired. Since then, they had kept casual contact and had visited each other a few times during that period.

Hratt informed Dreki of his desire to meet with Gwen in Pacem as soon as the three months were over. Dreki said that was fine with him and then allowed the conversation to return to what was being discussed before he arrived. He noticed that most of the talking was being done by Hratt, Slett and Vakandi with Elskandi mostly just listening and not saying much. He asked Elskandi if she usually came along on these visits and she informed him that this was her first time and that she felt a little out of place not being familiar with most of the experiences the others were sharing with each other.

Dreki asked her if she had ever made any longer trips anywhere. She informed him that she had only done short trips but would not mind an occasional long one as long as she went with someone who had made the trip before and knew what to expect along the way. She confessed that she was not really the adventurous type and preferred a quieter lifestyle. She said she knew a little about the rescue operation Hratt had helped in and that at least it sounded exciting rather than frightening. She also said that the people and places he talked about sounded interesting and made her wonder about them. She said she had caught a reference to Dreki and some evil person named Nequitia in one of the conversations but did not remember any details. She asked Dreki if he would mind telling her about it.

Dreki said it was a rather long story in its entirety and was wondering if she just wanted a summary instead. Elskandi said she was a "detail" dragon and would love to hear the whole thing but would settle for a summary since there was not much time before they would be heading back home. Dreki was noticing the sad expression on her face and came up with an idea. He asked her if she would be interested in going to Pacem. He said it was not far and that he knew Queen Gwen there. Pacem would have accommodations for them if they needed to spend the night and that Queen Gwen was the main person involved in the story. Getting a huge smile on her face Elskandi said that sounded great to her, but they needed to let the others know what they were going to do.

After informing the other dragons of their intentions they soon flew off side-by-side on their way to Pacem with Dreki telling Elskandi a little about Glyka and Vita. He mentioned some of the people there and that the general direction of the two kingdoms was westerly. He said that they were all part of the story and knowing a little about them ahead of time would help her in following the narrative. He asked her to tell him about herself and listened carefully as she filled him in on the details of her quiet life so far.

Landing in the castle courtyard Dreki started heading for the castle proper, asking the first person he saw to please let Queen Gwen know he was here. Since the girl he was talking with had seen him there before she responded, "Of course, Dreki, I would be glad to!" She headed off into the castle leaving the dragons in the courtyard. In a few minutes Gwen joined them there heartily welcoming them and asking Dreki to introduce her to the other dragon. After the introductions were completed Gwen said they were both welcome to join her for any meals and spend the night in the castle. Gwen said that since it was lunch time they could continue their conversation while they ate.

Further conversation and getting to know a little bit about each other were taken care of during lunch. When Gwen discovered that Dreki was going to tell Elskandi the complete story of Nequitia's overthrow she commented, "It is a very long tale if you want a detailed story. I would be glad to tell you part of it if you like, but a better option would probably be for the account in my annals book to be read. It is very detailed, and nothing would get left out that way. I had the royal scribe in Glyka make me a copy to keep here in Pacem since my original copy got passed on to Gwendolyn and was left in our old world." When Elskandi said that sounded great to her Gwen went into the castle and returned with the book in a short time.

Elskandi then looked at Gwen asking, "Would it be possible for me to read the book and ask questions when I have finished?"

"You could certainly do that, but I think a better choice would be to ask any questions of Dreki or myself if they come up while you are reading."

"Won't that be boring for you both just sitting there waiting for me to ask a question? I can see from the size of the volume that it will take several hours to get through."

"It won't be a problem at all if you sit and read near that bench by the tree over there. Dreki and I can go over to the one next to the fountain. I can sit on that bench with Dreki close by. We can quietly have a conversation of our own there without disturbing your reading yet be close enough to hear you if you have a question for us."

"That would be great! I really appreciate you both showing me such kindness and taking the time to let me do this."

"Don't be afraid you will interrupt anything if you have a question. Just go ahead and ask and one of us will try to answer it."

Elskandi then went over to the bench near the tree opening the book and placing it on the bench. She then seated herself comfortably in front of the bench and started reading. Gwen and Dreki headed over to the fountain and began updating each other as to what had been going on in each of their lives. Every so often either Gwen or Dreki would glance over at Elskandi and every time they saw that she was totally engrossed in the book. She had asked a few quick questions occasionally but was relying mostly on the book for her information. Since the accounts in the book were so detailed she did not require much clarification of events but mostly asked about how Gwen and Dreki were feeling or what they were thinking at the time the events occurred.

Walking over to Gwen and Dreki when Elskandi had finished the book she thanked Gwen as she handed the book back to her. Gwen asked if she had any further questions now that she had read the account in its entirety. Sighing she said no, but after reading the account she wished she could see some of the places and meet some of the people that Gwen and Dreki had encountered on their journey. Dreki then mentioned the upcoming trip to Glyka and Vita asking Elskandi if she would like to join them on it.

Elskandi was delighted at the possibility and instantly replied, "Oh, that would be marvelous! Are you sure that you two don't mind me tagging along?"

Both Gwen and Dreki said it was not a problem at all and they just needed to figure out the best way to coordinate getting Elskandi included in the party. Gwen said that because they knew the exact departure date Elskandi could just show up in Pacem the day before or she was welcome to stay there in the castle until the departure date. Gwen asked Dreki what he thought of either of these arrangements or if he had any other suggestions. Dreki said that either plan seemed fine with him, but that Elskandi was also welcome to stay with him for that time if she preferred that.

Elskandi thanked them both for their generosity but said that after thinking it over she would prefer to be with Dreki. She said that it would give her the opportunity to see his meadow and the Stone of Remembrance on its pedestal. She said that it all sounded very pretty in the account in the book, and she had been hoping for an opportunity to see them. She also said that she needed to let Slett and Vakandi know what the plans were so they would not worry about her.

Gwen suggested that they could all have supper in a bit and continue getting to know about each other during the evening hours. They could spend the night and Elskandi and Dreki could head out after breakfast the next morning. Elskandi said she thought that was an excellent plan and was looking forward to the evening conversation. They continued talking for a while mostly answering a few questions Elskandi thought of or expanding on some of the details recorded in the book. Continuing their pleasant conversation during supper, the meal and fellowship were enjoyed by all. The after-meal conversation continued until late in the evening when they finally all headed to bed.

Gwen had not been expecting any visitors and had been surprised when Dreki and Elskandi showed up. She enjoyed the short visit and getting to meet Elskandi. She now knew that the trip to Glyka would be right after the three-month period had expired and that Elskandi would be coming along as well. She liked Elskandi and was wondering if a stronger relationship between her and Dreki would develop. If it did not she was still hoping to keep up and develop a friendship with Elskandi and was looking forward to the Glyka trip to get better acquainted with her.

Finishing their breakfast Dreki and Elskandi were soon on their way. After letting Hratt, Slett and Vakandi know what their plans were they were off to Dreki's meadow. Gliding in for their landing Elskandi was commenting on how pretty a location Dreki had chosen to live in. Dreki asked her if she wanted to get some lunch right away or if she preferred a tour of the area first. She said she was hungry, but even more curious, so she preferred the tour first.

Dreki then proceeded to take her around the meadow showing her the lake, the path Gwen had taken and the Stone of Remembrance on its pedestal. He answered her questions as they walked noticing her smiling face and rapt gaze as she took in the surroundings. They then proceeded around the lake taking the wide path to Dreki's cave. After the cave tour they had something to eat. Elskandi remarked that Dreki really had a nice cave and that the surrounding area was very beautiful. She said it was going to be hard to wait until the upcoming trip to see all the exciting places she had read about in Gwen's book.

Dreki mentioned that before Gwen had arrived he had taken other trips in various directions searching for the missing Stone of Remembrance. There were some interesting things and beautiful scenery he had seen that he would be glad to show her if she was interested. She said that it would be great if it was not too much trouble for him to spend so much time and effort on her. He said that it was not a problem at all that it would be good for her to get in a few longer flights to get used to the feeling and that he enjoyed her company in any case. She said that she also enjoyed his company and was looking forward to spending the time with him.

During the time remaining before the trip to Pacem they made several of the other trips Dreki had mentioned. Elskandi was delighted to be able to enjoy seeing the new places and share the experiences with Dreki. She said it was much nicer than having to just wait the whole time and that it was much more enjoyable for her to be able to share the experience with someone rather than just experiencing it alone.

As they were packing and getting ready a few days before their trip to Pacem they spent a while talking over the time they had shared together over the past month and a half. The conversation started with them remarking about some of the interesting places and things they had seen on their trips together but then shifted to how much they had enjoyed each other's company on those trips. They both were realizing that their friendship had deepened to the point that they were wanting to spend the rest of their lives together.

Since dragons did not have any type of official wedding ceremony, but just solemnly pledged their fidelity to each other when they chose mates these pledges were given to each other at that time. They would let their friends and relatives know of their decision when they next saw them. They then finished their trip preparations and just enjoyed each other's company until they left for Pacem.

15

Fidem's New Duty

ENTERING the bow crafters' building Fidem was warmly greeted as usual. Fidem could see that Colonel Veren was conversing with Shauna, so she remained waiting for them to finish. Turning away from Shauna as he finished he gave Fidem a big smile when he saw her there. "I take it you have spoken with General Hapsom since you are here."

"He told me to report to you, and you would show me what to do and set my schedule. I am not sure how much actual shooting I will be doing as an apprentice instructor, so I may be requesting some practice time if the schedule allows."

"In the beginning what I would like for you to do is to change into comfortable shooting attire right after our morning assembly. Then I would like you to just follow me around and closely watch what I do. I will be doing a number of things to prepare for a class, during the class and afterwards. Feel free to ask questions any time other than during the class instruction time. If a question comes up during the instruction time please hold it until the class is dismissed unless it is a question of someone's safety. Are you ready to start now, Sergeant Fidem?"

"Of course, Colonel Veren, please lead the way."

Veren then told Fidem she would need to learn the location of where the various items needed for an archery class were stored. He then started showing her where she could find targets, target stands, bows, arrows, strings and several other things she would eventually need. He then took some time going over the general procedure to follow telling her that classes were taught on weekdays for three weeks and answering some questions that she had. He explained that there were some new very young students that had arrived that morning from Vita and had been given a short introductory class. Veren said that the students had been given bows, quivers and arrows and would begin the actual novice class tomorrow. He said that normally he would not be teaching classes at that low a level but felt that if he taught the first couple of classes Fidem would learn a lot watching and be able to ask him any questions that came up. He would then be turning the class over to another instructor and would be moving on to something else. Veren then told Fidem she was free for the rest of the day but should report to him in the morning.

Arriving at the archery supply storage area following the next morning's guard assembly Fidem saw that Veren was already there. Asking him if she could help him set up he told her what to bring to the range. After making several trips they had enough lanes set up for the tiny class of Vita students. Veren then led Fidem to a small classroom near the archery range which had a few tables set up with six students waiting for the class to begin. Walking up to the front of the class with Fidem Veren introduced her as his apprentice and helper. He noticed a few grins on some of the students' faces when they looked at Fidem, but he proceeded with the instruction mentioning that he would only be teaching the first class or two and then the class would be turned over to another instructor.

Veren explained the basics to the class while demonstrating himself or with Fidem doing the demonstration then having the students follow the example. The students were learning how to string and unstring their bow properly how to knock the arrow correctly with the fletching in the proper direction and how to anchor their knuckle on their cheek. The class then began making its way to the archery range. As the students were making their first attempts Fidem remembered her first experience and could sympathize with the ones who missed the target. After several shots the students seemed to be settling down and were able to usually hit the target but were not very consistent in keeping the shots close to each other or near the center of the target.

Veren then encouraged them to try to become more consistent. He said it was better to sight the same way for several shots seeing where they hit and then adjusting rather than trying to adjust after every single shot. They did improve a little by following this advice. None of the students had managed to get a bullseye and one of them said they did not see how it would be possible for anyone their age to get a bullseye.

Veren then said that it takes time and practice to perfect the art of archery. He then looked over at Fidem, so she spoke up saying that it was only a few months ago that she was at their level. She said that she had spent as much time as she could practicing to get to where she was today. She said that most archers did not progress that rapidly because not everyone had a natural aptitude for archery and some either could not or would not invest the time in practice.

One of the students asked Veren how good she really was. Veren then asked the students if it would be encouraging or discouraging if Fidem did well. They all said it would be encouraging because if she could do it, it would prove it was possible for them to do it also. Veren then had Fidem go to the shooting line on one of the lanes the students had just used. The students' eyes widened as she stepped up to the line confidently and put an arrow dead center in the bullseye. Several gasps were heard and Veren told Fidem to make two more shots so there would be no doubt that the one was not a lucky hit. Fidem's next shot was again dead center splitting the first arrow as it hit. Her third shot was the same.

Gathering the supplies to put away after dismissing the class Veren and Fidem were smiling at each other as they heard several students remarking that they had been about ready to give up at archery but now were going to stick with it even if they never made it up to Fidem's skill level. Veren and Fidem put all the supplies back with Veren explaining that tomorrow they would start keeping score for the students. Scoring was not done to rank the students as to who was best, but to allow each student to keep track of their own improvement as time went on. Veren showed Fidem where the scorecards were kept and they wrote the students' names at the top laying them out on the tables for class the following day. Veren explained that for higher level classes there would be an afternoon session as well as a morning one, but only a single class per day for novices. Since it was now lunchtime Veren dismissed Fidem telling her to report back to him after lunch.

The first part of the afternoon was spent with Fidem learning some of the less obvious aspects of instruction and having more of her questions answered. Veren then said that he thought she had learned enough for one day and asked if she wanted to spend the rest of it practicing since the general had not told Veren that Fidem was needed for anything. Thanking Veren she said yes smiling and heading off to the range with her equipment.

After supper Fidem spent the rest of the evening in her quarters going over the notes she had written to herself about the aspects of instructing that Veren had gone over with her. After reviewing them several times she finally went to bed. With all the new information to think about and all the archery practice time she had put in she slept very soundly that night.

Heading to the classroom directly after the morning assembly she double checked making sure each student had a scorecard on their desk. As she was finishing Veren entered greeting her. She was greeting him back with a smile just as the students started entering and taking their seats. She then joined Veren at the head of the class as he began explaining scoring to the students. Veren told them the purpose was not to see who was the best but for each student to record their own progress. He told them that it was better to be continually improving than to have one good score and the rest poor.

The students started gathering their equipment and began following Veren and Fidem to the archery range. As they were heading out of the building a guard approached telling Veren that General Hapsom needed to see him for about 10 to 15 minutes at his earliest opportunity. Fidem said it would probably take about that long just to get everybody ready and that she should be able to handle that aspect. Thanking her, Veren headed off with the other guard.

Fidem then had the students verify that they had the correct bow and string, the proper number of arrows in their quiver and their scorecard and pencil. When all of them finished acknowledging this she had them each go to their lane and begin stringing their bows. She stood watching making sure they did this correctly and only had to help one student who had a little trouble. When the student finally finished getting the bow strung Fidem asked the other students to please be patient for a minute or two. Fidem then had the student that had trouble unstring and restring their bow three more times. The last time the student did it without any trouble at all with Fidem complimenting him on a job well done.

Since Veren had not returned and Fidem did not want to waste time waiting she had the students ready themselves at the shooting line with an arrow knocked in the bow and standing ready to draw the string back. She then went verifying the arrows were knocked properly and the fletching was in the correct direction. She had to correct two of the students on the direction of the fletching but commended them all for correctly knocking the arrows on the strings.

Since Veren still had not yet returned she then had each student draw the string back anchoring it to their cheek aiming and releasing the arrow. She did this one at a time while watching each student's technique individually and making comments and suggestions. She then told the students to shoot five more arrows each sighting the same way every time and then putting their bows down and waiting. When the last student had finished setting their bow down Fidem then instructed them to take their scorecards and pencils to their targets and write down their score, but not to be removing the arrows until she had verified that the scores had been tallied correctly. She finished checking the scores, congratulating the students for scoring properly. She then reminded the students of the proper way to remove the arrows from the targets watching them as they performed this operation. Returning to the shooting line the students were preparing for another round when Veren came running up apologizing for the much longer than expected delay. Fidem said she was hoping he did not mind, but that she had done one round with them so they would not have to stand there waiting. Veren was impressed that Fidem had enough self-confidence to do that, so he asked Fidem to continue instructing two more rounds with him observing. She did this and she only once had to remind a student about the fletching direction. When the students were finished and the last scores recorded Fidem had them all bring their equipment back to the classroom for an evaluation of the day's shooting.

Once all the students were seated Veren then began by asking the class what they had observed or learned from the day's lesson. Several students said they observed that their first-round score was worse than the next two rounds. One student said that he remembered what Veren had said yesterday about not adjusting his aim after every shot and that his groupings were more consistent today. One girl confessed that she had made one shot with the fletching the wrong direction, but had corrected herself on the rest, but could not see that it made any difference.

Fidem asked Veren if he wanted her to demonstrate the difference or not and it would take about five minutes if she did. Veren said yes as he wanted to see what Fidem would do. Fidem then took her bow quiver of arrows a piece of black ribbon about a half inch wide and a foot long and a couple of pins and had the students follow her to the archery range. She then pinned the ribbon vertically on the face of a target moving the target further down range. She then approached the shooting line showing the students that she had four arrows of dark wood and two that were lighter. Explaining that she was going to aim the same way each time at the center of the ribbon, but that she would be knocking the two lighter colored arrows with the fletching in the wrong direction. Making her six shots she then went and brought the target back to the shooting line. The students could see that the dark arrows were exactly centered in the ribbon, but that the lighter ones were just to the side of it.

She explained that the incorrectly aligned fletching caused the arrow to deflect differently as it passed the bow. "Part of learning to be a good archer is doing your best to keep consistency in your shooting and properly aligned fletching is a part of that." The girl that had brought the issue up said she could now see that it *did* make a difference, and she now realized that the randomness of the deflections coming at different times would make it harder to correct her aim properly. She then thanked Fidem for taking the time to show her rather than just tell her what would happen.

The rest of the class time was spent with Veren explaining how to check to see if an arrow shaft was straight, if the fletching was becoming loose or too worn, if the arrowhead was not properly attached, or a bowstring was getting past its useful life. Veren then announced that they would be having a different instructor for the remainder of their class sessions as he had different responsibilities that needed to be attended to. Veren and Fidem were smiling at each other when they heard several sighs from the students. Veren then dismissed the class for the day.

Once the students had left Veren complimented Fidem both on her ability to assume leadership and start the class when he was delayed and her practical demonstration with the fletching direction issue. Veren then told her that he wanted her to keep teaching the remainder of the class sessions with these students. I will assign another instructor experienced at the lower levels to work with you, but I would like you to do the teaching and only ask for help if you need it. Fidem said she would be happy to do that and would finish out the class sessions with these students. Veren then said he needed to go and find the other instructor and left to take care of that.

Leaving her quarters the next morning Fidem heard her name being called turning to see Veren approaching her. She greeted him telling him she was on her way to the classroom. He said that her fellow instructor would be Dara and that she should already be there. Fidem thanked him before heading towards the classroom. Approaching the classroom, she could hear chairs being moved and the sounds of the students seating themselves. She then heard one student ask Dara if she was their new instructor. Dara replied that she was Dara and would be the new instructor's assistant. The student replied that she was hoping that the new instructor would be as nice as Veren and Fidem were. Fidem was smiling as she heard Dara tell her that the new instructor would be exactly what she wanted.

As Fidem was entering and Dara said, "And here she is," Fidem heard several happy exclamations and some hand claps as well. Fidem did well with the rest of the class sessions only asking for assistance a couple of times. The students also did well all passing the Novice level archery test with each student earning the black Novice pin.

When Fidem, Dara and Veren got together to discuss how Fidem did with the class it was decided that Fidem had done very well. Veren then told her that she should teach another Novice class with Dara as her assistant, but the time after that it would be a Marksman class. The Marksman class would be novice students hoping to move up to the next skill rank. Veren told Fidem that the differences would be that there would be no need to go over the basics again, there would be two sessions per day instead of one, and that the targets would be farther from the shooting line. The main things to work on would be proper technique and building consistency in their shooting.

Fidem taught two sets of classes at this level with no difficulty and had gotten her new stronger bow. After a few days practicing she found that she could now easily put all six arrows in the bullseye at the gold Expert level distance. Veren said he was very pleased with her ability as an instructor and that she was ready to move up to the Sharpshooter level. When she told him that she could put all six arrows in the bullseye at the gold Expert distance now Veren asked her if she wanted to try for the Expert Instructor qualification. Fidem said there would be no harm in trying. Even if she failed she would know what to work on to pass that level. Veren then explained that even her new bow was not quite strong enough for this level, but he felt that her skill would probably be enough to compensate.

Arriving at the range Fidem noticed that the target was at the farthest distance. Again, she was told that it took five bullseyes out of six shots to qualify. The first three shots were definitely in the bullseye, but the fourth one was just out. She put the next two in smiling at Veren saying that she did get five out of six in. Veren congratulated her as they went to retrieve her arrows then began pointing at the one that was out. As they started looking closer at it they could see that it had nicked the bullseye and they both smiled at each other. Veren then spoke, "Well it is not official until you hear it from General Hapsom, but congratulations *Lieutenant* Fidem!"

Veren then began leading Fidem to General Hapsom's office knocking on the door. When asked to enter Veren opened the door leading Fidem into the office. Explaining that Fidem had just qualified as an Expert Instructor Veren stood waiting for the general to reply.

The general stood up coming around his desk and facing Fidem. "It seems like your promotions cannot keep up with your skill and progress *Lieutenant* Fidem. When I first asked you to become one of the elite guards I knew that someday you would be a valuable asset to us I just did not expect someday to come so soon! By the way, I received a letter from King Kelan yesterday. He said that I should pass on compliments and appreciation to Sergeant Fidem for her excellent job instructing the novice class from Vita. The person in charge of the novice archers said that they performed better as a class than any previous group when tested."

Fidem thanked the general and then headed back with Veren. Veren led Fidem over to his office then began taking her down a short hallway to a small room at the end. He then started explaining to her that the rank of lieutenant was considered an officer and as such she would be having her own office. He further explained that due to her age and her not having actual rank with the guards except for dealings with archery she would have this room which had previously been a small storage area as an office. She said she had not been expecting anything so a small office would be great. She said it would be nicer to plan for the next class session here where it would be nice and quiet rather than in the classroom itself where she would hear sounds of the activities going on around her or possibly be interrupted. She thanked Veren then ended up spending the rest of the day getting her office set up the way she wanted it. She moved a few things from where they were located to a spot that she liked better and organized some of the files. She also checked the books on the shelves there noting which ones she felt she would not use and writing down a few she wanted to add to the collection.

Fidem enjoyed teaching her first sharpshooter level class and found it easier for her than the novice class had been. She could concentrate on honing the students' technique rather than having to teach several new unfamiliar concepts to beginners. Continuing her daily practice routine it did not take too much time before she got another stronger bow. She quickly got used to it and Veren said that since it was considered strong enough for the farthest target she could now start teaching the Expert level classes as well. He also told her that he felt her skill level was beyond his and it was only due to his higher rank that he was still assigning her classes to teach.

Taking advantage of a day off Fidem decided to see how Gwen and Gwendolyn were doing and went in search of them. She knew that Gwen, Dreki and Hratt had returned from their trip back to their homes, but she had not had the opportunity to get together with any of them since then. She was told that Gwen and Gwendolyn had gone to Vita for a few days to visit and would be returning this morning. They were planning to meet Dreki, Elskandi and Hratt for lunch in the small courtyard since it was a nice day and she could find them there at that time. Fidem then asked who Elskandi was as she said she was not familiar with that name. She was told that Elskandi had come back to Glyka with Dreki and that they were now mates. Thanking the person for the information she just went wandering about town for the rest of the morning.

She was not sure what was planned for lunch so she went to the courtyard a little early to ask the first person to show up what the plan was and if she could be joining them. She saw Gwendolyn approaching accompanied by a tall young man with curly black hair. Fidem greeted her with a wave and Gwendolyn introduced the man as Fergal. Fergal said he was glad to meet Dame Fidem as he had heard many good things about her. Fidem said that she was glad to meet him as well since she had also heard about him from Gwendolyn. Fidem then asked what the plan for lunch was and if she could join the party. Gwendolyn said that would be great as they were just going to have sandwiches from one of the town's vendors. Gwendolyn said that she and Fergal were going to pick them up and they were going to have to get a couple for Fergal since he was also joining them; they could get a couple for Fidem as well at the same time. They got sandwiches and a couple of jugs of cool fruit juice to go along with them. Carrying the items back to the courtyard Gwendolyn mentioned that they were also planning to get ice cream later for dessert.

The lunch was enjoyed by all and everyone appreciated being able to get updates as to what was going on in each other's lives. The dragons had made a trip back to their homes to check on things and all was well in both locations and Dreki now had a mate. Gwen had gone along to make sure things were alright in Pacem. Since things were fine there she had come back to Glyka with Dreki, Elskandi and Hratt. Gwendolyn had remained in Glyka and had spent a good bit of time doing things with Fergal. They both enjoyed the outdoors and had done a fair amount of hiking, horseback riding, some swimming and even a little archery. Fidem shared how much she enjoyed being an archery instructor. She said it was much nicer having a consistent duty to perform rather than just filling in with odd assignments like she used to.

Fidem then asked Gwen if there were any plans for the near future for Gwen, Gwendolyn and the dragons. Gwen said they had been talking about possibilities recently and she and the dragons felt that it was time for them all to head back to their own homes. Gwendolyn said that she planned to remain in Glyka with Fergal as their relationship had developed to the point that they were seriously considering marriage. Fidem noticed that she and Fergal were holding hands and smiling at each other when she said this. Fidem said she was glad that she was able to join them for lunch so she could have a good visit with them before Gwen and the dragons headed home.

Gwen said that she, Gwendolyn, Dreki, Elskandi and Hratt wanted to make a trip to Evimeria before heading back to their homes and told Fidem she should come along with them. Fidem said she would love to but did not know if she would be able to get out of her duties long enough to make the trip. Gwen said she had spoken to General Hapsom that morning and the general told her that King Firinne had just asked him if Fidem could make a trip there since she was an ambassador and it was important to keep good relations with allies. The trip would be considered one of her assignments and was planned for when she completed her present archery class at the end of the coming week. Gwen told Fidem that the general would not have had a chance yet to mention the assignment to her since he knew it was her day off and would not have disrupted it by having her sent for.

Since no one had plans for the afternoon the friends all spent it in relaxing conversation and enjoying their ice cream. There was some conversation about possible visits between different locations in the future, but no actual plans were made yet in that regard. Talking over aspects of their upcoming trip to Evimeria the one long leg where they had trouble due to the weather was brought up. They discussed the advantage of having a clearing midway between the two present ones that were so distant from each other. They tried to figure out a way to create a clearing in that spot on their upcoming trip.

Hiking from either present clearing to the midway point would take too long especially dragging the saws they would need through the woods. A dragon could hover, and the supplies could be let down on a rope, but the job of sawing trees to make a clearing was beyond the ability of Gwen, Gwendolyn and Fidem. Getting volunteer dragons transporting enough men and supplies and getting the job done was not practical for this trip either and would have to be implemented in the future if that plan were adopted. They decided that unless something presented itself on the trip a later expedition by the men would be necessary.

Gathering the supplies for the trip was not difficult since there was no quest or mission to accomplish. Fidem asked the general if it would be a good idea to have an official document signed by King Firinne and witnessed by Queen Gwen and Princess Gwendolyn affirming the acceptance of the peace treaty signed by Dame Fidem. The general thought that was an excellent suggestion and had Fidem follow him as he was leading her to the palace and asking for an audience with the king. King Firinne warmly greeted them both asking what he could do for them. The general then explained Fidem's suggestion and said that he agreed with it. The king also agreed but said he was thinking of a better idea. He then had Fidem come forward telling her she would receive a document stating that she was the official ambassador from Dartan to Evimeria. He explained that she could now sign agreements generated in Evimeria on behalf of Dartan due to her ambassadorship. He then said he would have the official document written signed and witnessed. She could then take that along and give it to King Lobarat to be kept in Evimeria.

Fidem thanked the king for bestowing this honor on her and putting so much trust in her judgment. She said if she was ever in doubt she would postpone signing anything in Evimeria until she had brought a copy back for the king's approval first. King Firinne then wished Fidem a safe journey dismissing both her and General Hapsom.

16

RETURN TO EVIMERIA

FIDEM having finished her duties for the week and the rest having gathered all their supplies, the travelers were now ready to depart. They got a good night's sleep leaving for Vita after breakfast. They spent a relaxing day in Vita heading on to Evimeria the next day. When they left on the long leg of their journey the weather turned rainy. It was not a stormy or heavy rainfall, but one of those steady soaking rains that plants love. Approaching the midpoint between the two clearings they started looking for less dense spots that could be used to make a clearing in. They had no thoughts of actually making the clearing on this trip but were just looking for likely spots for the future.

Suddenly Gwen thought of something from her first trip and asked Dreki if he breathed fire on a wet tree would it catch fire. Dreki said if he concentrated the blast on a single tree he could probably start it on fire, but the fire would go out quickly as wet as the trees were and with the rain still falling. What if he, Hratt and Elskandi tried burning a tree together then burning the one next to it and so on? Would they be able to eventually clear enough space to land? They decided to give it a try since there was no danger of the fire spreading with all the trees soaked the way they were.

Spotting a less dense section a little to the left ahead of them Dreki suggested that they concentrate on the large tree near the middle. The three dragons altered their course giving it a good blast while slowly gliding above it. With the combined fire the tree was quickly consumed. The dragons tried repeating the operation on about a dozen other trees and soon only the charred thinned trunks remained in an area that was plenty large enough for them to land and set up a camp in. The dragons then began concentrating on the charred trunks reducing them to ashes after a few more passes. They were now circling the area for a short time allowing any remaining embers to be extinguished by the rain. Landing in the new clearing they were soon setting up camp there for the day. Other than dealing with the muddy ash and remains of the stumps the clearing made an excellent campsite.

After setting up the tents they spent a relaxing time talking and congratulating each other on the success of the clearing operation. By late afternoon the rain had stopped, and the ladies did some exploring in the woods nearby. They found a small stream slightly to the south of the clearing and said it would be great for future stops. They had already collected enough rainwater for their cooking and cleaning and did not need the water from the stream for this trip. They did not find any puffballs but knew there was a good chance there would be some in the next clearing. Even though it had been raining for most of the day everyone was cheerful while eating their supper. It was nice to know that they no longer had the worry of having to make the long leg trip but now had a midway stopping point for lunch or if the weather turned threatening.

The rest of the trip to Evimeria was uneventful with the travelers arriving in Maith in time for lunch. Some of the townspeople recognized them as they were passing through and came up to greet them. After exchanging small talk and updating each other on news the travelers made their way to the restaurant with outdoor seating. Finishing a relaxing lunch, the travelers began heading on to the citadel and were heartily welcomed when they arrived. As soon as King Lobarat was informed of their presence he and Queen

Bonnie came to welcome them personally. When Lobarat discovered that Elskandi was Dreki's mate he declared her to be a Friend of Evimeria with the same privileges as the rest of the Friends. The travelers were shown to their rooms and invited to stay as long as they wished. Fidem presented King Lobarat the document from King Firinne declaring her as an official representative and told him the peace treaty was accepted as signed. The rest of the afternoon was spent in pleasant conversation with news updates on both sides.

Awakening to a beautiful day the travelers enjoyed a nice breakfast with the king and queen. They were then given a tour of the areas that had undergone significant changes. The most impressive of these was the dungeon. When they reached the end of the passage leading to the dungeon they were surprised to see a pair of ornate doors made of beautifully carved wood. They gasped when the doors were opened to reveal a huge ballroom with crimson hangings along the walls and chandeliers suspended from the ceiling. King Lobarat said that it was especially appreciated on hot summer days as it was always nice and cool down there.

The next stop was the stables and Fidem commented that she did not see the stallion, mare and filly that were there the last time. King Lobarat remarked with a huge smile, "That is because they are no longer here. We are only getting my horse to ride to their new home. You may follow me on dragonback once we get outside." Following the king as he headed across the bridge they were soon turning left once he got over the gorge. Topping a rise after about a half mile the small horse farm could be seen nestled amongst some trees. There was a nice sized pasture with a stream flowing along one edge of it and a modest barn and stables on the north side of the pasture. The stallion and filly could be seen in the pasture as the dragons were landing and the passengers dismounted.

King Lobarat said, "If you are wondering about the mare she is in the barn. She is expected to give birth any time now, so I need to check on her in any case. Come along and let's see how she is doing." Entering the barn, they saw a girl kneeling next to the mare who was lying in the hay.

When she saw them the girl exclaimed excitedly, "Hurry up, Your Majesty! She is just about to give birth!"

They all went rushing over watching quietly anticipating the event King Lobarat had been waiting for. When the foal emerged finally standing on its wobbly legs they were all smiling at each other. King Lobarat exclaimed, "Just what I was hoping for a healthy colt!" They were all congratulating him and asking if he wanted to stay and watch the colt or go back to give Queen Bonnie the good news. He said that as much as he would like to remain watching he felt it was best to tell Queen Bonnie the news so she could share in the experience. They all headed back to the citadel and the queen was informed of the mare's successful delivery of a healthy colt. She went riding back with King Lobarat and the travelers flew all arriving at the barn in short order.

Entering the barn this time they all saw that the colt was much steadier on his legs and was enjoying his first meal. Talking for a bit as they observed different things about the colt they spent about a half hour admiring it. They then made their way back to the citadel seeing a few more of the changes that had been made. The last stop on the tour was the main hall where they were admiring Dame Fidem's gold arrow. It looked very nice hanging below the target on the wall and was mounted on a beautiful dark wooden plaque with "Dame Fidem's Gold Arrow" written in gold letters below it.

King Lobarat then said that he had something for Dame Fidem picking up a box from the floor beneath the wooden plaque and handing it to her. When Fidem opened the box she gave a gasp as it contained a gold arrow identical to the one she had won in the contest. King Lobarat then said, "Just as you felt it would be a shame for you to have taken the original arrow out of the kingdom we also felt it would be a shame if you were not able to have it. We had this duplicate made so both conditions could be met."

"This is wonderful!" Gwen said excitedly, "Now we can show all the people in Glyka who were asking about the arrow what it really looks like!"

"I will treasure it always," remarked Fidem with reverence.

The travelers remained in Evimeria that day and the one following it but started heading back home the day after that. They decided on making a short stop in Maith on the way having breakfast there at their usual restaurant. The restaurant owner said that he was glad they had stopped in Maith again before heading back. He told them that word of their return to Evimeria had reached the ears of the Prime Minister. The Prime Minister had requested that if they were passing back through and had the time he was wishing to see them for a short visit. Obtaining directions to the Prime Minister's office after finishing their breakfast the travelers made their way there.

Entering the office building the travelers were enthusiastically greeted by the Prime Minister's secretary. He said the Prime Minister had instructed him to bring them to him and he led the way announcing them as he opened the door. The Prime Minister welcomed them and then said he wanted to officially let them know that their service to the neighboring kingdom of Evimeria was much appreciated and that they were to consider themselves Friends of Socair. Fidem asked him if he would be interested in signing a peace treaty with any of the represented kingdoms. He said that it would be very desirable and calling his secretary in asked him to draft the treaties and to sign them as a witness.

The secretary then made two copies of each of the treaties. Queen Gwen was signing the treaties for Pacem and Vita and Dame Fidem signing for Dartan stating that it was pending King Firinne's approval. She told him that she did not think there would be any problem as she had signed for Dartan when the treaty was made with Evimeria and King Firinne had approved of it naming her ambassador to Evimeria from Dartan. The Prime Minister said he had no problem with her signing. If her signature was good enough for King Lobarat it was certainly good enough for him.

The travelers then bid the Prime Minister farewell and taking their copies of the peace treaties headed back to Glyka. They had no problems on the return trip and really appreciated not having to deal with the long leg section any longer. Making their usual stop in Vita Gwen gave King Kelan the treaty with Socair telling him that they now had another ally to the west. They spent the night in Vita like always and spent an extra day there so that goodbyes could be said as most of them would be heading back to their homes from Glyka and would not be back any time soon.

Arriving in Glyka the next morning the travelers reported to King Firinne with Fidem giving him the treaty explaining that she had again signed for Dartan pending his approval. King Firinne said that it was fine and that he approved. He then rose asking Fidem to come forward and kneel. "Dame Fidem you are hereby appointed Ambassador to Socair from Dartan. And to save me from having to repeat myself in the future you are also appointed Ambassador to Pacem from Dartan. Unless Queen Gwen has any objection that is."

Gwen responded, "Absolutely none. And you might be interested to know Your Majesty that Dame Fidem was the one that suggested the peace treaties to the Prime Minister in Socair in the first place."

"That does not surprise me, but it does please me. Well done, Dame Fidem!"

"Thank you Your Majesty. I will continue to do my best to represent our kingdom when the opportunity arises."

"The General said I was to tell you that you were to have the rest of the day you returned as well as the following day off. He said for you to check in with Colonel Veren after assembly the day after that for your next archery instruction assignment."

"Thank you, Your Majesty. I will do that."

King Firinne then dismissed the travelers going about his normal business. Gwen found Royal Advisor Jenny in her official chamber asking if the travelers could all have lunch as a group with Jenny joining them. Jenny said that was a great idea and they should all meet at noon in the medium-sized dining room. Jenny then went to make preparations for the meal and the travelers relaxed for a bit before lunch.

17

Decisions Made

GATHERING in the medium-sized dining room lunch and conversation were enjoyed by all. After a bit, Gwen mentioned that she and the dragons needed to get back home and felt that it was time to do that. Gwen felt that two more days in Glyka should be sufficient for all the goodbyes she needed to say. The dragons all agreed that it was fine for them as well. When Gwendolyn was asked what she had decided to do she smiled before speaking.

"When we came here my original plan was going back to Pacem from here and then back to my own world from there. I don't think that is what I will do now. Fergal and I have been discussing different options for the future. Our relationship has developed to the point that we are now thinking of our future together. Fergal has asked me to marry him, and I have accepted his proposal, but no fixed wedding date has been set yet. We are deciding where we should settle and are leaning towards Glyka as he is familiar with the area and customs here."

Smiling at one another the travelers spent a pleasant time congratulating Gwendolyn on her upcoming marriage and talking about different possibilities for her future. Gwen mentioned that a side benefit of the marriage would be that it would further cement the good relations between Pacem and Glyka. With Princess Gwendolyn of Pacem marrying a citizen of Dartan it would help reinforce the already good relationship between the two kingdoms. Gwendolyn said that aspect had not even occurred to her but was glad it just happened to work out that way.

Discussion then turned to how Gwen and Gwendolyn could keep in touch. Since there were no dragons living in Dartan there was no practical way for Gwendolyn to travel to Pacem. Dreki said it was not a problem for him to be bringing Gwen to Dartan whenever she wanted to make another trip. Talking things over for a while longer someone suggested that for now Dreki could plan on bringing Gwen every three or four months and Gwendolyn's plans could then be checked and any changes implemented if need be. The one major drawback to this arrangement was that if for some reason Gwendolyn wanted to contact Gwen sooner it would not be possible.

Hratt spoke up at this point. "I don't know what the rest of you think or what King Firinne would say, but what if I stayed here in Glyka? I could then be available any time Gwendolyn wanted to visit Pacem."

The rest of the travelers all thought this was an excellent idea if Hratt did not mind relocating from his home in the East. Hratt said he would not mind at all in fact he said he had really enjoyed seeing this part of the country and being able to travel more. He also mentioned that he had really missed the companionship with Gwendolyn and the other people he had gotten to know. Hratt mentioned that he was not sure about where he would reside or how best to provide for himself.

Royal Advisor Jenny remarked with a smile, "That will not be a problem at all. As royal advisor the king has given me the authority to make these types of decisions without getting permission first, but I am sure the king would approve in any case. Hratt can stay in the room he is currently using in the palace, and the royal kitchen will supply his food requirements. The main reason I see this as acceptable is one that has not even been brought up yet. Hratt would not only be available for Gwendolyn's use, but more importantly for the kingdom of Dartan, he would also be available for Ambassador Fidem. Otherwise, she has no way to visit any of the distant places where she has been named as ambassador." Everyone enthusiastically agreed that this was a great plan and meant that only Gwen, Dreki and Elskandi needed to be saying their goodbyes as everyone else was remaining in Glyka. Fidem already had her quarters, and Gwendolyn was told she could remain in the room she had been using until she and Fergal were married. Hratt then mentioned that since he had only made the trip from Pacem once it might be good for him to go with Gwen, Dreki and Elskandi to get more familiar with the route and landmarks along the way. He could also go home and say goodbye to his fellow dragons at the same time. Everyone thought this was a good amendment to the existing plan and the rest of the conversation was spent sharing memorable events of their time spent together.

Saying goodbyes and preparing for departure kept Gwen, Dreki and Elskandi occupied for the next two days. Hratt and Fidem made a trip to the craftsmen so they could make measurements for Fidem's saddle. The craftsmen had plenty of time to work on it since Hratt's trip would be about two weeks long. Fidem would need some flight training when Hratt returned, but it would only require her to learn how to communicate to him through the reins and with her legs. About a week would be plenty of time since she was already familiar with all the other aspects of flying.

Heading to one of the courtyards after a leisurely breakfast Gwen, Dreki, Elskandi and Hratt prepared for their takeoff. They had been well provisioned for the trip and Abigail had made another two large pies for them so they would have enough to share with those they visited with on the trip home. Gwen told Elskandi that she was in for a treat as Abigail's pies were the best. There were a number of people gathered to wish them a safe trip, and they all waved as the dragons took to the air. The usual stops were made at Jim and Mary's and Daniel and Juliette's places and short, but enjoyable visits were made at both locations. Abigail's pies were greatly enjoyed by all and both couples remarked that they had never tasted better pies than Abigail's. Elskandi said that Gwen was right and that she also had never had a pie better than the ones Abigail had baked for them.

They were all in Pacem the day after that and after spending the night Hratt left the following morning to say goodbye to his dragon friends and let them know he was relocating to Glyka. Dreki and Elskandi spent most of that day visiting with Gwen but headed back to their meadow in the late afternoon.

In two days Hratt was back in Pacem. He told Gwen that he had said his goodbyes turning over the possessions he no longer needed to one of the other dragons. He spent the rest of the day there in Pacem starting his trip back to Glyka the next day. It was very different for him to fly alone, and he was missing the companionship he had appreciated on previous trips. He enjoyed talking with Daniel and Juliette and Jim and Mary when he made those stops along the way. Since dragons have a very good natural sense of direction and he had paid careful attention to the landmarks he had no problem finding his way on his trip back to Glyka. Entering the gates of the city late in the afternoon the porter welcomed him, "Welcome back, Sir Hratt! Royal Advisor Jenny said to tell you that the room you were in before is now officially yours and you should let her know you are here so that you will not miss out on the next meal." Thanking him for the information Hratt then made his way through town and into the palace grounds to find Jenny.

Finding Jenny did not prove difficult at all as he saw her coming out of the entrance just as he was approaching it. She asked him if everything was settled back home and he told her that he now considered Glyka as his home but may visit his old one sometime. He said if Gwendolyn or Fidem made a trip to Pacem he could easily make a side trip from there to pay a short visit. Jenny said they could have supper in the medium-sized dining room since that room could easily accommodate his larger size. She said that there should be time beforehand for them to check with General Hapsom and see if Fidem's saddle could be tried out.

Making their way to General Hapsom's office Hratt remained outside while Jenny entered the office and found him there going over some reports. He greeted her warmly and asked what he could do for her. Jenny then remarked that Hratt was now lodged in the palace to be available for either Gwendolyn or Fidem when the need arose and they were wondering if Fidem was available to give her saddle a check. He said that her afternoon class should be over and that most likely she was in her office. "If not," he said with a wink, "she will probably be at the archery range practicing."

Thanking him Jenny departed telling Hratt she was going to check Fidem's office to see if she was there. Hratt followed her and waited outside. Jenny found Fidem going over some notes she had written on the day's class sessions and asked if she had a few minutes to test out her saddle with Hratt. Fidem said that would be great but just wanted to jot down a few comments first while they were still fresh in her mind. Grabbing a clean sheet of paper she quickly had her notes written and went outside with Jenny to join up with Hratt.

They then went over to the craftsmen's building retrieving the saddle and taking it outside for the test. Fidem quickly strapped it on and climbed aboard. Hratt said that they would need to schedule about a week for her to work on the communication aspects of flying that she was unfamiliar with at this point and for the test he was just going to circle the area a few times to make sure the saddle felt good to her. The test flight was accomplished and Fidem said the saddle felt great and that she would speak with Colonel Veren and General Hapsom about getting the flight training time worked into her schedule. Jenny said that Fidem could join her and Hratt for supper if she did not already have other plans. Fidem said that would be great as she wanted to hear how Hratt's trip went and they all headed off to the dining area.

Once they were seated Jenny asked Hratt to fill them in on the details of his trip since Fidem had specifically said she wanted to know and Jenny said she was also interested. Hratt said that he would be glad to do that but wanted to hear what each of the ladies had been up to as well. They all took turns updating each other while they enjoyed their dinner. Fidem said she was looking forward to completing the flight training. She said that way Hratt could use the single saddle if either Fidem or Gwendolyn needed to get somewhere or the double one for whenever both Gwendolyn and she needed transportation to the same place.

The next day Fidem was informed that she should plan to complete her flight training with Hratt as soon as she had finished the instruction of her present archery class. She was told that Hratt would be told to put this on his schedule and should be ready and waiting for her in the field next to the archery range first thing on the Monday following the class completion.

Since Fidem had been eagerly anticipating the opportunity to complete her flight training she did not dawdle as she made her way to the field directly after the morning guard assembly. Hratt greeted her warmly as she was approaching and she soon had the saddle strapped on and was in place waiting for Hratt's instructions. They spent the first day going over each of the communication processes Fidem would be using to communicate with Hratt and practicing them a bit. The rest of the week was spent in fine tuning these as well as letting Fidem get used to the changes in flight Hratt may have to unexpectedly make and how to know what to do as a dragon rider rather than just as a passenger. All a passenger needed to do was to hold on tightly with their hands to avoid falling out, but a rider had to keep both hands on the reins, rely on their legs to stay firmly in the saddle, and not send any confusing signals with either their legs or the reins while doing so. Since Fidem had already made a number of long distance flights her time in the saddle had been considerable at this time and she was already familiar with using her legs to stay steady in the saddle and holding the reins while doing this was an easy thing for her to adjust to. By the end of the week both she and Hratt were feeling comfortable as a team and informed General Hapsom that they were ready to serve Dartan whenever the need arose.

18

Unwelcome News

FIDEM continued teaching her archery classes and was very much enjoying being an instructor. It was still a little hard for her to accept being treated by everyone as the top instructor in Dartan knowing that she was so much younger than any of the others. General Hapsom and Colonel Veren both really appreciated having her available as she could competently teach an entire class at any level as well as take over a class that someone else was teaching if that instructor became ill or injured. Fortunately, there had not been a time that she was unable to fill in due to her being in the middle of instructing a class herself.

Fidem was becoming a little worried about her mother though. On her last few visits her mother did not seem to be her normal energetic and cheerful self. When Fidem asked her about it her mother said she was not sure what was wrong and had just been feeling a little more tired than normal. Fidem asked her if she had changed her daily routine or diet. Her mother said that she was not aware of any changes that would adversely affect her and was going to ask Fidem's grandmother for advice when she visited her the following week.

Fidem mentioned her concern to Colonel Veren and General Hapsom asking them if they had any suggestions. They suggested that if Fidem's mother did not improve over the next few weeks that she could see the Royal Physician to make sure it was not something serious. Fidem thought this was good advice and decided to suggest it to her mother when she returned from visiting Fidem's grandmother.

The day after Fidem's mother returned home from her visit with Fidem's grandmother Fidem made a trip to see her and get an update on the situation. She noticed her mother did not seem to have improved but did not see a noticeable decline either. She asked if grandma had said anything helpful. Her mother told her that Fidem's grandmother had said something about a hereditary health issue on her side of the family.

Since her mother could see the anxious look in Fidem's face she continued with an explanation. It appeared that there was a possibility of having a weak heart. This was something that occasionally showed up in a relative but was not something that every person in every generation was subject to. It just happened every now and then. Sometimes several generations came and went with no issues and other times two cousins in the same generation would have issues. Fidem mentioned seeing the Royal Physician in a few weeks if no improvement was seen and her mother agreed to the plan. Fidem kept visiting about once a week for three more weeks and no change was felt by her mother or noticed by Fidem. Since General Hapsom was aware of the issue he had mentioned it to King Firinne who had in turn told the Royal Physician to be ready if Fidem's mother decided to be checked out. When Fidem asked General Hapsom about the possibility of setting up an appointment she was told that the doctor had already been informed of the situation and that Fidem should bring her mother to him the following morning.

Fidem had been given the next day off so had gone home the night before. After fixing breakfast for them both she and her mom enjoyed being able to chat during the meal. Fidem did the after meal cleanup and soon she and her mother were headed to the palace to visit the Royal Physician. Since they were expected, Jenny met them as they entered and escorted them to the Royal Physician's office. After thanking Jenny for her help, they went in to see the doctor. Before he began looking Fidem's mother over he started by asking for details about how and when the issue started, how it had progressed, anything different recently that may have caused or contributed to the issue, and for a family medical history. He then asked questions regarding how the issue was affecting her physically and mentally before starting the actual examination.

After checking the usual things and finding nothing abnormal he proceeded to do some tests based on the possibility of the issue being a weak heart. He checked her heart rate while she was sitting then had her stand up and checked it about a minute later. He then had her walk slowly around his office for about a minute and checked it again. He said that her standing rate was normal, but the rate was a little higher than normal after the walking. He then had her do a brisk walk around the office for a minute and made one more rate check. He noticed that her breathing was labored and her heart rate much higher than normal after this test.

He said that it appeared that she did have a weak heart and that care must be taken not to overwork it. He did mention that in some cases proper exercise could strengthen the heart muscles, but extreme care must be used if this was tried. He suggested that she should give it a try and see if any improvement was seen. He made a schedule for her to do a specific heart related exercise twice a day once in the morning and then once again in the evening. All she had to do was to check her heart rate before starting, walk normally for one minute and check it again. If the rate was below what he had written on the plan she should walk normally another minute and check again repeating the process and rechecking again after each minute of walking. Once her rate got above the number written on the plan she was to stop and lie down resting for five minutes. After that she could return to her normal activities for the day. She was told to do this for two weeks and then see him again with the results on her next appointment.

Fidem had again been given the day of the appointment off and had spent the night with her mother. Fidem was a little disappointed to learn that there appeared to be no change in her mother's condition after the two week trial exercise period but was hopeful the Royal Physician might be able to suggest something else that would help the situation. The Royal Physician said that he was sorry the exercise program had not proved beneficial and felt that she was just going to have to live with her condition as best as she could. He said that there was no way to know for sure, but in some cases if people with this condition were careful not to overexert themselves they could continue living a productive life for quite some time. He did say that in some cases a weak heart can just suddenly give out, but this was a much less frequent occurrence if the person was careful to avoid overexertion.

Fidem and her mother discussed what was the best plan on their way back home and decided that just living a normal life while avoiding overexertion was best. Fidem promised to keep making periodic visits and then returned to the palace and her normal duties while her mother got back into her normal routine at the farmhouse.

Now that Fidem's flight training was over King Firinne said it would be good for her to make a state visit to each of the locations where she was an ambassador. She could let them know that she now had the means to make periodic state visits on her own as an ambassador rather than just tagging along when someone else happened to be going that way. Her first trip was to Vita and on from there to Pacem before returning to Dartan. She had good visits in each of those places and spent time in enjoyable friendly conversation rather than any formal state meeting. Each was able to update the other on what had been happening in their lives lately and Fidem was able to spend some pleasant relaxing time sightseeing in each location as well.

Since the trip to Socair and Evimeria would take a good bit of time She worked out her archery instruction schedule with General Hapsom to take this into account. She would teach two sets of classes and then make her ambassadorial trip to the west.

At the end of her second set of classes the graduating students all wished Fidem a safe journey and said they were glad the schedule for their class allowed them to be taught by Fidem. Any archery student hoped to have the privilege of being taught by Fidem. She was not only respected as the most competent instructor in Dartan but was also loved for her courteous and encouraging teaching style. Even when correcting someone at fault she was able to do so in a polite and more importantly encouraging manner.

Fidem knew her ambassadorial trip west would be somewhat lengthy, so she spent a good bit of her free time the week before she left with her mother. She was getting used to her mother's somewhat slower pace of living but also wanted to make sure that there were no large tasks left for her mother to take care of while she was gone. Since Fidem was an only child there were no siblings to count on to help her mom while she was gone. She was able to do a thorough cleaning of the farmhouse as well as make sure the garden and yard were in good shape. She and her mother also spent time in the evenings just chatting about their lives in general or remembering fond memories of past events.

Fidem and Hratt decided to take their time during this trip and enjoy some of the beautiful scenery that they were passing along the way. Not only did they enjoy lunch by the waterfall as usual but took some time after finishing their meal to fly nearer and give the area right next to it a closer look over. They discovered a small grassy meadow next to the bubbling pool at the base of the waterfall and landed to make a more detailed inspection. There was a good bit of mist in the air from the waterfall and tiny rainbows could be seen in areas where the sunlight fell directly on the mist. They also found that the face of the mountain had been cut back over the years at the base of the waterfall and that there was plenty of room for them to get behind it. They were also pleased to discover that there was a wide flat ledge of rock there they could walk on and especially appreciated being able to look through the water and mist at the beautiful countryside beyond. Though the noise of the water hitting the pool was loud it was not oppressive, and it was well worth dealing with it to get such a spectacular view. After spending a few more minutes enjoying the experience they were again on their way. They were looking forward to sharing the experience with their friends the next time they all were in the area together. Since this waterfall had proved to be a good side trip they planned on checking out the larger one nearer Maith when they got to that part of the trip.

They made sure to stop by and greet both groups of forest dwellers on their way. They were able to give the forest dwellers an update on what was going on in the world in the areas Fidem and Hratt either lived in or had visited and the forest dwellers said they appreciated being able to get news from the outside and that they always looked forward to seeing a dragon come in for a landing. The larger group invited them to stay for the night and prepared a large feast for them with the entire community in attendance. It was a great time of getting to know each other better and sharing how things were going in each of their lives. They were able to share pleasant conversation later into the evening as the forest dwellers had made a small, cleared area near their cabins for the visitors to set up their camp so they would not have to hike back to the large clearing for the night.

Fidem and Hratt thanked the forest dwellers for their hospitality as they headed out after breakfast the next day. As soon as they had reached the end of the dense forest they had been traveling through and had emerged into the more open lands beyond instead of gently angling towards the highway as they had done on all the previous trips they made a sharper turn to their left heading in a more southerly direction. As soon as they caught sight of the river they altered their course slightly so that they were now headed directly towards the mist at the end of the river several miles away. When they reached the source of the mist they discovered that the landscape at that point appeared to be on two levels with about a 20 foot elevation difference. Since it was a good sized river with an abrupt 20 foot drop it was not surprising that there was so much mist produced.

They flew past the waterfall and dropped down closer to the ground at the lower level and circled back to get a good view of the waterfall from that direction. It was a very majestic scene due to the large amount of water cascading down from the upper to the lower level. They found a place to land and spent a while just admiring the grandeur of this larger and more powerful aquatic display. They smiled at each other and remarked that they would enjoy telling their friends of another "must see" side trip to take if their friends ever got the opportunity.

They made a stop in Socair to touch base with the Prime Minister and to inform him that King Firinne had approved the peace treaty and that Fidem was now the official ambassador to Socair from Dartan. She mentioned that even with the good relationship established between Dartan and Socair due to the distance involved her visits would necessarily be infrequent. He then said that he totally understood and that it was impossible for him to even make a visit to Dartan for the same reason. The Prime Minister then insisted on her and Hratt joining him for dinner as he felt that was the least he could do to show his appreciation for them making such a long journey to pay him a visit.

They had a very enjoyable meal, and each learned quite a bit that they did not know about each other's locations during the conversation held during the meal which continued for quite a while afterwards. It was a very relaxed and informal time together and both parties said they hoped to repeat the time together again sometime in the future. Eventually Fidem and Hratt excused themselves saying that they needed to get to Evimeria before it got any later. Since it was well after sundown and totally dark by then the Prime Minister agreed and bid them a fond farewell as they took off for the short trip across the gorge.

They landed in the courtyard and were enthusiastically greeted by one of the guards while another guard quickly headed into the citadel to inform King Lobarat and Queen Bonnie of their arrival. The guard they were speaking to suggested that they go to the large room reserved for the dragons and drop off their saddle and baggage. Once they had done this they could return to the courtyard. They quickly took care of dropping off the items and returned in very little time. The king and queen were there to greet them and invited them into the citadel. As they were walking along King Lobarat asked them if they needed anything to eat, if they would like to freshen up or if they were tired from their journey and just wanted to get some sleep. Hratt mentioned that he was fine and that they had eaten a large meal in Socair earlier but was not sure what Fidem's choice would be. When King Lobarat looked over at her she said she was hoping to have some relaxing conversation but would appreciate the chance to freshen up a bit first.

Since Fidem was well acquainted with the citadel layout she asked if she would have the room she had occupied on her previous visit and if not where her room would be this time. She was told she could have the same one and she headed off in that direction after being told to come to the small meeting hall near the throne room when she was ready. The king, queen and Hratt started making their way to the small meeting hall chatting as they walked along. Though the hall itself was not large it fortunately had a tall wide double door leading to a veranda outside which the three used to enter the chamber. The king and queen usually made use of the passage between the hall and throne room, but with Hratt's much larger size this was not practical for him.

The room was furnished for comfortable relaxing informal visits and was not intended for official state visits. The walls were of stone, but the individual blocks were of various shades arranged in an irregular, but very eye appealing pattern that had a calming effect when viewed. It reminded one of viewing gentle rolling hills or watching the waves of the sea while comfortably standing on shore. There was a fireplace with a small fire burning that was of just the right size to take the evening chill off without overly heating the room. The furniture was cozily arranged in a circular pattern so that a person never had to turn their head too far to the left or right to talk to someone else and the upholstery was of a soft leather with plenty of padding that gave you the feeling of resting on a cloud rather than sitting on a rock. They had just gotten themselves comfortable and were being served some refreshments when Fidem rejoined them. She smiled saying, "It looks like my timing is perfect!" as she gratefully sank into one of the soft chairs there with a contented sigh.

They shared a very relaxed evening and did not end up going to bed until after midnight. They were told to sleep in for as long as they wanted and to just open their door and ring the bell placed on the table just beside the door as soon as they were up. This would alert the citadel staff to start preparing breakfast for them. Many different topics were discussed and chatted about, but most were of a more personal nature, so they started with news updates from both areas to get them out of the way before proceeding to the more pleasant topics. Fidem and Hratt asked about the small horse farm and King Lobarat told them with a smile that both young horses were growing into fine specimens that should give the new crossbreed a good start. King Lobarat again thanked Fidem for coming up with the idea and said they could all check them out in the morning. Eventually everyone started yawning and it was decided that they should probably head to bed. Everyone had a peaceful night and Fidem was especially grateful for the nice soft bed after all the days of camping out on the trip.

Since Fidem had such a comfortable bed she got a really good night's sleep and woke very refreshed. It was not quite as early as she had been getting up while camping and traveling, but she did not just roll over and try to go back to sleep as is often done by some lazy people. She got up and rang the bell and then proceeded to get dressed and take care of washing her face, combing her hair and the rest of her morning routine before heading to the dining area for breakfast.

The king, queen, Hratt and several other citadel staff were already seated at tables there and Fidem waved to her friends as she entered and headed over to where the food was set out on a long table along one of the walls. She inhaled the wonderful aroma of the freshly prepared items that were placed on the table in buffet style so that one could choose whatever they desired and control the portion sizes to their liking. All of the choices looked good and there were many to choose from so she decided to take a very small sample portion of each one and then decide what she really wanted. After quickly trying the samples and deciding what she liked best she got normal sized portions of her favorites for her actual meal.

She then went over to join her friends at their table after she had filled her mug with Gwen's special coffee, as she really enjoyed it and took advantage of the opportunity to savor its light sweetness and wonderful aroma after the plainer variety she had been having while camping out on her travels. The camping coffee was very good, but if you have never had a cup of Gwen's coffee it will be hard for you to imagine how much of a treat it was for her! As she took her seat she said she was looking forward to seeing the horses at the small farm and anything else the king and queen wanted her to see. Queen Bonnie asked her if the golden arrow had arrived safely in Dartan after her trip back and what she had done with it. Fidem smiled and said it had arrived safely and was now mounted on the wall in her office behind her desk at eye level so that it was the first thing she saw while entering the room.

Queen Bonnie said she still marveled whenever she re-membered that day and how Fidem being the youngest archer there had hit the pea dead center. The queen also remarked that she was glad the contest allowed each participant three shots. If each only had one shot there was always the chance of a "lucky hit", but with three the luck aspect could either be confirmed or ruled out in almost all cases. In the case of two of the three shots being wide and the third one hitting the pea it was most likely luck that caused the win. On the other hand, as in Fidem's case when all three were very close the winning hit was obviously not just luck.

Fidem then just seemed to look off into the distance with a somewhat dreamy expression on her face remarking, "And I marvel to think that none of my wonderful experiences of getting to know so many people in the vast world around me and getting to go to places that most people in my country have only heard about, but never seen, would never have been possible if it had not been for the kindness of Queen Gwen to a sad little girl with a poorly constructed pretend bow!"

They continued chatting during their leisurely meal, but eventually everyone finished and they decided to give the horses a visit. Fidem said she was surprised at how big the young ones had gotten and agreed with King Lobarat that they looked like fine strong healthy animals. She then asked if any more foals were expected. Queen Bonnie told her with a smile that the original stallion and mare were expecting another and that the she had seen the two young ones getting to know each other a few days ago and was hopeful that they would have one as well. Fidem said that was good news and King Lobarat said that he agreed, but care would have to be taken now to make sure that the stallions did not get into any fights over the mares. He said he would probably keep the healthiest stallion there, another one at the citadel and either send any others to one of the other main horse farms or have them gelded and kept at the small farm or the citadel for riding purposes.

Fidem and Hratt spent another two days in Evimeria and got to see a few places in the kingdom that were not too far from the citadel, and they enjoyed picnicking with the king and queen as well as viewing the beautiful scenery. The day after that they headed to the courtyard after another enjoyable leisurely breakfast and were surprised at the number of people gathered there to wish them a safe journey home.

King Lobarat handed Fidem a rolled up document tied with a silk ribbon and with a royal seal on it. He said to give it to King Firinne when she saw him next. Fidem and Hratt then flew off as the crowd waved goodbye to them and had a safe and uneventful return trip to Dartan.

19

Events in Glyka

Fidem reported to General Hapsom first after landing in Glyka as his office was closer to where she landed than the palace. He said for her to take the rest of the day as well as a couple of more days off after she had reported to King Firinne. He said they would go over her schedule at that time and that she should report to King Firinne next and then go to visit her mother. Fidem thanked him and said she was anxious to see how her mother was doing but wanted to report in with the king first. She then said goodbye and headed on to the palace.

She happened to meet Royal Advisor Jenny as she was entering the palace and made sure to greet her and give her a quick update. Fidem said she needed to report to King Firinne but wanted to get together with Jenny later for a chat. She mentioned to Jenny that she would be heading to her mother's farmhouse after she finished reporting to the king, but that she should be free tomorrow afternoon if that worked for Jenny. Jenny told her that it was good for her too and that she was looking forward to it. Jenny told her that King Firinne had told her she was to announce herself and enter his chamber whenever she arrived, so Fidem made her way directly to the king's chamber. She announced herself and entered as instructed.

The king warmly greeted her and asked how her trip went in general and if she was ready to give him a report or if she needed another day to prepare it. Fidem said she was ready if the king wanted an oral report but would need another day if he needed a written one. The king said an oral report should be fine and he would only need a written one if anything unusual or concerning had occurred on her trip. She then gave her report adding a few more details when the king asked for them. She then handed the king the sealed document from King Lobarat.

When King Firinne asked her what it was about she confessed that she really had no idea. The king broke the seal and unrolled the document which turned out to be a letter. After reading it he looked over at Fidem, and she asked him if anything was wrong. He said with a smile, "No absolutely not! It is a letter thanking me for allowing you to remain Ambassador to Evimeria instead of replacing you with another more experienced individual. King Lobarat said that he much preferred having a good friend he could feel comfortable talking freely to rather than a representative that most likely would be more concerned with proper protocol than heartfelt communication."

King Firinne then told Fidem that he was very pleased with her service to the kingdom both as an archery instructor and as an ambassador. He said he valued her highly as a subject and looked forward to her continuing to serve well. He also said that he expected that Fidem was anxious to check on her mother and dismissed her. As she was about to depart he said, "By the way, if you ever need to see me at any time for any reason you now have that privilege by royal decree. Just announce yourself and enter as you did today if I am expecting you; but knock first announcing yourself and waiting for me to say 'Enter' if I am not expecting you. And be sure to say hello to your mother for me. Goodbye."

Fidem was indeed anxious to check on her mother, so she walked at a rapid pace on her way there. She greeted her mother warmly as she entered and they both shared a hug. Fidem noticed her mother was looking and acting about the same as the last time she saw her and was encouraged that she did not appear to be getting any worse. Fidem asked her mother if she was having any difficulty keeping up with the housework or gardening. Her mother told her no, but she was still having to adjust her expectations as to how long it would take to get something done. Fidem glanced around and was pleased to see the farmhouse looking neat and cared for like it had always been.

After breakfast the next day Fidem took a walk around the yard checking the condition of the flower beds by the farmhouse and then took a look at the vegetable garden to see what condition it was in. Other than pulling a few weeds that had recently popped up in the vegetable garden as weeds often do nothing else needed to be done and the plants in both areas were healthy and growing well.

After lunch Fidem told her mother that she needed to go see Royal Advisor Jenny so they could both update each other on what had been happening during Fidem's trip. She said she would be back home before dinner that evening. Her mother said, "I thought you had already given King Firinne a report. Why does the Royal Advisor need another one?"

Smiling at her mother Fidem replied, "This is not a formal report, but just two friends sharing events from their lives with each other. By the way, and before I forget, King Firinne said I was to be sure and say hello to you from him."

"He said that to you? That is not the way a king normally talks to one of his subjects. Are you now on such good terms with him?"

"Well, he did give me access to him any time I want by royal decree, so I guess so. I must admit that strange as it sounds I now feel as comfortable talking with him as I do with you. Quite a change from that day when I was seated next to him in the royal carriage outside our farmhouse. I was so hoping he would not address me as I had no idea if I would even be able to utter one word without fainting!"

They both shared a hearty laugh and Fidem departed for her meeting with Jenny. Fidem found Jenny and they both got a hot beverage before Jenny led them to a small table in a secluded area in one of the palace gardens. They enjoyed updating each other while sipping their drinks and relaxing in the quiet peaceful spot. Jenny remarked that this was her favorite place to retreat to if she wanted privacy to think something over or just get away to relax for a few minutes during the day. Fidem agreed and said as nice as her quiet small office was there was always the possibility of being interrupted there and this would be a great spot for her to get away if she needed to be alone as long as Jenny did not mind sharing it.

Jenny said, "Of course not! Besides I don't own or have control over it in any case. I do appreciate your thoughtfulness in asking though."

They both smiled at each other continuing their pleasant conversation. The subject eventually turned to Gwendolyn and Fergal's upcoming wedding which was now a little over a month away. Fidem said she wanted to know what Jenny thought about transporting King Lobarat and Queen Bonnie to the wedding using the dragons and the double saddles. She said that with her concerns over her mother's health it had slipped her mind, and she was sorry she had not brought it up sooner. Fidem said that King Lobarat and Queen Bonnie had both said they wished they had a way to get to the wedding the last time Fidem had visited them, but Fidem had not thought about the possibility of going to get them until later. Jenny thought it was a great idea but said they needed to get started quickly due to the limited time left before the wedding.

After a quick discussion it was decided that the best plan would be for Fidem and Hratt to make a quick trip to Pacem and see if Gwen and Dreki were available and willing to make the trip. They could have the craftsmen fabricate a couple more double saddles with larger passenger portions while she made her trip to Pacem and back. They already had the measurements for Gwen and Fidem and would just have to estimate the others. Fidem then got permission from both General Hapsom and King Firinne to make both the trip to Pacem and then the one to Evimeria. Jenny said she would take care of having Hratt and the saddle ready and Fidem went home to say goodbye to her mother and let her know about the two planned trips. Fidem then went back and met Hratt in the courtyard and climbed into the saddle. She was fully confident that Jenny had taken care of packing everything needed for the trip so she and Hratt immediately took to the air and were on their way to Pacem without delay.

They first made a stop in Dreki's meadow and as soon as Dreki heard what was planned he agreed to help and asked Elskandi if she wanted to come along to Glyka and wait for them there rather than waiting here by herself and flying to Glyka later for the wedding. She agreed to go with them, and they all headed on to Pacem from there. When they landed in the castle courtyard in Pacem it was not long before Queen Gwen came out and greeted them. When she learned of the plan she said of course she was willing to help and invited them all to join her for dinner and spend the night there. She said she could pack her things after dinner and they could all be on their way directly after breakfast the following day.

They spent the rest of the afternoon in pleasant conversation which was continued during the dinner meal. A bit more conversation was enjoyed as they all relaxed afterwards in one of the smaller halls in the castle. Eventually everyone headed to bed for a good night's sleep and were fully refreshed for their trip in the morning. Following a leisurely breakfast they all headed off for Glyka making their usual stops along the way arriving a few days later. They spent the next day in Glyka resting up and preparing for the longer journey to Evimeria.

The trip to Evimeria was made with meal stops at their favorite locations and nothing occurred during the journey to slow them down or cause any difficulty. They did make the two waterfall stops so Gwen was able to experience the view from behind the smaller one as well as enjoy the grandeur of the larger falls. Since they had made the trip several times by now they were not surprised by seeing anything new or anxious that they might miss something along the way. To add a little variety to the trip Fidem and Hratt decided to work on some of the unusual flight maneuvers they had been practicing lately as they proceeded along their route. They were not sure if they would ever need to use them but decided that it would be fun working on them in any case. Gwen enjoyed seeing the combinations of graceful swoops with energetic gyrations as she flew beside them and took pleasure in seeing Fidem's joy as she mastered them. By practicing these several times during the trip Fidem and Hratt were very comfortable doing them by the time they reached Evimeria and a couple of them were quite spectacular.

They arrived at the citadel courtyard after their usual midday meal in Maith and it wasn't long before King Lobarat and Queen Bonnie came out to greet them. When he saw that Fidem and Gwen each had a dragon with a double saddle he got a confused expression on his face and asked why they did not just come together on one dragon.

Gwen smiled and said, "As ambassador to your fine country and the person who came up with the idea I will give Fidem the honor of explaining it to you."

Fidem then explained the plan for transporting them both to Glyka for the upcoming wedding if they were able to be out of Evimeria for that amount of time. She also mentioned that it would be best for King Lobarat to ride with her and Queen Bonnie to ride with Gwen as that would give a more even weight distribution for the dragons. Both the king and queen enthusiastically accepted the invitation with thanks and said they could be ready whenever the transport team had rested up enough for the return journey.

Two days later the trip to Glyka was underway. The king and queen were both experienced equestrians and had no trouble adapting to travel by dragonback. They said the only thing that was a little unsettling was the first few takeoffs and landings as the fairly rapid changes in altitude was something they had not experienced on horseback. They were shown most of the interesting spots along the way and said they really appreciated being able to finally see the places that they had only heard about previously. When they finally came in for a landing in the palace courtyard in Glyka they both remarked that they had not realized how long and far a journey the trip between the two locations actually was.

The dragons had been spotted while they were still a good way off as King Firinne had lookouts posted keeping a watch for them. He had started posting the lookouts once the minimum time for getting to Evimeria and back had passed so he and the queen as well as several of the kingdom officials would be there waiting for them to land. As they landed the crowd there cheered the arrival and King Firinne and Queen Unestita stepped forward to be the first to greet King Lobarat and Queen Bonnie and officially welcome them to the kingdom of Dartan. They were then escorted into the palace shown the room they would be occupying during their stay and made comfortable in one of the smaller halls similar to the one in the citadel in Evimeria by King Firinne and Queen Unestita.

Meanwhile Gwen, Fidem and the dragons took care of unpacking and putting things away from the trip. Once they had the saddles stored, which was the last item on their list, the dragons headed off to Hratt's quarters telling Gwen and Fidem they would be there the remainder of the day resting if they were needed for any reason. Gwen and Fidem then headed toward the palace to see if they were wanted and decided to rest in their quarters as well if they were not needed. Jenny met them at the entrance and told them that Fidem was free for the rest of the day and should take the following day off as well. Since Gwen was also a visitor she was told she could do whatever she wished and to make free use of the room she had occupied on her last visit.

Gwen and Fidem thanked Jenny and gratefully headed to their rooms to get some rest. The kings and queens spent a small amount of time conversing and getting to know each other better, but the visitors were allowed to go to their room after a short time for some much needed rest as well. Since it was still several days before the wedding nobody felt rushed to get something done and they all met including the dragons in the medium sized dining room for dinner and conversation.

After getting fully rested King Lobarat and Queen Bonnie went on a day trip to Vita to get better acquainted with King Kelan and Queen Rachel. They had made the usual one day stop there and been given an introduction and quick tour but wanted to spend a bit more time getting better acquainted and having a lengthier tour where they could ask more questions. Gwen, Fidem and the dragons went along as chauffeurs and Gwen went on the tour to answer any questions about the battle. Fidem decided to check out the orphanage since she had not spent much time there the last time she was in Vita.

Fidem was warmly greeted by Angela when she knocked on the door and was invited in for a cup of coffee. Fidem was smiling as she gratefully accepted the invitation. Fidem noticed that some of the children kept looking at her and talking quietly to each other. She mentioned it to Angela and Angela said that the children had heard about her and had been wondering what she was really like.

Fidem told Angela to call them over as she would be glad to talk with them and answer their questions. The children all sat quietly waiting for Fidem to speak and several hands went up when Fidem asked if there were any questions. She spoke with each child one at a time answering their questions.

"Is it scary to ride a dragon?" a young girl asked.

"The first few times it is a little bit, but the dragons are very careful not to swerve or dive until a rider is ready for it. Once you have become used to it even the swerves and dives are not scary; in fact, they can be quite fun!"

A slightly older boy then asked, "How were you able to beat all those big strong soldiers in the archery contest? We all saw the golden arrow you had so we know you were not just making up a pretend story for us."

"Archery is more about skill than strength. There is a certain amount of strength required, but any normal person can build up their arm strength to that point with perseverance. The skill requires practice time. Some people, like myself, have been gifted with the ability to excel at archery. If a gifted person does not practice though they will not excel. On the other hand, a person who is not particularly gifted can excel if they put in enough practice time. In my case I have both been gifted and spent a lot of practice time."

The last question came from a girl about Fidem's age. She asked, "How could you have killed that wolf at your age without the time to build strength and skill?"

"It is hard to explain actually. I think it must have been a combination of instinct and my desire to protect others from harm. I was not consciously even thinking about it. It happened so fast that I don't remember my actions in actually shooting the wolf as well as I remember looking around afterwards to see if there were any more wolves nearby."

Queen Gwen then poked her head in the door saying, "Sorry to interrupt, but I am afraid Dame Fidem is wanted by two kings and queens, and we better not keep them waiting!"

Fidem then excused herself meeting Gwen outside the door. Just as they were heading off they heard one of the children remark in a loud voice, "We are so lucky! We have gotten to meet both Queen Gwen when she was ruling here and now Dame Fidem the wolf slayer herself!"

Gwen and Fidem smiled at each other and chuckled as they were heading off to meet the others. It was nearing lunchtime and since Fidem had been at the orphanage she did not know of the picnic lunch plans that had been made in her absence. They had all decided that a picnic lunch in the clearing where Gwen and Dreki had landed on the day of the battle would be great. The rest of the group was waiting just inside the castle by the drawbridge and they all headed out together as soon as Gwen and Fidem had joined them. The path through the woods to the clearing had been made wide enough for a dragon so the entire group was able to make the expedition.

It was a quiet peaceful spot which was ideal for just enjoying nature along with a good lunch. King Lobarat and Queen Bonnie thanked Fidem for having shared with them a lot of the things they were now seeing. They said Fidem had done an excellent job as ambassador in describing Vita and Dartan, but they were glad they had now been given the opportunity to actually see these places in person. After they had finished their lunch they all felt a good long walk would be desirable and decided to take the road leading from the front of the castle and going over the mountain into Dartan. They did not plan to travel the entire way as they knew it was farther than they wanted to hike and there was also not enough time to complete the journey. They hiked as far as the point where the road started to go up the mountainside and explored the area there a little envisioning the diverters breaking away from the rest of the army at that point and heading to the south. By this time, they decided to hike back to the castle and return to Glyka so they would not miss the evening meal. They arrived in Glyka with plenty of time to freshen up a bit before meeting Elskandi and heading to the medium sized dining room for dinner.

After dinner they relocated to the smaller more comfortable hall for pleasant conversation and light refreshments. The next day was pretty laid back and the only event worth mentioning was an afternoon tour of the town of Glyka for King Lobarat and Queen Bonnie with Gwen and Fidem for their tour guides. The king and queen were dressed very casually as they said they hoped to avoid having to acknowledge all the bows they would receive dressed as royals. They felt that not acknowledging a bow with at least a nod and a smile would make them appear conceited and that was definitely not the impression they wanted to make.

When they entered the shop where Gwen, Gwendolyn and Jenny had gotten their necklaces the shopkeeper greeted them warmly. He then said with a smile, "Queen Gwen, it looks like you and Dame Fidem have brought me a couple more customers."

When Gwen introduced them as King Lobarat and Queen Bonnie of Evimeria the shopkeeper bowed deeply and said, "I apologize and humbly beg your Majesties pardon for speaking the way I did. I certainly meant no disrespect and would not have addressed you like that had I known who you were. I am so used to Queen Gwen's openness and down to earth manner that I spoke without thinking." He remained bowing as he waited for a reply.

King Lobarat then spoke up, "My good man, please rise!" When the shopkeeper stood straight again King Lobarat continued, "Neither the queen nor I wish to stand upon ceremony. Had we been that type of king and queen we would have had Queen Gwen announce us formally before we entered your building. We are merely visitors to your fine country and city and as you jokingly spoke to Queen Gwen do wish to be customers. We wish to take a couple of souvenirs back with us to remember our trip, but it appears that from the obvious quality of the items we see not your usual souvenir."

"Is there any particular type of jewelry you are interested in or a certain style or gemstone color? If so I can show your Majesties where they are displayed."

"You can drop the 'Majesties' and just refer to us as Sir and Madam. Since Dame Fidem has a golden arrow from Evimeria I think it would be nice if I had one from Dartan to remember her by once Dame Fidem's Gold Arrow is no longer in the citadel." He then asked his wife, "What about you dear do you have a preference?"

Queen Bonnie replied as she looked at the shopkeeper and pointed at Gwen's necklace, "I would like something in the style of what Queen Gwen is wearing if you have anything like that."

"I have quite a few items in the style Madam is looking for. If you look in the walnut case to your left you will see a number of the better examples and some less expensive ones in the case next to it."

The ladies then headed over to the walnut case and began examining the items on display there. The shopkeeper then addressed King Lobarat, "It may be a bit more difficult to find something for you Sir. All the arrow jewelry I have is fairly small and designed mostly for ladies, but I can show you what I do have and see if anything interests you."

The shopkeeper then led him over to a wall with several cases mounted on it. He pointed to the leftmost case and said that one and the next two had quite a few arrow themed pieces in them. He also told King Lobarat that he could have Dame Fidem's Gold Arrow duplicated and sent to him at a later time if he would like. King Lobarat said that he would prefer something actually from Dartan rather than a copy of something Evimerian and began looking over what was in the cases. He asked to look closer at one piece he was interested in and the shopkeeper removed it from the case and handed it to him.

The shopkeeper then noticed the ladies looking at a particular piece with interest and asked if they wanted a closer look. When they answered in the affirmative he took it out and handed it to them before going back over to see if King Lobarat had made a decision. King Lobarat said that of all the choices he had seen this was the one that he liked best, but added, "It is a shame you do not have anything larger. I was hoping for something a bit longer than two inches."

The shopkeeper then hit himself on the forehead exclaiming, "I just remembered something! Let me get it from the back." He returned holding a golden arrow with a diamond arrowhead and emerald fletching that was about six inches long. "I was trying to come up with a trophy for an archery contest a while back and this was one of my ideas that was not used. I totally forgot about it as I did not consider it jewelry due to its larger size and had just left it there in the back."

King Lobarat smiled broadly at him exclaiming, "That is absolutely perfect and is just the sort of thing I was looking for!"

Queen Bonnie then said, "I found something I really like as well!" as she held up a necklace for him to see that was a very close match to Gwen's. It was a gold filigree heart with the alternating rubies and emeralds around the edge and the heart shaped cut diamond in the center. The only difference was that Gwen's was thin around the edge and thick in the center like a pillow while Queen Bonnie had chosen one that was flat and about $\frac{3}{8}$ of an inch thick.

They made their purchases and headed back towards the palace. On the way Queen Bonnie asked King Lobarat what he was going to do with his arrow once they got back home. He said he would keep it on his desk as a pleasant reminder of Fidem and also where anyone approaching him there would be able to see it. They then remarked that they were looking forward to tomorrow as that was the day of the wedding. They then left the shop and continued their town tour.

20

The Wedding

THE day of the wedding had arrived at last, and everyone was excited about the event. It was the first time a wedding would be performed between a citizen of Dartan and someone from another kingdom. It was also the first time anyone from the kingdom of Evimeria had attended a ceremony there and to have the representatives from Evimeria being the king and queen made it extra special.

The ceremony was similar to the ones you are familiar with in our world, but there were some interesting differences. The king would perform the ceremony, and it would take place at the palace. Don't forget that the kingdoms in Dreki's world are much smaller than those in ours so the king did not have many weddings to perform throughout the year. The ceremony had the exchange of vows and rings just like we do, but instead of the bride being escorted down the aisle both the bride and groom walked down the aisle side by side without touching each other. They remained about two feet apart as they did this to represent their status as individuals before the ceremony. At the end of the ceremony, they walked back down the aisle holding hands to represent their status as a united couple now.

The most striking difference was when the man and woman were from different countries. The woman would wear a veil in the color and traditional style of the country she came from.

After the exchange of vows and rings and the pronouncement of the couple now being man and wife, but just before the kiss the man would remove the bride's veil and replace it with one in the color and traditional style of his country. He would then lift the veil and kiss his new bride. The veil exchange represented the transfer of the wife's loyalty from her old country to that of her husband.

Since the weather was fine and mild it was going to be an outdoor wedding. All of the attendees were seated in the largest courtyard and waiting for the bride and groom. The largest courtyard was chosen due to the number of people attending. Since Princess Gwendolyn was closely related to Queen Gwen who was considered a hero of Dartan for defeating Nequitia and herself had participated in the overthrow of Sordibus in Evimeria helping to secure it as a valuable ally in the western lands she was well loved and respected by all the people residing in the kingdom of Dartan. Instead of a "wedding march" or other musical number for the entrance of the bride there was one long blast heard from a single trumpet high upon the castle wall. The location of the trumpet was chosen to give a clear signal without its being so loud that people would be startled and jump at the sound. Everyone rose at the sound of the trumpet and remained standing until the bride and groom had reached the front and turned to face each other. At this point the people seated themselves and the formal part of the ceremony began. It was obvious that there was much love between the bride and groom as they smiled warmly at each other throughout the ceremony and that this was not a marriage of convenience or a political alliance between two countries. After the kiss and as the bride and groom headed back down the aisle holding hands the people all stood cheering and clapping. Once the couple had reached the back row of people there was one more trumpet blast to indicate the end of the ceremony.

The bride and groom continued walking hand-in-hand for about 50 feet past the last row and then turned around to face the attendees. Those that wished to congratulate the bride and groom formed a line and those that did not feel comfortable doing so moved to the sides of the courtyard. The groom received handshakes and the bride hugs as the line progressed with the people moving to the sides of the courtyard after meeting the bride and groom. Once the congratulations were completed King Firinne announced that the reception meal was about to begin and gave thanks for the meal.

There were two long tables one on each side of the courtyard placed about six feet from the walls. This allowed four lines of people to fill their plates at the same time. Many delectable choices were available to pick and choose from and there were sufficient quantities of each so that nobody had to worry about someone coming after them not getting what they wanted. A large number of rectangular tables had been set up in an irregular pattern, so guests had the feeling of dining in a fine restaurant rather than a school cafeteria. The tables could comfortably seat ten people with ease so most families could sit together if they chose to do so.

Partway through the meal a large bell that had been placed near the center of the courtyard was rung once. Everyone stopped eating or talking and looked toward the table where the bride and groom were seated. The bride and groom then rose and gave a short speech. They went back and forth sharing thoughts about when they first met, what had attracted them to each other, events they had shared together and plans for the future. Some things shared were touching and others were humorous. When they had finished everyone clapped and then resumed their meal.

When most of the crowd had finished eating and were just enjoying conversation a musical ensemble began playing. Everyone waited until the bride and groom had danced the first dance together, but then quite a number of couples took to the floor and joined them. The dancing continued for several more hours with the number of couples participating slowly dwindling as the night progressed.

About an hour after their first dance the bride and groom left the dance floor to participate in a tradition that Gwendolyn found unusual, but interesting. Fergal had explained it to her one night as they were discussing wedding plans and Gwendolyn asked if gifts were given to the bride and groom like in her world. Fergal had her tell him about what it was like in that place, and he said it sounded a little boring after hearing her explanation to him. Once I tell you what they did in Dartan you will see why he said that.

They went over to the "gift table", but there were no gifts there. What was there was a stack of cards from the gift givers. Each card had instructions on where to find the gift as all the gifts had been hidden somewhere in the accessible areas of the palace. Some of the instructions were very clear and easy to follow and that gift was soon found and unboxed. Others were a bit more cryptic and that gift took a while to locate. The bride and groom got to choose how much time to spend searching and after an hour and a half of hunting they took the remaining cards for gifts that they could not locate to Royal Advisor Jenny who had a list of all the gifts and their locations. She would then hand them new cards with clear and simple instructions so that the remaining gifts were quickly located and added to the rest. Gwendolyn admitted that this tradition made it much more fun than the way she was used to it being done in our world.

The bride and groom then left for their honeymoon while the dancing slowly came to an end. Once the musicians stopped playing everyone headed back to their homes except the cleanup crew who would be busy for about another hour. The relocation of all the chairs and tables and the grounds cleanup were left for the following day, so the cleanup crew did not have to deal with them and just took care of washing the dishes pots and pans and taking all the table linens to the laundry and dropping them off there.

Fidem and her mother were discussing how beautiful the wedding had been as they slowly walked home afterwards. As soon as they had entered the farmhouse Fidem helped her mother get ready and into bed. Fidem was soon in her own bed as well and sleeping soundly. Fidem was up early and had breakfast ready when her mother got up a little later. They enjoyed breakfast together and Fidem made sure everything was in good shape at the farmhouse. She knew that she and Hratt as well as Gwen and Dreki would be taking King Lobarat and Queen Bonnie back to Evimeria so she said goodbye to her mother explaining that she would be staying at the palace to get an early start in the morning.

Nothing unusual occurred on the trip to Evimeria and back to Glyka so Fidem was back in a couple of weeks. Gwen, Dreki and Elskandi headed home after Dreki had rested up for a couple of days and Fidem went to check on her mother. Her mother seemed to be moving much slower and seemed to tire very easily so Fidem got permission to stay with her for a few days.

Fidem's mother said she felt alright except for the tiredness so Fidem took care of any tasks that needed doing around the farmhouse. The next day Fidem did all the outside chores as well as inside ones. She fixed breakfast but helped her mother into bed afterwards as her mother said she needed to rest. After resting for an hour or two her mother got up and slowly made her way out on the porch and sat there reading in her favorite rocker until lunchtime. Another rest was needed after lunch followed by another reading session in the rocker. After dinner her mother just wanted to go to bed early and fell asleep shortly after climbing in bed and starting to read her Bible.

The third day Fidem's mother said she did not feel that she had enough energy to get up and just wanted to rest in bed. Fidem said OK and then headed to the palace to get the Royal Physician to check on her mother. When Fidem and the Royal Physician arrived at the farmhouse Fidem went into her mother's bedroom to see if she was any better. Her mother said she was still too tired to get up. Fidem had the Royal Physician come and check her over and he took her pulse and listened to her heart for a bit. He motioned for Fidem to join him in the other room and Fidem knew the news was bad as she followed him there.

Fidem closed the door and looked over at the Royal Physician. He told her that her mother's heart was much weaker than the last time he checked and that she would not be able to handle any exertion. She should remain resting in bed and have her food brought to her there. The doctor gave her a bedpan stating that her mother would not be able to use the normal bathroom as the strain would be too much if she tried to get there and back again. He said that it was just a matter of time before her heart gave out completely. He said, "It could be any minute or she may hold out for a few more weeks. There is really no way to say for sure." He then departed and Fidem went back to her mother and asked her if there was anything she wanted. Her mother said no and Fidem just kept close and took care of her throughout the day. At the end of the day Fidem again asked if there was anything she wanted.

Her mother said that she liked reading her Bible before going to sleep but felt too tired to do it. She asked Fidem to please read to her until she fell asleep. She told Fidem she would probably drop off pretty quickly as tired as she felt and that Fidem should just start where the bookmark was and read from there. Fidem started reading and noticed a peaceful smile on her mother's face as she continued. After only a few minutes she heard her mother say in a quiet voice just above a whisper, "Thank you dear." Her mother then give a soft sigh and was gone.

Fidem wept for several hours but finally got the courage to go to the palace. Just as she entered she met Jenny. When Jenny saw Fidem's sad expression and red eyes she asked, "Is it your mother?"

Fidem managed to say a weak "Yes", before bursting into tears.

Jenny immediately held her and let her sob onto her shoulder for some time. When Fidem had cried herself out Jenny said, "I know it will be hard, but we need to take care of your mother's body."

"I know, that is why I am here. What do we have to do now?"

"We need to find the Royal Coroner and the Royal Undertaker as well as a few guards to transport the body. I will go take care of that at once. Do you want to go back home yourself or do you want to wait for me to go with you. It will only take me about ten minutes to gather the men."

"I will wait for you here as I would really appreciate your company heading back."

Jenny squeezed Fidem's hand then quickly departed on her errand. She was back before the ten minutes had expired and putting her arm around Fidem walked her back to her farmhouse with the men following them. Fidem led the Royal Coroner and the Royal Undertaker to her mother's room and then went back outside and waited with Jenny. In a couple of minutes, the coroner and undertaker came out and asked the men to carry the body out and place it on the cart they had brought. Fidem watched them carry her mother's body covered by a sheet out and place it on the cart.

Fidem watched the men slowly roll the cart down the lane toward the palace and just stood there as the cart went out of sight around a bend in the road. Jenny asked Fidem if she wanted her to stay with her for the night and Fidem gratefully accepted the offer. They both went inside and Fidem got ready for bed. Jenny said not to worry about her; she would just sit up for a while on the couch and sleep there when she got tired in a bit. Fidem thanked her, then crawled into her bed and cried herself to sleep.

The next day Fidem felt a little better and had breakfast with Jenny. They talked for a bit and Jenny asked Fidem if she was ready to discuss any plans yet or needed a bit more time. Fidem said she had figured a few things out but did not want to try and process too much right away. She said she planned to stay at her barracks and continue her archery instruction for sure. She was not sure about making any trips soon and what to do about the farmhouse and wanted to wait a while before tackling those.

The funeral for Fidem's mother was attended by a very large number of people. Very few of them were acquainted with Fidem's mother, but Dame Fidem was well known and respected in the kingdom. The service itself was not lengthy but was beautifully done and very meaningful to all those attending. Rather than standing next to the casket to receive condolences Fidem was seated in a chair. This was done due to the large number of people wanting to say words of comfort to her. The time spent after the service in giving condolences was quite lengthy as there were so many people wishing to do so and Fidem was very grateful that the chair had been provided for her.

There was a short graveside service at the cemetery and Fidem's mother was finally laid to rest there. Fidem wept a bit more as she said her final goodbye and Jenny helped walk her back to her mother's farmhouse. Jenny offered to spend the rest of the day and that night with Fidem if she wished it, but Fidem thanked her and declined the offer. Fidem said she just wanted to spend the next few hours alone wandering about the farmhouse and grounds fondly remembering the good times she and her mother had shared there. Jenny then left heading back to the palace.

Fidem slowly walked from room to room noticing things in each location that gave her good memories of her mother. She also spent time down by the garden remembering helping her mother to plant some of the things that had grown up so nicely now. She spent a little time on the porch sitting in a comfortable chair with her eyes closed thinking of the times she and her mother would sit there talking on cool evenings while her mother rocked in her favorite chair. Lastly she got ready for bed picked up her mother's Bible from the table next to her mother's bed where it had been placed on the night her mother had died and taking it to her room read for a while until she fell asleep. She could imagine hearing her mother's comforting voice as she read to herself and finally fell asleep with a smile on her face. The next day Fidem took the Bible with her to her room at the barracks and left it there so she could continue reading it before bed each night.

Fidem gradually got back into her routine as an archery instructor over the next week and found that her practice time was very therapeutic as it gave her time to think while doing something relaxing and enjoyable at the same time. As more time passed, Fidem got used to life without her mother around and after a few months had gotten over her initial grief and settled back into her normal routine.

21

AN UNEXPECTED THREAT

THINGS were going well in the kingdom of Dartan at this time. Gwendolyn and Fergal had returned from their honeymoon and were getting settled in Glyka. Fidem had asked them if they wanted to move into her mother's farmhouse instead of having a room in the palace. They said that it would be great for them to have the privacy and a place they could call their own but asked Fidem if she was sure that was what she wanted and did not want to keep it as her own. Fidem said it would be inconvenient for her to live there and have to make early daily trips to the palace to be there in time for the guards' assembly first thing in the morning. She also said she would not be able to keep up with the gardening and other tasks around the farmhouse and teach her archery classes at the same time. Trying to do all that on her time off was not practical either. She knew Gwendolyn and Fergal would take proper care of the place and that was all she wanted for her mother's property. She said she was hoping that she could visit on occasion and they told her she could visit any time she wanted.

Since there were no major upcoming events and the kingdom was peaceful and running well King Firinne decided to make a trip north to visit his cousin King Eagna who was reigning in the kingdom of Fredelig some distance away. Prime Minister Liganth came along as he had relatives and friends there as well. The king had General Hapsom as well as a troop of palace guards accompany him and Queen Unestita in the unlikely event that they ran into a band of robbers along the way. Since Fredelig was a fair distance away he planned the expedition to last about a month. That gave them roughly a week to get there two weeks to visit and another week to get back home. He left Royal Advisor Jenny in charge and left knowing the kingdom to be in capable hands.

They ran into no difficulties on the way there and enjoyed camping out along the way. The weather was excellent for travel and the country they traveled through was very scenic. They arrived safely in Fredelig and were warmly welcomed by King Eagna and entertained and feasted lavishly. They were enjoying themselves immensely totally unaware that trouble had been brewing in Dartan.

A few days after the king's party had departed on their trip, the guards at the city gate of Glyka were surprised to see a fair sized army approaching, led by what appeared to be a king. They were all dressed in battle array so the guards quickly closed and barred the gates until they could determine whether or not this was the threat it appeared to be. The leader boldly approached the gates and stopped in front of them. He then proclaimed in a loud voice, "I am King Mektig of Sterk and demand that you unconditionally surrender! If not you will all be slaughtered. You have until sundown to respond." He then returned to his troops which were waiting just beyond where he said the range of the archers should be.

The guards quickly informed Royal Advisor Jenny of the problem, and she gathered those leaders remaining at the palace for a council. She had gotten representatives for guards, archers and soldiers in case a defense was planned. Fidem had been asked to join the council as she was most familiar with the capabilities of all the archers and Colonel Veren was included because he knew how best to apply those capabilities militarily. Jenny also found cooks and those in charge of stored goods in case a siege needed to be endured.

Once the council had gathered discussion began in earnest. Each leader gave his or her expected outcome of a conflict based on the number and skill of the combatants in their area of expertise. They all came to the conclusion that they would not be able to defeat this enemy with the forces remaining in Glyka and it was uncertain what the outcome would be even if King Firinne and the soldiers with him were added to their forces. They had allies in the west, but it would take months for them to reach Dartan due to the terrain they would have to traverse. Pacem was much closer but lacked any armed force. The few guards and soldiers there might be able to defend the castle there from a band of brigands but would not be enough to make any difference in Dartan's case. Vita did not have near the number of soldiers that were there when Nequitia was reigning and was in a similar situation to Pacem. They had enough to defend themselves if attacked by a small force, but not enough to make a difference for Dartan either. Besides there was no practical way to even contact Pacem or Vita and get a response before the sundown time limit was reached.

The cooks and those in charge of stored goods said there were enough supplies to feed all the castle occupants for several months, but that if the entire town had to be supplied they would run out of provisions in less than two weeks.

The council came to the conclusion that unless some unusually effective plan could be thought of there was no hope for them and that surrender was the only viable option. Jenny said that she thought the only thing that might work would be to trick the enemy into believing that Dartan's military strength was much greater than it actually was but had no suggestion as how to accomplish that.

Fidem then said, "Well. . . I have a rather risky idea, but if it fails we will be in no worse condition than we are now."

Jenny quickly responded, "We don't have much time left so please tell us what you are thinking!"

"You all know that many years ago someone brought a Bible here from Gwen and Gwendolyn's world and there were quite a few copies made of it. My mother had one that she often read especially before retiring for bed. She would read out loud to me until I fell asleep and then read to herself until she got tired and went to bed. One of my favorite parts was about a young boy named David who fought a huge enemy giant named Goliath that everyone else was afraid to face. Goliath and I am guessing most of his fellow soldiers as well all made fun of David's small size. When David killed Goliath the rest of Goliath's fellow soldiers all ran away in fear."

Jenny looked puzzled and replied, "I don't see the connection. They don't have a Goliath, and we don't have a David."

Fidem smiled and said, "In a way we do so please hear me out. I will be our 'David' and treat King Mektig as their 'Goliath'. What we need to do is make him believe we are not afraid of him, we have superior forces and we are merciful, but our patience is limited. If I go out the postern door dressed in common clothes rather than armor or a military uniform and stand in front of the gates he will think he sees a little girl standing there that is well out of bowshot. I will tell him that he and his men are in great danger, but that we are offering them all the opportunity to retreat before they suffer loss of life. While I am exiting the postern door and speaking every archer, guard and soldier should be given a bow and line up on top of the city wall with an arrow knocked and a grim expression on their face. He will see many more archers than he was expecting but will not be worried because of the distance. He will also likely assume that with that many archers the number of soldiers is also more than he expected. I will inform him that Dartan is famed for their archery skill and that if he does not retreat or returns at a later time he will sorely regret it. I am assuming he and most of his men will have a hearty laugh and say something insulting. I will then tell him to have one of the men standing behind him hold up one of their round shields. I will shoot an arrow into the center of the shield explaining that I am too young to be trained as a soldier and am considered such a poor shot that I am merely used as an arrow retriever for the practicing soldiers. I will tell him to leave immediately and never return. I will then come back in without waiting for a reply."

The council agreed that such a bold plan would be totally unexpected and might actually work. They were very worried about Fidem and asked if she was sure she wanted to risk herself this way.

"As I said before we will be no worse off if the plan fails. Since they did not storm the city but asked for surrender first they appear to be rational people rather than barbarians. I expect the worst that could happen to me would be I would be taken prisoner, but I doubt if any of his men would be brave enough to approach after my archery demonstration. Besides I will be well inside the city again before they have time to even act."

The plan was then immediately put into effect and all the archers and available soldiers and guards were given a bow and some arrows. The archers were properly equipped, but some of the soldiers and guards had bows and arrows that were not the right size for them. At the distance the enemy had kept back they would not be able to tell the difference anyway.

It was about an hour before sunset and some of the enemy soldiers were becoming restless as they tired of waiting. King Mektig called them to order and had just turned back around to face the city when movement was noted all along the top of the city wall. The enemy watched as the "archer army" lined up with their bows ready and looked uncertainly at each other when they saw how many there were. They were so intent on this that most had not seen Fidem exit the postern door. A few had noticed and shouted this to King Mektig.

King Mektig spoke loudly to his men, "Look at the tiny person they sent to inform us of their surrender!" All the soldiers as well as the king laughed heartily and he said, "Well little maiden what have you got to say for yourself?"

Unlike what he expected Fidem stood straight and tall and spoke in a clear commanding voice, "Dartan is famed for our archery skill as well as bravery in battle and if you do not retreat or you attempt to return at a later time you will sorely regret it!"

He was thunderstruck and stood gaping with his mouth open for a few moments. Some of the soldiers became uneasy as they did not know what to make of the situation either. He recovered quickly however and said with a sneer, "Talk is cheap! I see nothing to fear!" He then gave another laugh, but it was not quite as confident sounding as the first one.

"Have one of the men behind you hold his round shield above his head and you might change your mind."

He turned quickly and rapped out, "I don't see what that will do, but go ahead soldier and do what she says!"

The soldier lifted his shield while chuckling. Fidem raised her bow and knocked one of her special hunting arrows with an extremely sharp point on it. She then immediately fired hitting the shield dead center with enough force that the arrow protruded about two inches on the other side. The chuckling stopped abruptly.

Many gasps were heard as the soldier hid behind his shield and ran for it to try and get out of range. The shield would not have actually been of much help as the soldier had to keep it at his side as he ran leaving his back exposed, but he was operating in total panic mode running for his life. There were a few "That's impossible at that distance!" and "Oh no, run for it!" comments heard as more soldiers rapidly moved back as well. King Mektig's horse felt the king's nervousness and began to fidget, which encouraged Fidem greatly.

"I am too young to be trained as a soldier and am considered such a poor shot that I am merely used as an arrow retriever for the practicing soldiers. You need to leave immediately and never return or suffer the dire consequences of your folly!"

Fidem then turned her back on him and slowly walked back to the postern door. She closed it again after she was inside then hurriedly made her way to the top of the wall. What she saw made hear heart leap with joy! All the soldiers were making a rather hasty retreat and seeing the panicked way they were running King Mektig soon joined them.

After the enemy was well out of sight down the road and a dissipating dust cloud was the only evidence of the enemy having been there a huge cheer went up in the city! Everyone was congratulating each other on the narrow escape and Fidem's ingenious plan and bravery in executing it. After several minutes had passed Royal Advisor Jenny asked for another meeting of the council to discuss the event and to get it recorded in the annals.

The councilors no longer had those worried expressions on their faces like the last time and were still congratulating each other when Jenny called the meeting to order. She made sure the event was recorded accurately and completely with no detail left out. The council then went back to the congratulatory talk for a while, but eventually Jenny asked to make a comment.

"What if King Mektig changes his mind and convinces his army to give it another try? We need to prepare for that. Once King Firinne and General Hapsom return plans for our future defense can be worked out; it is right now that worries me. I am a little concerned that after coming all this way he may want to try again before going home and possibly make a sneak attack instead of actually heading home."

"I can't think of anything else we could possibly do!" said one of the soldiers.

"If he does return soon we are doomed." remarked an archer.

A cook added, "We will only starve if we try to wait out a siege!"

Jenny raised her hands for attention and smiling at Fidem commented, "Fidem came up with a plan that sent him running because he believed we were stronger than we actually are. We need to come up with a way to keep an eye on him making sure he does not return here. We also need to come up with a strategy to cause him to continue believing we are stronger than he is in the event he starts to waver in his belief. Does anyone have a suggestion for doing this?"

Fidem suggested that she and Hratt could follow the retreating army at a distance to make sure they got all the way home. Everyone thought this was an excellent idea and solved the first of the concerns. What would they be able to do if Fidem came back telling them the enemy was returning? This was a much harder situation to deal with. A lot of negative "We can't. . ." comments were made, but nothing positive had been suggested after several minutes.

Fidem spoke up, "What about this. My telling him my archery skill was poor compared to the soldiers' helped the first time because he assumed the soldiers' skill to be much higher than mine. If he turns back Hratt and I can land in the road facing him. We could land far enough away for Hratt to breathe a large blast of fire. I can then tell him not to make the fatal mistake of thinking he had any chance at all of defeating Dartan. Hopefully the thought of Dartan having dragons in their army as well as soldiers riding them will be enough to send him on his way. Again, we have nothing to lose by trying."

Everyone agreed that this was a good plan and Fidem quickly located Hratt and got him saddled. Since his saddlebags already contained the items Fidem usually took on her ambassadorial trips the cooks only needed to gather some food and take it to the courtyard. When Fidem and Hratt showed up in the courtyard the food was quickly loaded, and they were on their way.

Jenny called another meeting of the rest of the council to see if they could do anything to help the situation in case Fidem was unsuccessful on her mission. The only thing they could come up with was for several large hunting parties to be formed to make forays into the nearby woods for game and a few other parties to go to any outlying farms and harvest what produce was available. If the parties were successful that might give them enough supplies to hold out under siege long enough for King Firinne and General Hapsom to return in about three weeks with reinforcements.

The parties were formed and headed out early the next morning on their expeditions. By the late morning both parties had had a good bit of success and returned with much appreciated food. It was not enough to guarantee that they could withstand a siege, but it was enough to give them some hope and lifted their spirits considerably.

Meanwhile Fidem and Hratt followed the retreating army from quite a way behind. They could easily see the dust cloud produced by the horses and tramping foot soldiers noting that a steady retreat was being made. When the army stopped for the night Fidem and Hratt landed making camp. They were far enough away that their campfire would probably not be seen, but just to be safe they found a low spot with a hill between them and the enemy army and made their camp there.

Fidem and Hratt were up at dawn and again took to the air after a quick breakfast. They saw no movement of the enemy army, so they flew back and forth for a bit watching remaining low and far enough away to not be seen. Apparently King Mektig had second thoughts and had convinced his army to go back for another try because the dust cloud now started moving towards Dartan rather than towards Sterk.

Hratt shook his head and said, "It appears they need more convincing. How about if we land with that roll maneuver we worked out on our recent trip to Evimeria? That followed by a good fire blast should impress him!"

"Excellent idea!" said Fidem with a smile and adding, "We will have to see how they respond before deciding what to do next, but hopefully they will at least go home first before making any other attempts to attack. If nothing else this would gain us a little more time to try and figure something else out."

They then flew off towards the approaching army but stayed low and slightly to the side of the road so that their appearance would be quick and dramatic. They suddenly popped into view and as they came in to land Hratt tucked in his wings and made a roll so that the army observed a rider so skilled that they remained firmly in the saddle even when flying upside down while spinning. Fidem and Hratt watched the army come to a complete standstill with their mouths agape as he landed. Hratt had taken a much deeper breath than normal, so his fire blast was an extremely large one. This caused all the horses except the one King Mektig was mounted on to bolt down the road towards home with their riders barely able to stay in their saddles. It was all King Mektig could do to keep his mount from bolting as well and it took all his skill and effort to do this. Even though it only took a short time for King Mektig to calm his horse to where he could keep it under control some of the foot soldiers took this opportunity to follow the bolting horses. He shouted to his remaining troops, "Stand! If we ever do retreat it will be orderly and not a panicked rout!"

Fidem and Hratt could see the troops uneasily holding their ground, but they were trembling and most were poised for flight. King Mektig's horse, although under control, was shifting uneasily as well. Fidem was carefully observing King Mektig's actions as she knew that he was a strong leader and that his men would follow his lead. She could see that though he spoke with authority he moved uneasily and made a couple of glances at his troops to see what they were doing. She knew that a leader that was confident enough in his men following his lead would not have looked back. If Fidem could have heard the talk passing back and forth in the troops she would have been even more encouraged.

Several shouts of, "Dragon riding warriors! Oh no, we're doomed!" were made.

One soldier said to his neighbor, "Look! That is that little arrow retriever!"

The second man replied, "You're right! If that little girl has her own dragon and is that accomplished a dragon rider we don't stand a chance against their armed forces!"

Another remarked, "I don't know about the rest of you, but I am not going to throw my life away in a country that did not attack us first!"

There were many soft agreements murmured amongst the soldiers as well. Even the commanding general was shaking his head and muttering to himself, "I am afraid if the king decides to pursue his folly he will be doing it alone!"

Fidem could see them speaking in low tones to each other with very worried expressions on their faces. She decided to speak boldly but was going to use tact instead of blustery threats, but she also wanted to make it clear that Dartan was not to be messed with.

Fidem looked King Mektig directly in the eye and said slowly, "Do not underestimate Dartan's military strength. If any evidence of another attack is even heard of your kingdom runs the risk of being totally decimated."

King Mektig had just come to that conclusion himself and was fearing that Dartan might just decide to wipe them out to prevent any possible future threat from Sterk. He was actually debating with himself the merit of surrendering there and then when Fidem continued, so he remained silent to hear what else she would say before making any further comment.

"You are fortunate that Dartan is a peaceful country and prefers to have good relations with others. I am Dame Fidem and come from a very respectable family in Dartan and though I am not qualified as a soldier the king has graciously appointed me as an ambassador. I have pen and paper with me, and I am offering you the opportunity of signing a peace treaty with us, but with certain stipulations attached. If Sterk attacks any other kingdom unprovoked Dartan will side against Sterk with that kingdom. Dartan will however come to Sterk's aid if it is attacked without provocation by another kingdom. Sterk will be expected to come to Dartan's aid if we are attacked unprovoked. Will you agree to these terms?"

King Mektig looked over at his soldiers noticing that all of them were nodding their heads at him. He also heard several comments like, "Do it!", "Say yes!" and even a, "Don't be a fool! Accept!" from someone near the back.

He quickly thought over the situation reasoning in his mind. The possibilities seem to be either to accept the terms or face possible annihilation. Returning defeated would be humiliating, but returning with a treaty with a powerful country promising to be an ally if Sterk was attacked would be a positive thing. He decided to agree.

King Mektig then dismounted and slowly approached Fidem. He held his sword out to her hilt first saying, "I accept your terms. Please draw up the treaty for us to sign."

Fidem accepted the sword and then retrieved the necessary items from one of Hratt's saddlebags asking King Mektig to choose one of his soldiers as a witness. As Fidem was writing two copies of the treaty clearly stating the terms King Mektig had his commanding general come over to sign as a witness. Fidem noticed that the general removed his sword from its sheath and left it with a subordinate before approaching. The treaty copies were soon written and signed by the principals and witnesses. Hratt had dipped one of his claws into the inkwell and made an X for his signature as the witness for Dartan.

Once the ink had dried Fidem rolled up her copy, tied it with a ribbon and placed it into Hratt's saddlebag. She then rolled up King Mektig's copy, tied it with a ribbon and handed it to him. She then returned King Mektig's sword to him saying, "I am pleased to return your sword to you as an ally rather than keeping it as spoil from a defeated enemy."

King Mektig accepted the sword bowing deeply and saying, "Your graciousness in this matter overwhelms me. I wish you long life and prosperity." He then mounted his horse and prepared to lead what was left of his army back home.

Fidem then smiled at him saying loudly, "Go in peace! I now return to gratefully inform our citizens that we need no longer prepare for war!"

King Mektig galloped off and soon caught up with the retreating foot soldiers. He slowed to a trot and had them follow him at a quick march until they met the troop of soldiers that were still calming their frightened horses. They all remained there until the horses had been finally calmed down. This allowed time for the troops that were following behind him to catch up with them. Since the morning was somewhat advanced by this time and King Mektig did not want to give his men the opportunity of conversing together before he had the chance to address them himself he had the troops halt at that location to regroup. Explaining that they now had a peace treaty with Dartan and would be returning home with a valuable ally they would remain where they were until their ranks could be properly reformed. They would then have their midday meal and return home. The reforming was taken care of while they made their meal preparations. The troops were extremely relieved by this news especially those that had not witnessed the signing of the treaty and had feared that Dartan might just wipe them out before they even had a chance to retreat home.

Meanwhile, Fidem had climbed into the saddle, and she and Hratt had flown back to Glyka. When they landed in the courtyard. Jenny approached with a worried look on her face that soon changed to one of relief as she saw Fidem's broad smile.

"Did they actually go all the way back home?" Jenny asked hopefully.

"No, they attempted to return to Dartan."

"Then, were you able to scare them into retreating back home?" Jenny asked her uncertainly.

"Well. . . not exactly." Fidem replied with a grin but continued after seeing the puzzled expression on Jenny's face, "We did scare them sufficiently to do so, but I felt it was better to come up with something more permanent." She then removed the peace treaty from Hratt's saddlebag and handed it to Jenny.

Jenny stood with her mouth open as she read the document and remarked, "This is incredible! I would not have thought it even possible. King Firinne is going to be so pleased that he can celebrate having another ally rather than having to prepare for war when he returns! We need to get busy! We should have a huge welcome home celebration prepared for King Firinne's return. A large feast is always part of a celebration of that sort, and we can surprise him with the news and peace treaty after everyone has finished eating. It will be great to use all that food just collected for the feast instead of during a siege! Fidem why don't you and Hratt follow me so we can update the annals with the new information. Once that is done we can concentrate on the upcoming celebration."

Everyone was kept busy over the next two weeks preparing for the event. Since the reception area for Gwendolyn and Fergal's wedding had worked well for a large crowd the same basic plan was implemented for the feast. They skipped setting up all the chairs as they would not be needed. They used the extra area to set up some more tables just in case as they were expecting even more people than had attended the wedding. A huge welcome home banner was stretched across the road just inside the city gates and many smaller vertical banners were along the sides on the entire route from the gates to the palace entrance. All was in readiness, and everyone was just awaiting the King's arrival, which was expected any day now.

The day of King Firinne's return he dispatched a rider shortly after breakfast to arrive several hours ahead of the main party to inform those at the palace of his return. The rider was totally surprised by the banners and remarked jokingly to Jenny as he entered the palace, "Did you really miss us so much that you went to all this trouble just to welcome us back?" When he was informed about what had transpired he looked incredulously at Jenny saying, "She did what?! She faced a whole enemy army by herself. . . twice?! I know that the king speaks highly of Dame Fidem and that she has proved to be a good ambassador as well as being very dedicated to her guard duties, but this goes far beyond dedication! It is definitely a cause for much celebration!"

Jenny said, "Now that we know the King's party should arrive in a few more hours we can get everyone and everything ready for when he arrives." She then went off to make sure all was in readiness for the King's arrival.

22

THE CELEBRATION

WHEN the king's party entered the gates they were very surprised by the decorations and even more surprised that so many Dartan citizens were lining the way cheering their arrival. Royal Advisor Jenny met them as they entered the palace and asked them to please follow her to the celebration feast. She said she knew they were a little tired and dusty from their journey as well as being very hungry, but what was being celebrated was of such importance to the kingdom that it could not wait. She was sure the king would agree and not mind waiting to freshen up until afterwards. They would first eat and afterwards the celebratory news would be shared. Since the king had full confidence in Jenny's judgment he followed her marveling that something of this magnitude could have occurred during his brief absence and was wondering what could have transpired.

Jenny led the king and queen to a special table at the front and told the rest of his party that there were a couple of reserved tables for them nearby, but they were also free to be seated at any vacant place they chose. Most of the party took advantage of a nearby table, but a few had seen vacant places at a table with family or special friends and chose those instead. The king and queen were seated in the two central positions at the head table. The other positions were occupied by various palace officials, and one place was occupied by

263

Fidem and there was an open spot there for Jenny. All of the regular tables already had their occupants seated and quietly waiting.

The feast was greatly enjoyed by all and the king's party felt much better after relaxing over a good meal. Jenny then spoke to King Firinne, "Your Majesty you would normally be the one to address the attendees at a function like this and you certainly may do so if you wish, but since you are unaware of the reasons for the event and the details involved I can take care of that and then turn the platform over to you if you like. What does Your Majesty wish?"

"I am overwhelmed with curiosity. Please go ahead and inform me of what occurred to cause such a huge celebration!"

"Very well, I will now read the account as recorded in the *Annals of the Kingdom of Dartan*." She then opened the volume to the correct page and began reading. As she read the king's face took on several vastly different expressions at different times and although he felt like speaking up he did not want to disrupt the narrative and allowed Jenny to read the account all the way through to the end.

At the beginning the king's face showed anger at being threatened for no cause and remorse for not being present. It then changed to happiness and pleasure as Fidem's actions were related and absolute delight when the peace treaty terms were read. Jenny then turned to the king gesturing with her hand and saying, "Your Majesty."

King Firinne rose and began to speak slowly, "When I left for my trip I knew the kingdom was in capable hands; I just did not know how capable they would turn out to be. I am so sorry I was not here to deal with this threat, but you must admit it was unprecedented and totally unexpected. The way the situation was turned around is indeed a cause for celebration and I declare the date of the treaty being signed as an official Dartan holiday from now on. It shall be called the 'Day of Thanks' and will be celebrated by a public feast like this one."

Much clapping and cheering occurred at this point and King Firinne allowed it to die down before continuing. He then called Fidem up to stand next to him, and more clapping and cheering accompanied her walk. Once she was standing next to him and the cheering had died down he went on, "The kingdom owes much to this young lady. Her resourcefulness and bravery in a very dangerous situation is the only reason we are all able to celebrate here today. If it were not for her we might be languishing in a prison cell or forced into slave labor. The laws of this land are the same as in Vita with a provision for a commoner defeating an enemy in single combat becoming the king or queen. Since that is what Dame Fidem in effect has done she would have that right if I and the queen were not living. The queen and I have been discussing something lately that might eventually bring that about depending on what Dame Fidem decides."

Everyone there, especially Fidem, had puzzled expressions on their faces as nobody had any idea what could happen to make Fidem a queen without the king and queen abdicating and why King Firinne and Queen Unestita would not continue to reign. They were all waiting intently for King Firinne to continue and were hoping he would give some explanation as to how this could occur without the abdication.

King Firinne then turned to face Fidem and spoke to her directly, "Dame Fidem, you are aware by now that the queen and I remain childless with no prospect of producing an heir. Had we produced a daughter I cannot imagine being prouder of her or loving her more than we do you. We have been talking for some time about wishing to have a daughter like you. It was not possible while your mother was alive, but we now wish to adopt you as our own daughter if you are willing."

Fidem got a huge smile on her face and replied with tears streaming down her cheeks, "I don't have any knowledge of my real father as he died before I was born; but your kindness to me after I became a palace guard and then an ambassador and concern you showed for my mother at the end of her life

made me wish for a father like you. I would be very happy
to call you father and would very much like to be adopted!
Do you mind if I call you and the queen dad and mom now?
And can I continue teaching archery classes?"

The queen quickly rose and joined her husband. They both
wrapped their arms around Fidem and the queen said, "Of
course not dear! And you may absolutely continue to teach
those classes for as long as you wish until you are crowned
queen."

The cheers and clapping had been loud before, but now
they were almost deafening. The entire crowd was on its feet,
and the noise went on for some time. Eventually King Firinne
raised his arms above his head and the crowd quieted back
down. The king and queen remained standing with Fidem
between them as he addressed the crowd once more.

"I will have all the necessary paperwork completed tomorrow and the event shall be recorded in the annals, but the
queen and I are fatigued from our journey and still covered
with dust and need to get cleaned up. We will now retire
accompanied by Princess Fidem. You are all dismissed. Good
night."

Taking Fidem's hands they both led her out of the courtyard
and into the palace.

Epilogue

PRINCESS Fidem had moved from the barracks to her own room in the palace and had been sure to bring her mother's Bible as well as a few other items that she wished to keep. She also retrieved her gold arrow and a few more personal items from her office. She was now enjoying the luxury of the palace's amenities and privileges of being royalty. It did not go to her head though and she was still the same Fidem she had always been.

When she had reported to General Hapsom the day after the feast he had been startled and said with a bow, "Princess Fidem, what on earth are you doing here? Now that you have been adopted you are no longer a guard under my command and have no responsibilities here!"

Fidem had said that she realized that, but teaching archery was a joy she did not want to give up. "I understand that I am no longer a palace guard, but is it not possible for me to continue teaching? I do not expect to have the continual classes that I had before, but could we not work out something where I could teach a set of classes say once a quarter? I would not be at the morning guard assembly; but could I not meet the students at the classroom for the normal time spent with them and just return to the palace when the class was dismissed?"

"Well having the Royal Princess teaching archery classes is certainly unusual, but if it is done the way you described it I see no reason that it could not be worked out. You will just have to let me know ahead of time when you would like to teach a class and Colonel Veren will work it into the schedule."

General Hapsom had smiled and continued wistfully, "I will miss having you as a normal instructor, but some of your former students have progressed far enough that they are competent instructors now and they appear to be able to pass that skill on to their students as well."

Fidem had thanked the general and waved goodbye as she headed back to the palace thinking to herself, "It seems a little strange to wave at the general instead of saluting, but I suppose that I'll get used to it eventually."

Early one afternoon a lone rider approached the city gates. He was a handsome young man who was richly dressed in fine clothes. His horse was obviously not a working animal either. He had a confident relaxed and very polite manner as he asked the first person he met after entering the gates the way to the palace. He was told to just follow the road he was on, and it would lead him there. He thanked the individual and continued down the road at an unhurried pace.

When he reached the palace entrance the guards stopped him but politely asked him to state his business within the palace.

Smiling at them he replied, "I am King Klok the son of Mektig from the kingdom of Sterk to the south. Our two countries have a peace treaty signed by my father the previous king, and Dame Fidem. I come in peace and wish to have speech with her."

The guards bowed and asked him to please come into the grounds and wait in the shade of a nearby tree while his message was conveyed to the palace proper. A messenger was then sent inside to deliver the message to Royal Advisor Jenny. She asked about the visitor and when she heard a description of him and his horse and the fact that he came alone dismissed the messenger and went to find Princess Fidem. When she found Fidem in one of the gardens and had told her King Klok of Sterk was requesting an audience with Dame Fidem, Fidem was intrigued and asked Jenny if she wanted to accompany her to meet the gentleman. Jenny was also curious and agreed immediately. As they approached the visitor King Klok dismounted and bowed to the two ladies.

He repeated what he had said earlier, "I am King Klok the son of Mektig from the kingdom of Sterk to the south. Our two countries have a peace treaty signed by my father the previous king and Dame Fidem. I come in peace and wish to have speech with her. Are either of you ladies Dame Fidem?"

Fidem could tell by his speech and manners that King Klok was quite a different person than his father. She wanted to find out a little more about him and his business before she revealed too much so she said with a smile, "I was the one who signed the peace treaty with your father. Since you introduced yourself as king can I safely assume that your father is dead?"

"Yes. I am not like my father though and that is why I came. I could tell from the way the treaty was worded and from my father's most likely embellished account that there was still some tension felt between our countries even after the treaty signing. I was never in agreement with my father's desire for conquest and feel countries should be content with what lands they have. They should have the right to defend what is theirs but not have the right to take something from someone else. I would like to hear your thoughts on this and your account of the incident, Dame Fidem."

Fidem was a good judge of character and could tell by body language, word choice and the way he was unafraid to look her in the eye while he spoke that he was being sincere, open and honest with her. She decided to afford him the same courtesy asking Jenny if she would bring the annals book and read what was recorded as Dartan's official account.

While Jenny was getting the book Fidem also looked King Klok in the eye and began, "I appreciate you taking the time to visit and especially your trying to better the relationship between our two countries. We also feel a country should have the right to defend itself if attacked but not have the right to try and conquer another country and take what was theirs. I sense your honesty and therefore will also be honest with you. As you will find out when the recorded account is read we succeeded in convincing your father that we were much stronger than we really are. Also, I am no longer Dame Fidem. That was my title when the treaty was signed, but since then I have been officially adopted into the royal family and am now Princess Fidem, which accounts for the nicer clothes I am now wearing than what I had on when I met your father. I also sensed on the day that the treaty was signed that your army as a whole did not desire conquest but were reluctantly following your father as the leader of your country."

By this time Jenny had returned and Fidem asked her to read the account from the annals for King Klok. The reading took only a few minutes, and King Klok was nodding his head at the end. He remarked to Fidem as Jenny closed the book, "I thought so. Even had I not spoken to you and gotten to trust you, your account is much more believable than the... I said embellished account earlier, but now fairy tale seems more appropriate... account my father told. I am glad you brought about the treaty without the shedding of any blood. After seeing the shield with your arrow through it I realized you could just as easily have put that arrow through my father's leather armor right into his heart to make your point, yet you chose fear rather than violence as a weapon. I greatly respect you for that! I feel much more comfortable now with you as an ally and am no longer uneasy with the relationship. I hope we can continue to improve relations as time progresses. I should return now and let my people know the happy truth about our ally to the north!"

"We would be pleased if you would join us for dinner and rest overnight here in the palace. You could then return tomorrow in good time rather than arriving fatigued in the middle of the night. One of the staff can take your horse to the stables for the night."

"I graciously accept your kind offer of hospitality. Lead on."

Fidem then took him into the palace introducing him to the king and queen. He was warmly welcomed and enjoyed a hearty meal with good conversation, slept well and was off for home after a good breakfast in the morning.

As Fidem and Jenny were waving goodbye to him Jenny remarked, "Well, I would never have thought we would be on friendly terms with *anyone* from that country but leave it to Princess Fidem to find a way!"

They both shared a hearty laugh as they headed back into the palace smiling at each other.

www.ingramcontent.com/pod-product-compliance
Lightning Source LLC
Chambersburg PA
CBHW051553030726
47592CB00001B/275